THE MERCENARY

Also by Paul Vidich

An Honorable Man
The Good Assassin
The Coldest Warrior

THE MERCENARY

PAUL VIDICH

NO EXIT PRESS

First published in 2021 by No Exit Press,
an imprint of Oldcastle Books Ltd,
Harpenden, UK

noexit.co.uk
@noexitpress

ISBN
978-0-85730-445-2 (Paperback)
978-0-85730-446-9 (Ebook)

2 4 6 8 10 9 7 5 3 1

Typeset in 11 on 13pt Minion Pro
by Avocet Typeset, Bideford, Devon, EX39 2BP
Printed and bound in the UK by Clays Ltd, Elcograf S.p.A.

For Ryder, Juniper, and Leo

He had two lives: one, open, seen and
known by all who cared to know...
and another life running its course in secret.

– Anton Chekhov
'The Lady with the Dog'
(translated by Constance Garnett)

1

RED SQUARE

GEORGE MUELLER KNEW THAT the night ahead would be about stamina. Stamina for waiting, for worry, and stamina for fear. He understood that he had to be ready for the moment, when everything would suddenly change and he would be a man on the run. He wouldn't get off that roller coaster until the mission succeeded or his luck ran out. Hardened nerves, cold resolve, and a tolerance for nausea were things he would have to possess if he was going to get through the night. He had memorized his route through Moscow and took care to anticipate what could go wrong, knowing that he was no longer a young case officer who could jump off a cliff and hope to find his wings on the way down.

Five minutes after four o'clock in the evening, December 31. Mueller noted the time and date for the report he'd later write. The Agency's new rules made it important to document an operation, and failure to do so was a poor mark on any case officer's career, but date and time were important to Mueller for an entirely personal reason. At sixty-three, he was a few months from voluntary retirement. He didn't want to end his storied career with a failed mission.

The cable from Headquarters that came into Moscow Station had been succinct. The walk-in Soviet intelligence officer who had approached Mueller, throwing an envelope in the open window of his car when he was stopped at a traffic light, was potentially the most valuable Soviet asset to ever offer his services to the CIA. Recruiting the man known only as GAMBIT took precedence over all other activity in Moscow Station.

Knowledge of GAMBIT's existence was limited to Mueller and John Rositske, his deputy chief of station, who was at the wheel of the Lada. They were next in line to exit the embassy parking lot, and they waited for the marine guard to raise the barrier for the lead car. Neither of the junior officers in the Lada – Ronnie Moffat, who sat in the back next to Mueller, or Helen Walsh, in the front – knew the details of the night's operation, nor did the case officers in the decoy car being waved through.

Mueller lit a Prima and cracked open his window. The top floor of the embassy's French Empire façade was singed with dusk's streaking light, turning the pale stucco an ochre red. Its height set it apart from neighboring Georgian homes along Tchaikovsky Street. Soviet militia stood in guard shacks on both ends of the embassy, using their telephones to call out the comings and goings of embassy staff to nearby KGB surveillance teams. Mueller's eyes moved to the left, beyond the militia's shack, toward two parked Volga sedans, exhaust pluming into the bitter cold. Across the street at the bus stop he saw two Russians in quilted-cotton jackets and shabby wool caps drawn over their foreheads sharing a bottle of holiday vodka. *KGB?* he wondered. *Or members of the million-man-strong army of Russian alcoholics?*

Gusting wind drove a light snow across the wide boulevard, which was empty of traffic at that hour as Muscovites left work early to celebrate the new year. Streetlamps went on one after another, illuminating the embassy like perimeter lights along a prison wall. Moscow was a city of elaborate privileges for foreigners with hard currency, but to Mueller and the other CIA officers in Moscow Station, it was a denied area – a dangerous place of provocations and surveillance. Mueller alone knew his destination that night. Two vertical chalk marks the day before on a postal box by the tobacco kiosk outside Kievskaya Metro Station had told him the meeting would go on.

Mueller was tall, and his knees hit the back of the small car's front seat. He wore a bulky Russian overcoat that he'd purchased at a flea market, a pair of thick-soled shoes, and an old fox *shapka*. He struck a match and relit the Prima, cupping his hands against the breeze coming in his window, and exhaled pungent tobacco smoke.

Mueller had joined the Agency out of the OSS and witnessed firsthand the burgeoning bureaucracy's reliance on new technologies, but he understood that spy satellites and code-breaking algorithms didn't substitute for the intelligence that came from the solitary man who gathered secrets at the risk of his life. Mueller's hair was gray and thinner, his lower back kept him from a good night's sleep, and he started his morning with a regimen of pills, but he admitted to no one that he was too old to play at the young man's game. He had circled his retirement date, but he had done that before, and there was no certainty he'd follow through this time. The job had defined him, shaped him in ways he hadn't expected, and he found it hard to imagine life on the outside. Doing what? Quietly writing a memoir? Fishing? Reading Shakespeare? Looking for ways to stay relevant?

The marine guard raised the barrier. Mueller met Rositske's eyes in the rearview mirror, and he confirmed that it was time to go operational. John Rositske was Mueller's physical and personality opposite – shorter, heavier, Catholic, and a man who liked to talk even when it was wise to shut up. He had joined the Agency when it was no longer an exclusive club for eager young minds from the Ivy League. He was in his early forties, coming to the end of his two-year tour, a burly man with a big voice and an outsize confidence. He had red hair and a West Texas tan, which had paled in the long Russian winter, and his eyes, lively and kind at times, were grim coals and relentlessly skeptical on the job. He'd picked up his gruff voice as a teenager working weekends as a ranch hand, and it had served him well during his two tours in the Mekong Delta commanding a marine platoon. He'd led forty-two men on a risky night helicopter assault, which had earned him a Bronze Star and left half of his men dead.

Rositske lowered his window for the marine guard, who checked his State Department ID and glanced in the car.

'What's that?' The guard pointed his flashlight at a cardboard box on the back seat.

Ronnie showed off covered porcelain dishes holding a holiday dinner: aspic, *pirozhki*, chicken with potato *sloyami*, and meat patties. She was prepared to give the address of the New Year's party they were attending, and she also had an explanation, if one was needed, to account for the compressed air canister at her feet.

'Ready,' Rositske said after they'd been waved through. Rositske tapped the gas pedal twice to make sure the notoriously unreliable product of Soviet engineering didn't stall, and he moved the stick shift with his knuckled fist. 'Rock and roll, gentlemen. Moscow Rules.'

There was only one rule in Moscow anyone could remember, but the plural had survived. *Trust no one.* Assume every taxi driver, every drunk on a bench, each traffic policeman, and every shy girl in a bar looking for companionship worked for the KGB.

Rositske turned onto Tchaikovsky Street, and in his rearview mirror he saw two black Volgas pull away from the curb. 'Tics.

Far left side.' He kept to the speed limit, making the second right turn into a neighborhood of narrow streets and once-elegant homes, and he continued at that speed, slowing only to make another right turn and then a left, altering course, and with each turn he confirmed the Volgas still followed. He knew their advantage – high-powered cars equipped with encrypted radio transmitters.

'Next turn.'

Ronnie threw a blanket off her lap and pulled a deflated, life-size sex doll from the floor, arranging it on the seat, slumped forward. Mueller tested his door handle, rehearsing in his mind a sequence of moves.

Suddenly, the Lada sped up, accelerating into a right turn, and Rositske followed with another immediate right turn, and then a third. As he came out of the last turn, he pulled hard on the hand brake, slowing the car without its brake lights glowing red.

'Now!'

Mueller pulled the handle, opening the door, and he rolled onto the pavement, hitting hard. His momentum brought him to his feet, and in a split second he had taken cover between a stunted bush with prickly thorns and a parked car. Mueller pressed against the car, gulping air, and he looked at the accelerating Lada. The inflated life-size doll was propped in his seat, the glowing tip of a Prima dangling from her mouth and a fox *shapka* on her head. Technical Services in Langley had come up with the trick. They purchased the doll and two back-ups in a Washington, DC, sex shop and shipped them to Moscow Station via diplomatic pouch.

Mueller saw the two Volgas speed past unaware of the deception and breathed deeply to prepare himself to go dark. He looked at his watch: 4:17 p.m.

*

Mueller moved along the dark street, keeping to the center of the sidewalk, and passed through circles of light cast by widely spaced streetlamps, just an older man carrying a cloth bag with his holiday meal. He had three hours until his rendezvous with GAMBIT, and while it had once seemed like an unnecessarily long interval, he was glad he had the time to dry-clean himself.

Mueller moved from shadow to shadow in his bulky overcoat with the slack step of a Party apparatchik returning to his one-room apartment to eat dinner alone. His cloth bag held a fresh orange, parsley potatoes, herring, walnut *rogaliki*, and a small bottle of plum brandy. Under his pensioner's dinner was tightly wrapped brown paper of the sort used by butchers, and inside a T-50 miniature camera fitted into a ballpoint pen, film cartridges, a tiny burst radio transmitter, and a thick stack of rubles. The cloth bag swung at his side as he walked and from time to time he blew on his gloved hands for warmth. The falling temperature stung his cheeks.

Mueller made his way along grim streets and through drab apartment blocks dotted with lights, beacons of joy for families gathered to celebrate a secular holiday that the Communist Party had elevated over Christmas. He crossed the Moscow River at Borodinskiy Bridge and then doubled back on Kalininskiy Bridge, headed toward Moscow Center. He was alert to movements in his peripheral vision, but he resisted the temptation to look. He had learned not to meet another person's eyes. If he looked, he knew the stranger would look away. Muscovites kept to themselves, and they knew to mind their own business.

But coming to the end of the second bridge, Mueller happened to stop to light another cigarette. As he shielded his match against the wind, he glanced around. If the KGB were there – on foot or in a car – they had mastered the art of being invisible, and that was the fear of some case officers in Moscow Station. It had been a bad season. A dozen of the Station's best assets had been arrested, their networks rolled up, and years of patient work wiped out. Everyone had a theory for the loss. Rositske believed the KGB's new ghost surveillance was a ploy to demoralize Moscow Station. Teams of KGB would wait beyond the visual horizon for hours, giving the appearance there had been a break in surveillance, and then suddenly they would converge in cars or on foot, when the case officer was confident he was dry-cleaned and could go operational.

Rositske advised Mueller not to take an operational role that required a young man's reflexes and a chess master's mind. At sixty-three, Mueller had his best years behind him, but the evening's success depended on more than fitness – it depended on GAMBIT's trust, and Mueller alone had that.

Mueller flicked his cigarette over the edge of the bridge and watched it fall to the river's pack ice. He fixed his eyes on Kalinin Prospekt in the distance and beyond that the metro station. *Ready*, he thought.

The Arbatskaya Metro Station entrance was empty of the usual crowd, and he joined the few people moving down to the platform level. He let himself be pushed by a big, bustling woman who smiled until she got a better look at his face. Mueller was alert to watchful militia teams nearby and the footsteps of passengers rushing to beat the metro's closing doors. He moved through the vaulted lobby, becoming another submissive Soviet Russian who knew to keep to himself. He shuffled his worn shoes to give the appearance of a diminished older man, someone the militia would judge to be a person of little interest. In this way Mueller passed through the station, emerging on the street at a separate entrance. He glanced back. *Clean*. It was time.

*

Mueller entered Karl Marx Prospekt on the northwest corner of the Kremlin. Cold darkness lay across Red Square, and he slapped his gloves to warm his hands and prepare for what lay ahead. Not since he'd parachuted behind Nazi lines at night in Occupied France had he been this nervous.

He moved clockwise around the medieval fortress and entered the open square, where the enormous clock and bells of Spasskaya Tower inside the Kremlin wall announced the time. A horizontal band of snow obscured the spire's red star.

Mueller saw the honor guard goose-stepping out of an archway in the wall, proceeding to Lenin's Tomb on their hourly rotation. He gazed across the scattered pedestrians who crossed the square, hunched against the wind, trying to stay warm. Mueller looked for a man like himself, dressed in a tired overcoat and *shapka*, holding a cloth bag in his right hand. GAMBIT had set the time and place of their brush pass, thinking – Mueller assumed – that an open place with people to overwhelm the militia's watching eyes would be a good spot to converge. This was an amateur's mind at work, and Mueller knew that GAMBIT's choice could put them both at risk.

In spite of the bad weather and the late hour, groups of visitors looked toward Lenin's dark granite mausoleum. Tourists from the provinces and a few foreigners endured the cold to catch the changing of the guard, while others had taken up positions to watch the evening's fireworks display.

'Smoke?'

Mueller was aware of the man before he heard his voice, but what unsettled him was the question in English. He turned to face an Interior Ministry militiaman wearing a high-crown cap with the seal of the USSR. He had the stern, self-assured face of a man aware of his authority. Mueller gave no hint that he understood, and his eyes opened slightly. Confusion. The militiaman pumped two fingers to his lips.

Mueller obliged, hitting the red pack of Primas on his sleeve, offering a loosened cigarette.

'*Spasibo.*'

Mueller continued toward the Monument to Minin and Pozharsky in front of St. Basil's Cathedral's candy-striped domes. Mueller had gone a few steps when he saw the man he knew must be GAMBIT. The time was right, the spot agreed, and the man carried a cloth bag in his right hand. He was dressed like Mueller, so they could pass as doubles – two older men who looked alike on a vector to cross paths by the benches. If all went as planned, they would exchange bags in their brief moment of contact and separate. Only the most vigilant observer would notice that the cloth bags had been switched, Mueller carrying another man's dinner and GAMBIT carrying camera, film, radio, and rubles. The brush pass would happen in the blink of an eye.

'*Amerikanets!*'

Mueller cursed his luck. The militiaman was having fun with him because the night was cold and there was no one else to harass. He continued toward the monument and considered whether to abort.

'*Ostanovis!*' Halt.

Mueller's world got very small. His choices were usurped by the sudden appearance of a black Volga that emerged rapidly from a side street by the GUM department store. A second Volga entered the square farther away, its wheels skidding on the thin covering of fresh snow, swerving wildly until its driver regained control and headed for Mueller. Third and fourth cars swept in from behind St. Basil's. Tourists and foreigners gathered at Lenin's Tomb looked at the four vehicles that raced toward the old man with his cloth bag.

Mueller stood perfectly still. It would be a fool's errand to run. Plainclothes officers emptied from their cars and advanced on him in a tightening circle. *Fuck!* It was as if they had known he would be there. Mueller considered GAMBIT, now drawing the attention of a militiaman, and in that moment, he prepared himself mentally for the diversion he knew he must create.

He sprinted toward a narrow opening in the encircling net in a hopeless bid to escape. He was easily apprehended, but he continued to put up heroic resistance, cursing the men holding his arms. He continued his indignant objections until the officer pinning his arm kneed his lower back. A second blow struck the back of his skull. His head began to spin, and he dropped to the pavement. He breathed deeply to shake off the nauseating pain and gather his thoughts. His glove was pulled off and his palm grazed with a handheld black light, revealing dim, amber fluorescence.

'Mr Mueller.'

A pair of polished black leather boots filled Mueller's field of vision, and he raised his eyes. As he did, he glimpsed the *shapka*-capped man with his cloth bag by the Monument to Minin and Pozharsky. The man passed a few more benches and turned for a second, watching the commotion. He looked toward Mueller, a quick glance to take in the scene, and then turned again, walking away, beginning to hurry.

The officer standing over Mueller was of average height with bony cheeks scarred with pockmarks, calm eyes, and a gaunt frame that made him look menacing. Mueller recognized the high-crown gray cap of a KGB lieutenant colonel. Mueller had not met the officer, but he knew the face from Moscow Station's files. Lieutenant Colonel Viktor Talinov, first deputy to the head of the Second Chief Directorate. Mueller knew he was a brutal man who had been trained by the Soviet system to be a tool of repression. He was known to be precise and quick in his methods – like a good butcher.

Talinov removed the contents of Mueller's cloth bag and handed them to the KGB officer at his side – the orange, the plum brandy, herring, parsley potatoes, and finally the walnut *rogaliki*, briefly savoring the dessert's candied aroma. He complimented its perfection with a knowing nod.

Talinov removed the brown paper package from the bottom of the bag. He undid the twine, unfolded the paper, and looked at the contents. He presented his discovery to his prisoner like an offering.

'*Dolboyob*.' Fuckhead.

Talinov removed his stitched leather glove by pulling one finger at a time, until his long, delicate pianist's hand was open to the cold. He slapped Mueller's cheek with the glove.

'I have been looking forward to meeting you. Unfortunately, these are difficult circumstances.'

Mueller felt the slap's sting as a prelude to a bruising night. He said what he would repeat many times, in those and similar words: 'I am an American diplomat. I demand to speak with my embassy.'

2

GREENWICH VILLAGE
TWO DAYS LATER

THE MOMENT ALEKSANDER GARIN opened the front door of his West Village walk-up, he knew that his wife was gone. He stood in the vestibule, attaché case in hand, and he felt the dark silence of the empty apartment. Her coat was missing, her purse not where she usually placed it, and there was an envelope pinned to the corkboard where she knew he would see it – the care of a person making sure to tie up loose ends. She had written his name in her big, loopy script.

He moved into the small living room and dropped the envelope on the round dining table. He was reluctant to open it but also eager to know what she'd written, those opposing feelings tugging at him at the same time.

It was snowing outside again. Through the casement window he could hear plows scraping the pavement on their rumbling way down the quiet street. A week earlier they had celebrated his birthday at his favorite restaurant in Little Italy, and he'd commented that the neighborhood had changed, the old places now drawing patrons from the suburbs, but they had still enjoyed the meal, sharing a bottle of Chianti, and they'd made love when they got home. It had been a brave effort to hold on to their intimacy, but when they finished, they lay apart on the bed. They fell asleep without talking.

The next day, he'd gone to work, as usual. When he left the apartment, she was at the round table writing an outline for an article she was pitching to editors, and she hadn't looked up to say goodbye even though, as previously planned, she would be off to visit her parents in Los Angeles for the weekend. She had returned from Los Angeles on the Sunday night red-eye, missing him before he left for the office, but she'd been waiting for him in the kitchen when he got home Monday night. They had talked, and then the argument had begun. It started with a small thing, as all their arguments did, and he couldn't remember what had taken them down the path of blame and recrimination, but once there, they were unable to stop. Heated emotion eventually exhausted them and, just before going to bed, she had said it was over.

*

'Sophie?' He didn't expect her to answer, but he thought it advisable to confirm she was gone before he read her note. He lifted it, holding it like an unwanted gift. She had written *Aleksander* on the envelope, addressing him as she occasionally did, but only when she was being formal, or serious, or when *Alek* wouldn't get his attention. She had used Aleksander in their marriage vows, in heated arguments, and once when he'd been hit by a taxicab.

He opened the envelope. When he finished reading, he refolded the stationery and placed it back in the envelope and laid it on the table, as if that was where it belonged. He made himself a gin martini and drank half. Looking up, he happened to see his reflection in the beveled wall mirror above the breakfront. He was a little stunned, a little tired, but there was no surprise on his face and no sadness in his expression. He knew that would come later. After all, the end of a relationship was a kind of death, and sadness accompanied death. He finished the martini and made another.

Things between them had not been good for some time. His hours were long, his absences unpredictable, and his work a black box that he didn't discuss. When they'd first met, he had laid out the reasons why he would be a terrible partner, but she had ignored his warning, believing she could change him. They had discovered the challenges of day-to-day living in the first months of marriage – lost weekends, urgent calls, and the mystery of his sudden out-of-town trips. What had seemed acceptable in the fresh blush of romance became unbearable in marriage. He believed that she cherished him, and she said she did, and there was a time when his privacy was safe from reproach. They had loved, made love, enjoyed the fullness of their feelings, and seized carefree moments. God, how he had wanted a normal life with her.

Garin turned away from the mirror. He walked to the bedroom and switched on the light. Everything was in order. The bed perfectly made, each vacation photograph squared on the wall, fluffed bed pillows arranged as she liked them. It was an odd thing, he thought, to leave the room in perfect order at the moment of her flight. There was a part of her he'd come to discover that needed predictability, order, safety. His work had none of that. When they understood this, they both knew the marriage was doomed. For a long time they refused to admit they'd made a mistake. He had known her as well as he'd known any person, but now, seeing her gone, he wasn't sure he'd known her at all.

She had taken some clothes, and when he checked her jewelry box, he saw that she had taken a pair of heirloom earrings and her pearl necklace. There were empty hangers in the closet, and her rolling suitcase was missing.

He opened his desk drawer and felt underneath. Tape fixed

the hidden manila envelope to the bottom. She hadn't found his documents, or hadn't looked. He removed the envelope and confirmed that the seal was unbroken. He tossed it on the bed.

Garin moved to the kitchen and stood at the sink, looking out into the dark, snowy night. He drank a glass of water and saw his reflection in the mirrored smokiness of the window. His hand was trembling. The glass fell, shattering in the porcelain sink, and a shard pierced his palm. He bled out the cut under the faucet's cold water.

Suddenly, the telephone rang, startling him. On the second ring, he lifted the receiver.

'Sophie?'

'Alek Garin, please.'

'Yes.'

'I'm James Slattery. I am with the Agency. I'm calling on a secure line. Are you alone? Can we talk?'

'I'm alone.'

'I'm calling at the request of the deputy director. Sorry to bother you at this hour. There has been a problem in Moscow. Your name came up. We have a request for you.'

Garin's eyes came off the snow falling out the window. His silence was a sort of consent.

'Is there anything that will keep you from flying out of JFK the day after tomorrow?'

Garin closed the faucet and put pressure on his cut, cradling the phone against his neck. Sophie's sudden departure and the surprise call combined to create a surreal sense of displacement. He knew he couldn't live alone in the apartment. Memories in the familiar place would be a terrible reminder of their failure. His mind went over the half-dozen ties that would prevent him from going. 'When do I have to decide?'

'Now, actually. On this call. It's an urgent matter. The Air

France flight leaves at 5:00 p.m. We can have a car pick you up Wednesday afternoon. The driver will brief you.'

'How long?'

'Stopover in Charles de Gaulle for a further briefing. From there, you will fly to Sheremetyevo. You'll be in Moscow in seventy-two hours.'

'How long will I be gone?'

'We're not sure at this time. Weeks, certainly. Months, perhaps.'

'The money?'

There was a pause. 'We are prepared to deposit twice your usual fee in the account you've used in the past.'

The offer surprised him, not simply because of its size but because the amount implied the seriousness of the matter, and possibly also the risks. One day earlier, the danger would not have appealed to him.

He looked around the apartment. This was to have been his new life, but there had never been an end to work's demands, and never enough money. Contract jobs paid well enough, but they were unpredictable. He'd stuck with it because the work had never been just about the money. He had a figure in mind – the amount he needed to start over in another city.

Garin wrote two numbers on the notepad that hung by the wall telephone. He gave Slattery the larger number and was prepared to accept the lower, but that wasn't necessary. When the call ended, Garin placed the handset in its cradle and considered all that would now follow.

Garin entered the bedroom and lifted the manila envelope, tearing the seal. His American passport was the logical choice for the job – the name matched his driver's license, and it was the name on his marriage certificate – but there was also good reason to use the name that appeared on his Soviet passport and his birth certificate. He looked at both passports, considered where he was going, the risk of being stopped at immigration, and made his choice.

3

MOSCOW STATION

SHEREMETYEVO INTERNATIONAL AIRPORT'S WEATHER was unseasonably warm the morning that Garin stepped off Air France 1744. Winter fog was deep and gray on the tarmac, and it turned aircraft into ghost machines. His overnight flight from Paris was the last to land before air traffic controllers announced a ground stop. Passengers walked in the light mist from the plane's remote location to the new terminal under the watchful eyes of armed border guards. Garin was alert to the surveillance, becoming for the moment another fatigued passenger happy to get out of the rain.

When it was his turn at immigration, he presented his American passport and forged visa to a stern, middle-aged officer with bloodshot eyes, a loosened necktie, and a mysterious badge on his uniform. He looked twice at Garin's visa, matching photo to face, comparing the likenesses with the inscrutable expression of immigration officers everywhere, looking for a single reason to doubt the documents. Garin followed the example of other passengers, who did as they were told, moving from one queue to the next, until they extracted their bags from the carousel's conveyor belt. He opened his bag for the customs agent, who poked through his underwear and then waved him through to the glass lobby.

The embassy driver sent to collect Garin stood beyond a roped perimeter that held back eager parties waiting to greet arriving travelers. Garin nodded at his handwritten name on the driver's card and let the driver take his duffel bag.

Garin didn't talk on the drive in. His mind was preoccupied by the view from the car's window. The dense fog had lifted enough for him to see landmarks he thought he'd never see again – the brutalist architecture of grim apartment blocks, wispy coal smoke that rose straight into the air, and the sameness of the cars. How many times had he driven this route, the exact drive? There was something illusory about time and space that in the moment made him feel as if he'd never left the Soviet Union. The low visibility darkened his mood and reminded him of the morning he had been forced to flee. It still haunted him that he hadn't seen, or chose to ignore, the obvious dangers. His wishful thinking had blinded him to the treachery of men he trusted, and it was only when he'd gotten out that he had time to reflect on what had gone wrong. On instinct, he looked behind and saw a black Volga following.

'They've been there since we left the airport,' the driver said, catching Garin's eye in the rearview mirror.

Nothing has changed, he thought. *But things were different.* He was older, with a scar on his neck, another name, and a new assignment.

*

Garin was six feet, and slender for his age, which made him appear younger than he was, and his knees hit the front seat. After thirty-six hours of airport lounges and coach travel, he was exhausted, and he looked it. His cheeks had the rugged shadow of a hiker just back from a four-day trek. It was a masculine face but not a tough face, and fatigue had darkened his preoccupation. His slacks had lost their crease, his shirt was gray with perspiration, and his wide tie was loosened at the neck and fell across his chest like a lanyard. When he saw the embassy, he tightened the necktie's knot and swept back his hair.

'We've been expecting you,' Ronnie Moffat said when Garin stepped from the car at the embassy's side entrance. 'I'll bring you up.' She hustled Garin past the marine guard.

Moscow Station was a cramped suite of rooms on the seventh floor. Bricked-up windows gave the vestibule they entered from the elevator a claustrophobic feeling. The small room served as a kind of air lock in which non-Agency personnel were allowed to read classified material. They moved toward a door without a handle or keyhole and no opening except a peephole for those inside to see who wanted to enter.

'Listening devices were found in the beams,' Ronnie said, noting his wandering eyes. 'Two years ago, an electric typewriter had to be quarantined. We found a KGB microprocessor under the typewriter's keypad that recorded each stroke and sent the data to the power cord, which transmitted it wirelessly.'

She swiped her badge against the electronic wall pad, causing the door to swing open automatically, and they entered a long, crowded area of cubicles and cramped offices. Overnight cipher clerks transcribed and decrypted coded messages from Headquarters, working reverse shifts to accommodate the time difference. Little had changed, Garin thought, as he stepped into Moscow Station, calibrating what he remembered against what he saw.

Ronnie pointed to a conference room that was encased in inch-thick Plexiglas. 'Secure conversations take place there. We call it the Bubble.'

'Aleksander Garin,' she announced, opening the conference room door.

George Mueller sat at one end of a long conference table, and next to him was another man Garin did not recognize. Garin nodded at each one, but he settled on Mueller. Mueller's right eye was a purpled spider web, which gave him the look of a man who had been on the losing end of a fistfight, and his left hand was splinted and bandaged. Mueller's overcoat draped a chair, and his bulky garment bag leaned against the wall. An airplane ticket, his black diplomatic passport, and an open file lay in front of him on the table.

'Your car is ready to take you to the airport,' Ronnie said.

'When I'm done here,' Mueller replied, and then he looked at Garin. 'Sit down. You keep looking at my face. You've never seen the KGB's handiwork? It could be worse. I'll have it looked at in Washington.' He nodded. 'Yes, I've been declared persona non grata and expelled. This is my deputy, John Rositske.'

'Long trip?' Rositske said.

'No more than usual.' Garin met Mueller's eyes without acknowledging that they knew each other. He turned to Rositske. 'Just the two of you?'

'For now,' Mueller said. 'Surveillance?'

'One car. They dropped back when we crossed the bridge.'

'Immigration?'

'No trouble.'

Garin saw Rositske stare at him like a bored house cat watching a sparrow through a window. 'What?'

'Your name?' he said. 'I drew a blank when your name came through on the cable from Headquarters. I read that you're a native Russian speaker. That surprised me. I'm familiar with all the case officers in the division who work on Soviet affairs. I've never come across your name. How is that possible?'

'I don't work in the SE Division.' Garin took a measure of the two men opposite. He flattened his accent to rid it of clues of who he was or where he was from, and he gave an account of the phone call and the details of his departure from New York, leaving out only personal details that weren't germane. Garin had mastered the art of separating life and work. He spoke about the trip with the calm of a man who long ago had surrendered his will to the sudden demands of unpredictable covert work. 'I was told there's a mess to clean up.'

'We *don't* have a mess,' Rositske said in his Texas drawl.

'There was another breach,' Mueller interrupted. 'The KGB knew I would be in Red Square.' Mueller folded his hands on the table solemnly. He nodded at late-arriving staff coming through the peephole entrance door. 'That's why we are in here. It's just the three of us for now.'

Coffee was brought in. Garin took his black with four sugars that he measured carefully, stirring slowly counterclockwise, and then he drank it all at once. He listened to Mueller describe the Station's loss of MOBILE, PANDER, and two others he didn't identify.

'We can't afford another loss,' Mueller said. He described the few details they had on the man known only as GAMBIT. 'He took a terrible risk when he slid the note into my car. I'm a known intelligence officer who is watched by the KGB. He was visibly nervous in our first meeting but clearly aware of what he is doing. He refused to give me his name or his position. But he knew a lot about me, and he had knowledge of our operations, so I assume he is high-ranking KGB or GRU. He brought excerpts of military weapons specifications to prove his value. The Pentagon confirmed the documents are authentic. They are eager to get their hands on his intelligence. The Soviets are building weapons that we haven't figured out how to design.'

Mueller adjusted his splint. 'GAMBIT asked me to be his handler, but I said that was impossible. I'm too visible. He was adamant that he didn't want a randomly assigned handler.

He also doesn't speak English, so he wants a Russian speaker. In our first meeting, he threw out several names. I got the impression that he's been planning this for some time. Before I was blown, we agreed on communication protocols – drop points, signals, meeting places – and he gave me the person he wanted to be his handler – the man who handled General Zyuganov.' Mueller looked at Garin. 'That must be you.'

Garin didn't respond. 'What does he want?'

'Money.'

'They all want money. What else?'

'We haven't gotten that far.'

'Defect?'

'Yes, he'll probably want to be brought out.'

Garin clapped his hands slowly twice. 'Perhaps we can have a band play farewell when he boards Aeroflot and waves goodbye.' Garin leaned forward and growled, 'You have *never* exfiltrated a KGB officer from Moscow.' Garin grunted his skepticism. He went for his coffee, but he put down the cup when he saw that it was empty.

'You're not with the Agency, are you?' Rositske said.

'I left.'

'What have you been doing?'

'Whatever I'm paid to do. Contract work.'

'What does that mean?'

'White papers,' he said dismissively.

'On?'

'Counterintelligence,' he snapped.

Rositske smiled. 'Who thought a guy with a desk job was the right man to run a covert operation in Moscow?'

Mueller placed a restraining hand on Rositske's arm. 'John.'

'No,' Rositske said. 'I want to know the answer.'

Garin leaned back in his chair, exciting a creak. 'I am quite certain of my qualifications.'

'What are those qualifications, besides speaking the language?'

'Talk to GAMBIT. He seems to know.'

'Zyuganov was compromised,' Rositske snarled. 'How does a spectacular failure qualify you?'

Garin stood. 'I don't need this.' Garin had known men like Rositske, who wore their toughness with a superior attitude. Men who believed difficult intelligence problems were better solved with brute force than the puppet strings of psychology. 'I am happy to leave this problem in your capable hands.'

'Sit down,' Mueller said. He turned to Rositske. 'I'd like a minute alone with Alek.'

*

Garin's cup had been refilled. He stirred in the four sugars in the same slow counterclockwise motion, and when he was satisfied the sugar was dissolved, he sipped, looking over the cup's lip at Mueller.

'He'll be a problem going forward,' Garin said.

'He doesn't know anything about you.'

'As it should be. What do you know?'

Mueller made sure the conference room door was closed. 'I know you left the Agency. I know General Zyuganov was executed. I've heard the rumors. Ambitious men distance themselves from failures to protect their careers.'

'You get used to it.'

'You never get used to it. If you say you do, then you're fooling yourself.'

Garin said nothing.

'How's Sophie?'

'It's over. We're finished.'

'No one tells you that side of the work,' Mueller said. 'Never

32

having an ordinary life. There is nothing ordinary about this work. The best of us burn out, drink too much, or leave.'

'Don't lecture me.'

Mueller looked at Garin. 'Why did GAMBIT ask for you?'

'I said I don't know. This job came out of nowhere. Three days ago I got a call at midnight and I was on a plane forty-eight hours later. I was handed my visa when I landed in Paris.' He looked at Mueller. 'Things haven't changed, have they?'

'When were you blown?'

'Carter's term. Revolutionary Guards had taken the embassy in Tehran. Then General Zyuganov was lost. I was undercover with the Second Chief Directorate, gathering shit on Moscow Station. Then the leak happened.'

'Their side or ours?'

'We never knew.'

'Were there grudges? Is GAMBIT a lure to reel you in?'

'There are always grudges. They lost assets in Washington. Networks were rolled up. It was a bad time for them. Maybe they're smarter now.'

'You're a risk.' Mueller's eyes drifted to the hallway, where Agency staff getting off the elevator pretended not to be aware of the two men sitting in the Bubble. 'But you're an outsider. That qualifies you.' Mueller leaned forward. 'I was compromised by someone inside Moscow Station. Black lights showed a phosphorescent chemical on my hands when I was picked up. My guess – METKA. I was tagged, probably here in the embassy.' Mueller met Garin's eyes. 'And there's another reason why you're suitable for this assignment.' He slid a black-and-white photograph across the table. 'Talinov.'

Garin studied the official portrait – the grim, unsmiling lieutenant colonel with his chest of medals and a high-crown cap with a single red star. Garin remembered the slightly ascetic face. Thinking eyes, thin lips, and a long, beaked nose that gave him a predatory visage. It was a face that was hard to forget.

'He interrogated me,' Mueller said. 'He knows we're working an asset, and he knows the asset is senior. His questions were vague and speculative, but he found the package I was carrying – money, camera, radio transmitter. He knows enough to make your job dangerous.'

Mueller paused. 'GAMBIT will reach out. Check a postal box on your way here in the morning and look for his chalk mark. I've arranged a desk on the second floor. You'll be working in the consular section as a temporary, non-diplomatic liaison to Helsinki Watch. You are on your own. This is the last time you come to the seventh floor, understand?'

'How many people know about GAMBIT?'

'Rositske. Me. Now, you.'

'Was he the leak?'

Mueller looked away. 'John is a good case officer, but as you saw, he is a man shaped by his experiences, and he plays his chess game one move ahead. That's not good enough.' Mueller wrote down two phone numbers in Washington, DC, and pushed the paper across to Garin. 'Contact me by pouch or, if necessary, encrypted telephone. You'll work for Helen Walsh, who is our MI6 liaison operating as commercial counselor with the State Department. She's not in the loop – keep it that way. Ronnie will get you what you need.'

Mueller stood. The meeting was over. He gathered his files and stuffed them in his attaché case. 'You will need to make Rositske your ally. He controls staffing and money. You may not like each other, but this operation won't succeed unless you work together. He is subtler than he appears, and you, I suspect, are more violent than you make out.'

Mueller stuffed an arm into his big winter overcoat and hefted his garment bag. At the door, he turned to Garin. 'Life rarely offers second chances. Don't squander this one.'

Later, on the plane home, Mueller made a note in his diary, a random entry that he consulted when he wrote up his account of the whole episode: *Meeting didn't go well. I knew him in the past. Moody. Sullen. Drank too much. When his mood improved and his drinking slowed, he did good work. He was never good with authority or women. Let's see what happens.*

*

It surprised no one when a memo announced that Aleksander Garin had joined the staff as Consular Officer, Human Rights. The news was largely ignored by harried staff, who struggled with the urgent political demands of the Soviet Union's long war in Afghanistan. Great political significance accompanied America's attack on the Soviet Union's treatment of ethnic minorities, gypsies, artists, intellectuals, writers, and Jews, but he was met with mild indifference when he introduced himself as the new man. Garin was happy with their response. The best cover was to be *visible*. Men without purpose attracted attention. All he had to do was draw attention to a purpose that distracted the observer from his real work. Garin's visit to the seventh floor on his first day was noted but ignored. Every newcomer to the embassy was required to visit Moscow Station and be lectured on KGB surveillance, life in Moscow, and the danger of Russians wanting to befriend Americans.

The process of establishing his cover could have been protracted, but Garin had no time for that. In full view of his supervisor, Garin joined a fast crowd of junior staff. He put himself forward as the slightly older, amicable fellow who shook hands, remembered names, and could be counted on to tell a good story. People found it easy to like him and easy to dismiss him – another overqualified consular officer doing missionary work. They let off steam after work in bars friendly to the city's diplomatic corps or in private apartments. He became a gregarious drinker, and he made sure to fit in, often going in the company of Ronnie Moffat, who became his sidekick. A few nights of loud, boisterous drinking quickly established a notoriety that got around. Smart, well-spoken, until he'd had too much to drink. Then he developed a kind of stupidity, the sort found in men who drank too much and, being unaware of themselves, began to speak loudly and make inappropriate advances. He was aware of the impression he was creating, and for a meticulous man who had those tendencies, he easily acquired the reputation of a dissolute malcontent.

It was that way in the embassy as well. He arrived late for meetings and told anyone willing to listen that he'd been taken off a distribution list or had not gotten a response to his memo. Helen Walsh's secretary didn't return his calls and admonished him when he arrived late. With time, even Helen, who covered for him and indulged his lapses, began to avoid him. He arrived with goodwill and quickly squandered it. Little by little he was politely laughed offstage and became a man in whom no one took much interest. He ate alone in the cafeteria. He became a solitary figure who belonged to the sad class of ambitious, middle-aged men politely excluded from the mainstream – an eager runner at tryouts banished from the team. That's when the rumor started. Although he was newly arrived, he would be gone soon.

*

Garin had been in Moscow four weeks when he found GAMBIT's signal: two vertical chalk marks on a postal box. He had left his apartment before nine, as he did every day, taking a route that passed by the tobacco kiosk outside

Novokuznetskaya Metro Station. He was careful to avoid the neighborhood haunts of his previous Moscow life, and that morning he crunched across the rutted snowbanks into swirls of bus exhaust.

The chalk marks were where he'd been told to look. White chalk on the side of a red postal box. There was a note with the details of a meeting waiting for him in the lobby of a building.

Garin entered the metro station. He stopped to light a cigarette, failing until he turned his back to the wind, and then he casually looked for the single surveillance officer who had sporadically followed him during his first weeks in Moscow, but he was gone.

4

VVEDENSKOYE CEMETERY

GARIN STOOD OUTSIDE THE cemetery's iron gate, having stopped to purchase a red rose from a peddler whose only business was to sell twenty-kopek plastic flowers to the occasional visitor. Garin, feeling generous, had placed a fifty-kopek coin in the old woman's hand and received a startled reaction.

He entered the cemetery holding the artificial rose in his right hand and the day's paper under his arm. He moved along the narrow stone path that lay under a canopy of frost-stiffened branches. Even at noon, the winter sun was low on the sky and cast long shadows on the rows of untended graves.

Garin looked for the man who, like him, would be carrying a red rose. The cemetery was an old, neglected place with a few mausoleums built for dignitaries who had died before the October Revolution, and newer crypts of simpler socialist design. He glanced at the names on the graves and saw pithy inscriptions on several that had meant something to the dead or to the one who had paid for the crypt. Everywhere there was a light dusting of snow. On the path ahead, footsteps of another visitor were being filled with gently falling powder, which also covered the graves' names, and when he thought he was at the right spot, he wiped away the snow.

But a young woman in a black shearling coat, who stood a

few meters away, had no doubt about the deceased's identity. She was tall, with raven hair, a leather handbag, dark glasses, a scarf wrapped around her head, and a cigarette in her mouth, which she threw to the ground before saying, without turning her head, 'General Zyuganov.'

Garin saw a rose in her hand, but it was white not red. He'd assumed he was meeting a man, but he couldn't recall whether he had been told to expect a man or had simply assumed that GAMBIT was a man. And the rose was wrong. He waited for her to ask the time, and in the moment that followed, he recognized her rudeness and the annoying Russian insistence on one-word answers, and then too, when she added, 'The traitor,' he heard in her voice the casual sarcasm that passed for polite conversation in Moscow.

She stood at the neighboring crypt. 'Maria Yudina,' she said, seeing Garin's interest. 'The pianist.'

It was not until the winter sun had sunk a few degrees, touching the treetops, and the cold had begun to numb his fingers, that Garin knew that the woman wasn't there to meet him – and she wasn't going to leave. She had lit another cigarette, and taken one long, nervous draw, releasing smoke from the corner of her mouth, when she glanced at Garin. Their eyes met, but she quickly looked away. Silence lingered between them.

'The gate closes shortly,' he said. 'You might want to be gone before you're locked in. The guard sleeps off his vodka lunch. It will be hours before he comes back. You'll freeze to death.'

She nodded and smiled.

'Muggers know the guards leave at noon,' Garin said. 'They prey on visitors like you.'

She shot a sideways glance. 'This is Moscow. There is no crime here.'

'That's a nice leather handbag you've got. It would fetch a good price.'

She clutched her bag protectively.

'People are the same everywhere,' Garin said. 'The same appetites, the same diseases cured by the same medicines, attracted to the same fine leather bags. There was crime before the Party, and there will be crime when it's gone.'

She gasped. 'Only a foreigner would speak like that.'

'Or a thief,' he said. 'Don't worry, I have no interest in your bag, as nice as it is, and I can see that it is well made.' He looked again at his watch, cursing the meeting time that had already passed. 'It's a three-minute walk to the gate. If you leave now, you'll still get there before the guard locks up. You're not dressed like a person who wants to climb the fence.'

'The gate,' she said, bristling, 'closes for me at the same time that it closes for you.' She nodded at him. 'You keep looking at your watch. Perhaps you are the one who is worried about the gate.' She suddenly turned. '*Izvinitye.*' Excuse me. She stepped forward so she was beside him. 'If you don't mind.'

He stepped back. She brushed away twigs that had fallen on General Zyuganov's crypt, tidying the grave of debris fallen from trees in the last storm. She placed her white rose on the top of the crypt, aligning it respectfully.

'Even traitors need to be remembered,' she said.

Her voice was brusque but polite, a soft, stern voice. She contemplated the general's framed photograph fixed to the stone. A memory. She removed her mitten and ran her fingers over the name cut into the marble. Her eyes closed, and her lips moved soundlessly.

Then she stepped back and used her knuckle to wipe a tear. Abruptly, she pulled her mitten onto her hand and whispered, 'A traitor to the Party.' Her expression was once again cold and remorseless.

She nodded at the adjacent grave. 'Like her.' Faded flowers and a field of spent candles had turned Maria Yudina's grave into a shrine. 'We honor our heroes and our artists, but not our traitors.'

'You knew him?' Garin asked, nodding at Zyuganov's portrait.

'What do you think?' she snapped. 'I'm standing here.' She looked at Garin. 'And what brings you to this spot?'

Garin used the moment to put his mind around an answer that wouldn't seem obviously false. He stepped forward to Maria Yudina's grave and laid his plastic rose among the others along the foot of the vault. 'I've heard the stories. I came to see for myself.' Garin had placed his plastic flower when he heard the sharp crack of a twig breaking nearby and a cough, and he saw that the woman beside him was suddenly agitated. She looked nervously toward a gap between two ponderous mausoleums, but when he followed her eyes, he saw nothing.

'A man,' she whispered in an urgent voice. 'I must leave. It is not good to be seen here. It is better that you let me go ahead, and better still that we not be seen together. And the best thing is to forget that we met. It would be the kindest thing, if you have any respect for the man in this grave. Good day.'

She didn't wait for his response and began to walk quickly down the path. She was gone in a moment, having turned a corner and disappeared between two mausoleums. Garin saw only her long striding footprints in the snow and heard, farther off, the sounds of her footsteps.

How quickly one becomes aware of silence even in so silent a place as a cemetery.

Another cough. The man who had driven her off emerged from his hiding place. He was a big man who walked lightly and gave the impression of bulk without weight. He looked at Garin with an intense agitation, and his hand was shoved in his pocket as if holding a weapon. He didn't look like a KGB officer. He looked like a professor, or somebody's father, a well-dressed, well-fed man graying at the temples who had an air of uncertainty about him and a look of trepidation.

Garin hesitated. Was this a KGB officer sent to chat him up and then *'Amerikanets! Ostanovis!'*? The hand on the shoulder, the other motioning for backup to make the arrest? Garin took in the man all at once, judging the threat and wondering if the woman had been part of an elaborate ruse. But then the stranger revealed a red rose under his right arm. He approached slowly, and when he stood beside Garin, he placed the flower at the base of General Zyuganov's crypt.

'Any chance you know the time?' the man asked.

'It's past midnight.'

'Finally.'

Garin met GAMBIT's eyes. The two men took each other in, cautious, tentatively curious. Strangers joined by conspiracy.

'Who was she?' GAMBIT asked.

'A grieving woman. She couldn't take a hint.'

GAMBIT grunted. 'This place isn't safe now.' Quiet for a moment. His eyes darted between the marble mausoleums. 'Come,' he said. He directed Garin toward the exit. 'You plan for everything, but you can't count on bad luck. I have another spot. We can talk without an audience.' He nodded at Zyuganov's grave. 'My wife's idea to meet here. She said no one would guess.' He paused. 'You're alone?'

'Yes.'

'Surveillance?'

'I lost them in Arbatskaya Metro Station.'

'You're sure?'

'Yes.'

'So it was only her?'

'Are you worried about her?'

'I worry about whatever I want to worry about. We'll take my car.'

5

SOKOLNIKI AMUSEMENT PARK

BLISTERING COLD MADE IT an afternoon like many others in February. GAMBIT had made Garin wait behind a palomino on the merry-go-round, and he waited an ungodly amount of time for GAMBIT to return from the park's administrative office, closed for the winter except for two guards who had put on large winter coats at GAMBIT's direction. They took the bottle of port GAMBIT held out.

'Hurry up,' GAMBIT said, ushering them out the door. 'She'll be here any minute. Your two ugly faces will scare her off.'

Garin watched the two men disappear behind the rusting Ferris wheel, idled like a junkyard memory, and emerged when GAMBIT waved him forward.

'Friends from my hometown,' he said. 'Quick. Inside.' He closed the door, and Garin found himself in a spare room with a small woodstove, empty shelves, a table made of plywood, and one small, dirty window that provided the room's only light. Red-hot coals warmed the room.

'I give them a bottle, and they go away for a few hours so I can meet my girlfriend. It's good they didn't see you. They'd suspect I was *goluboy*.' Queer. GAMBIT shrugged. 'Married fifteen years. I've never cheated once, but it's guys like me that those two would think, yes, it's possible, he's a deviant. Vlad, the older one with the limp and a pig's nose, is a distant cousin. The other one, Alexei, is smarter. Hates the Party, hates anyone from Moscow. He's a *muzhik*, like me, but I'm a KGB lieutenant colonel and he's a *muzhik* guard at Sokolniki Amusement Park. He is smarter than me in all ways but one – he never learned to keep his mouth shut and his opinions to himself.'

GAMBIT removed his bulky overcoat for the heat of the stove. His first question cut short any further small talk. 'Vodka or whiskey?'

'Vodka.'

'Good.' GAMBIT pulled a bottle from the cupboard and placed it on the plywood table with two glasses. Then he laid out a package of brown waxed paper, which he proceeded to unwrap, revealing a selection of cured meats. He removed a loaf of black bread from a cloth bag.

'*Zakuski*,' he said. 'Talking is better if we eat and drink first. There's blood sausage, pig's knuckles, smoked white fish. I told them to leave it. I said I needed something tasty for the girlfriend.'

GAMBIT cut a slice with his pocketknife and carried the morsel to his mouth on the blade, all the while keeping his eyes on Garin. 'So, who are you?'

'An American.'

'The hell you are. Your accent. A deserter or a refugee. Those guys are all *nashi*. Native Russian speakers are all collaborators.'

Garin took a slice GAMBIT offered on his blade. 'Who do you think I am?'

'You look Russian, but you don't act like a Russian. What I can't figure out is how you learned Russian.'

'One day I'll tell you.'

GAMBIT laughed. 'You're an émigré. That's my guess. Taken

out as a child by nervous bourgeois parents. How old are you? Forty-five?' He pondered Garin. 'Forty?'

Garin ignored GAMBIT's speculation, saying his age didn't matter, and eventually GAMBIT tired of the silence. He laid his knife on the plywood. 'What happened to the other who was taken on Red Square?'

'Expelled.'

'I heard the rumors inside the directorate. It was too close. I could smell the shit in his pants. They were waiting for him. Where is he?'

'Don't worry about him. I'm the only one you'll be dealing with.' He looked at GAMBIT. 'You requested me?'

'I asked for the one who lost Zyuganov.' GAMBIT made a generous pour of vodka and raised his glass, but he stopped, hesitating at the point where his lips tasted the liquor. 'So you're him?' He threw back the drink and poured a second glass.

'Yes.'

GAMBIT raised his glass in a toast. '*Na zdorovye.*' To your health. 'We'll need it.'

Garin emptied his glass, recognizing the metallic taste of local alcohol, and he went drink for drink on his way to establishing trust during their first meeting. 'So,' he said, 'why me?'

'Why you?' GAMBIT smiled a self-satisfied smile, like a cat who had cornered a mouse. 'Why a man who failed General Zyuganov? You must know he was executed.' GAMBIT's finger rose to the nape of his neck. 'He was shot in a basement cell in Lubyanka. Made to kneel, head forward. One bullet. Yes, why a man responsible for that?'

GAMBIT judged Garin. 'It doesn't make sense from your point of view, but if you are me, the thing that makes no sense is to put my life in the hands of a new man with no experience who only wants to advance his career. For him, failure is expulsion and a long flight home. For me – and for you – it's our lives. KGB officers don't survive two failures, and I think the CIA is the same. We both succeed, or we both fail. I trust a man who has as much to lose as I do. You are such a man. Am I right?' GAMBIT waited for an answer, but when he didn't get one, he added, 'I see doubt in your eyes. You think I'm playing you. If that were true, the KGB would be at the door already.'

Garin felt the workings of a self-conscious intelligence that could easily be mistaken for an amateur. In their roles, he was the handler, but he felt himself being handled. It didn't matter if GAMBIT was wrong because there was no going back.

Garin slowly poured himself another drink, watching the clear alcohol rise in his glass, and lifted it in a toast. '*Za vashe zdorovye.*'

'We should introduce ourselves,' GAMBIT said. 'What's your name?'

Garin slid his laminated identity card across the table: name, recent photograph, title. GAMBIT looked at it and then slid his own card across the table. 'Take a good look. It's as phony as yours. At least the idiots who created yours didn't name you Lenin.'

'Okay,' Garin said, taking back his card. 'Then who the hell are you?'

'First business. I want the camera, radio, and money I was promised.'

Garin removed a cloth bag from his overcoat's pocket and placed it on the table. He knew that when money entered the conversation, it was likely that money was GAMBIT's motive, no matter how much political gloss he daubed on his reasons for working with the CIA. It was a sort of fraternity between them. Money served many purposes, established understanding, and each man had his own reasons for wanting it. He stared at

GAMBIT counting the stack of rubles, flicking the bills with his wetted finger.

'I asked for two hundred thousand. This is shit.' He pushed the money back. 'You think I'm joking.'

'Why so much? Where would you spend it?' Garin had objected to Rositske, who had insisted on cutting GAMBIT's down payment in half to keep him on a short leash.

'I don't need to spend it. Understand?'

'So why two hundred thousand?'

Garin recognized in GAMBIT a man who engaged with other men on the principle of advance and retreat. When challenged, he stepped back from an outrageous request, and when he felt weakness, he pushed forward. He was the type who didn't respect weakness in other men, and he reserved his esteem for men who challenged him.

'To judge how serious you are,' GAMBIT said. 'To see how much I'm worth to you.'

'I'll recommend it. The rest will go into a Swiss bank account in your name. It's yours when the job is done.'

'So, you're just the errand boy. The CIA,' GAMBIT scoffed. 'A bureaucracy of permissions.' He stared. 'I am not putting my family's safety in the hands of a Washington deskman who folds up work early and goes to a hotel to fuck his girlfriend. Do you understand?'

'You'll have the money.'

'Good.' GAMBIT tossed back his drink. 'Let's start.'

'What's your name?'

GAMBIT hesitated, and then smiled. 'The point of no return.' He took a red leather wallet from his jacket and removed an official identity document issued by the Chief Intelligence Directorate of the Komitet Gosudarstvennoy Bezopasnosti. Garin compared the embossed photograph to the man sitting opposite – Lieutenant Colonel Viktor Semyonovich Petrov, forty-eight-years-old. He committed the identity number and birthplace to memory and handed it back. He knew he was looking at an authentic document: worn paper, crisp embossing, good ink.

'*Khorosho.*' Okay. Garin had what he'd come for. If GAMBIT got cold feet, his name could be used against him: blackmail, threat of exposure, the point of no return.

'What's your position?'

'Deputy head, Third Department, Fifth Chief Directorate.'

Garin went down the list of questions he'd been given and recorded answers in his spiral notebook. It was a standard list of questions – overseas postings, positions held, personal background, names of colleagues. Standard material to confirm Petrov's bona fides.

'Where do you work?'

'Seventh floor, KGB Headquarters. Dzerzhinsky Square.'

'Lubyanka?'

'Have you been there?'

'No.' *A lie.*

'It has the best view in Moscow,' he said, and laughed. 'From the basement, you can see all the way to Siberia.'

Garin saw he was more comfortable now, opening up with an old joke.

'I work on the DOM1 side, on the seventh floor, which is inconvenient, because the passage to DOM2, the place where I copy documents, is on the fifth floor. It is a marvel of Soviet misplanning. DOM1 is from before the Revolution and the other was built by Stalin, but they don't quite line up.' Petrov's hands widened a short distance. 'I have to walk down the stairs, then across, and then back up, and in the whole process I am carrying secret papers. So, you can imagine what people ask. "Viktor, what are you doing, walking up and down?" I have to be clever with my answers. The stress is not good for my heart.' Petrov took a deep breath and lightly patted his chest.

'By the way, for our next meeting I want you to bring ginseng root. It's good for stress, my wife says. Moscow shops don't carry it. Can you have it shipped in via diplomatic pouch?'

'Of course.' Garin watched Petrov finish his second glass of vodka. *Drinking and stress*, he thought. *A bad combination.*

'What do you call me?' Petrov asked. 'We give every asset a cryptonym. You must do it, too. What's mine?' When he saw Garin pause, he added, 'Look, I'm not just being nosy. From time to time, I see the encrypted cables that we intercept. If a cable with my cryptonym comes across my desk, I need to know if I'm in it. What if the KGB commentary on the cable is "We're close to uncovering this sonofabitch"? You should want me to know to protect myself.'

'GAMBIT.' Garin spelled it. 'A chess term, but it has no meaning here.' Codenames were taken from a sterile list of random words that had no rhyme or reason, and no connection to an operation.

Petrov presented a hand-drawn sketch to Garin. 'This is the lobby of the building where I will drop exposed film. There is a radiator. I will leave an envelope between the radiator and the wall.'

Garin demonstrated the camera he'd brought. It was the Agency's most sophisticated miniature camera, one-sixth the size of a Minox and small enough to be concealed in a Montblanc pen. He had brought two – one as a backup. The film, lens, and shutter were housed in an aluminum casing and the eight miniature ground-glass lenses were stacked vertically to enable high-resolution photographs of technical drawings in low light. Garin showed Petrov how to place the end of the pen thirty centimeters over the document and click once.

'With this, you won't need to use the copier.'

Petrov wagged his finger. 'Don't tell me how to work. You think I can walk out with the originals.' His brow creased, and his eyes narrowed. 'Don't tell me things you know nothing about, and I won't reject your suggestions. Those are my ground rules. If you agree, we'll make progress. And by the way, I need more film.' He held up the dozen tiny canisters. 'There are hundreds of documents, the entire cache of Soviet weapons in development. I will copy as much as I can by May 28.'

It was the first time Garin had heard the date.

'It's Border Guard Day,' Petrov explained. 'Many guards take the day off, and those who are on duty drink. It is the best day to cross the border. I will have most of the film on me. It will be me, my wife, and our five-year-old son.'

Garin looked hard at Petrov. 'You're crazy. You will be hard enough to get out. A five-year-old? We'll send for them.'

Petrov stood. 'Fuck off. Those are my terms. My family comes with me, or you can walk out the door.'

Garin stretched out his long legs and gazed up at the big man with his weak heart. He respected Petrov's concern for his family, but emotional attachments, he had learned, were the jeopardy that compromised an operation. Still, the purpose of this meeting was simple – get to a second meeting.

'Which border?' Garin asked.

Petrov sat down. 'Two choices. Uzhgorod is on the Czech border. A lot of smugglers cross there, but it's a long train ride. Raja-Jooseppi on the Finnish border is two hours closer and the terrain is remote. They might expect that, but sometimes it's better to do what they expect.'

Petrov looked around the room. The glow of burning coals had dimmed during the meeting as the coals became dark embers. 'This is a good place to meet,' Petrov said. 'There are no safe houses in Moscow. People listen. Neighbors talk. This will do. The lunkheads you saw won't suspect anything, and if you do your part, they won't see you. They'll think I'm having a good time with my girlfriend. I know their gripes. They hate the Party.'

Petrov drew a sharp breath, and his eyes settled warily on Garin. 'It was Talinov at Red Square. I recognized him. I don't believe in coincidence. How many people will know my name?'

'Me. Two, maybe three, in Langley.'

'Moscow Station?'

'One.'

'One too many.' Petrov wrapped the leftover meats for the guards. 'One more thing,' he said. 'I need medicine for my son. It is not possible to get the medicine in Moscow.' Petrov wrote the name of the medicine on a piece of paper, which he handed to Garin. 'I need this for his seizures.'

Petrov looked around the room. 'Yes, this shithole will do for now. You pass for a Russian. You speak Russian. I've met Americans who don't understand how much they stand out.'

Petrov had stood, but feeling the warmth of the bond they were forming and reluctant to go into the cold, he sat once again. He poured himself a smaller glass of vodka and threw it back. 'There is a joke about Americans who come here thinking they know us. One day the Second Chief Directorate was going crazy looking for an American illegal. The American had been thoroughly trained, his identity documents were flawless, he dressed like a Russian, and he spoke fluent Russian. But his work in Russia was never successful. One day this illegal – let's call him Peter – drank with another American illegal, a friend, and he complained about his failure. "Dimitri," he said, "what's my problem? I speak fluent Russian, I sing ballads like a Russian, and I go man to man drinking with Russians." "Yes, you do," his friend said. "So, what's the problem? How is it that I don't fit in?" Peter asked. The friend said, "Peter, you're black."'

Petrov's eyes sparkled, enjoying the joke. He carefully

measured another glass of vodka and swallowed it at once. 'Here's another,' he said. 'Then we will go. Same idea. There is an official meeting in the KGB's Dzerzhinsky Club, where higher-ups go. There are one hundred officers in a room facing a dais where a few important colonels are making speeches. The junior officers sit together in the audience, chatting during the speeches, which, as usual, are long and tedious. The first junior officer says to his neighbor, "Lyosha, we spotted a CIA mole among us." "Really?" the second officer says. "Which one is he?" "Row ten, just on the aisle, with a red tie. Can't you tell? He's the one paying attention."'

Petrov's smile vanished when he looked at Garin. 'You laugh when we make fun of ourselves. That's the thing about you Americans. You're dull, serious, smug, but easily fooled, and you underestimate us. We have perfected look-down radar systems that are a generation ahead of your best technology. We are many things, and we have many failures, but we are not stupid.'

Garin saw that Petrov had drunk too much. He saw in Petrov the struggle of a man who disliked America but who felt himself an outsider in the Soviet Union, holding dangerous opinions. They both stood and were at the door.

'What can you tell me about Zyuganov?' Garin asked.

Petrov was suddenly alert, and his eyes narrowed. He looked at Garin warily. 'He was executed. No one believes the official story. He was Andropov's man heading up the KGB's anti-corruption crusade – and you don't make friends that way.' Petrov was close to Garin. 'He worked with you.'

'Who betrayed him?'

Petrov cupped a match against the wind in the open door and drew on his filterless Prima. He blew gamy smoke from the corner of his mouth and eyed Garin. After a second quick pull on the cigarette, he tossed it to the ground. He thrust one arm into his overcoat but kept his eyes on Garin. 'Who said he was betrayed? Caught? Yes.'

Petrov shoved his other arm in the sleeve. He had the expression of a man who was done with the conversation. He turned sullenly and walked toward the Ferris wheel. But having gone a few meters he stopped suddenly and turned. 'It's in the past,' he said. 'Leave it there.'

6

TOWER 324
VERNADSKY PROSPEKT

Doubt wasn't new to Garin. He'd lived with doubt for years, and with doubt came fear. His childhood fear had been crippling, but he had trained himself to confront his demons. He tested himself against the dark, sleeping in his bedroom without the night light, trembling and afraid to close his eyes but unwilling to surrender. As a ten-year-old, he had stood at the edge of an abandoned quarry, inching toward the precipice, feeling the nausea of vertigo. He had closed his eyes, feeling the lip with his toes and imagining the hundred-foot drop. He made fear his companion, and he came to understand that men who weren't afraid were either lying to themselves or colossally stupid. These experiences had shaped the one true thing he knew about himself: his need to do the opposite of what was expected of him was often stronger that the threat of harm that might befall him if he went ahead.

Garin didn't see the prostitute at first. He felt a presence on the sidewalk when he was outside his apartment block, but she was there when he looked a second time. She wore high heels, a fur scarf, and gaudy red lipstick, and she had wide eyes that invited him to join her. Of course he was tempted, and of course he knew the last thing he should do is let himself be fooled by a local prostitute. He smiled at her air kisses but shook his head.

Garin stood at his ninth-floor apartment door. The hallway was quiet, but he knew that even at a late hour there would be curious, or frightened, neighbors who would crack open their doors at a hint of trouble.

Garin placed his hand high on the doorjamb and found the single strand of hair still in place. He'd fixed it with egg white in the morning, and it had held fast. He undid the mortise lock, turned the key to open the bolt, and entered.

He'd been billeted in temporary housing arranged by a nice woman in the embassy's personnel department. The small apartment was dark when he entered. The embassy had provided used furniture from storage – a white cotton sofa with wine stains from someone else's party, unmatched dining chairs, chipped plates, and a greasy saucepan.

There was nothing personal about the apartment, nothing that made it belong to him. He preferred it that way. It would be easier to leave it. There was nothing to attach to, and when he left, it would all stay behind. The blank walls and empty windows didn't depress him. They were a reminder that he was there to sleep, and when his work was done, he would move on. Nothing in the apartment would help investigators establish who he was.

The refrigerator had moldy cheese, four dozen eggs, and three beers, and he took one. He undressed in the dark and drew a bath. Electricity for the water heater shut off at 9:00 p.m., so the water was cold, almost shocking, but he slipped into the porcelain tub until only his head was above water. This too was a test he gave himself. His chest tightened, and his member shriveled, ridding him of fatigue and urges. He thought briefly of the prostitute, but then he closed his mind to concentrate on all that he needed to accomplish by May 28. As he did, his thoughts drifted back to the night he lost General Zyuganov, trying to find the conducting threads of that labyrinth.

He opened his eyes and stepped out of the tub. He was cadaver white, and his hands were wrinkled like a newborn's, but his mind was sharp. He began his handwritten note to Mueller at the small desk that faced the dark Moscow skyline. This note, and the ones that followed, would later serve Mueller when he assembled his account, but when Garin put his pen to paper, shaping his thoughts, he had no intention of creating a self-conscious record.

Every time you get a walk-in, he wrote, *he is observed, doubted, and interrogated until there is a good answer to the question: Why is this man turning against his country? In GAMBIT's case, it is a combination of things. Money is important, but he's not just trading secrets for a bank account – at least that's not the whole picture. He has a five-year-old son who suffers seizures. He needs medicine for the boy, but the medicine he needs is only available in the West. After three vodkas, I saw another side of him. He is opinionated about the Soviet Union. The more he drank, the darker his humor became, and I saw a disillusioned man, maybe even a desperate one. He talked at length about growing up in the provinces, and he was proud that he was the first in his family to earn a commission in the Soviet Army, and then privileged to enter Frunze Military Academy. He believes in the greatness of Russia, but he has contempt for the Communist Party and the Soviet system. His litany of complaints went on for twenty minutes: corruption, red tape, the queues, empty shelves, filth in the public bathrooms, police rudeness, and the impossibility of getting proper medical care for his son. And he resents his privileged Moscow colleagues who hold his peasant background against him. He went on about the miseries his family suffered under Stalin.*

Garin looked up from the page. Then he added a final sentence: *He occasionally uses French words, which I assume he picked up when he was stationed in Belgium.*

He set aside his report to Mueller and opened his spiral notebook. He had begun to record his activities. His notes were brief, often no more than reminders, and he made little effort to expunge names or references that could compromise his work if the diary fell into the wrong hands. It was a way of talking to himself. He wrote down concerns and opinions that he was not comfortable sharing with Mueller: *What I disliked about John was his obviously colored hair with the gray roots clearly visible. There is something annoyingly vain about a middle-aged man unwilling to accept his age. I don't trust him.*

Then he added another random thought: *The child will complicate things.* He underlined the passage. He knew that it was always the human element that was hardest to predict and most difficult to accommodate. A spy took terrible risks, but a spy with a family was a different challenge. Garin needed to better understand Petrov's character – his fears, needs, moods, and family loyalty – in order to unlock his complex psychology. Petrov was managing a three-dimensional world, lying to Garin in ways that Garin didn't yet know, lying to his wife certainly, and possibly lying to himself. Garin knew that a traitor lived under tremendous pressure and if he wasn't handled properly, he had the potential to spontaneously combust.

He's on the fence, Garin wrote. *Let's see if he goes through with this.*

He dated the entry. There were ninety-five days until Border Guard Day.

Garin woke at dawn and composed a report for Rositske on his Remington manual typewriter. He had an obligation to keep Rositske informed, and it was that requirement that helped him communicate with a man he preferred to keep in the dark. He knew that the report would be encrypted and sent to Langley, and eventually Mueller would read it. He didn't write anything that contradicted what he said in his handwritten note, but he added answers to questions he knew would be on senior minds at Headquarters. The report would go to the head of the SE Division, the DCI, and, if Mueller was correct, the Oval Office, where the president had taken an interest in GAMBIT.

He claims he has access to top secret documents held in a classified library used by Sergei Churgin in his role as deputy chairman of the Committee for State Security, Garin wrote. *Churgin is a front-runner to head up the KGB if his boss succeeds Chernenko as chairman of the Presidium. He is testing his power by having different institutes send him reports on their military technology research. Information comes into the classified library from places around Moscow, including the Scientific Research Institute of Radio Engineering. GAMBIT has exploited a gaping hole in the security system. He can sign out documents so long as he returns them by 6 p.m. Backpacks, attaché cases, bags, coats, and jackets are searched when officers leave the building at night so he works inside. He copies documents during the day, and at night he photographs the documents in a small closet near his office.*

It gave Garin a sense of power to think of his readers, and like a good actor who played to his audience, he exaggerated where necessary. *He has seen schematics of stealth aircraft designs with details on speed, radio frequencies, weapons capabilities, avionics, and look-down radar systems.* Desk bureaucrats who demanded unreasonable quantities of intelligence had always rankled Garin, and when he reread his report, he underlined the last three words.

Garin thought intelligence bureaucrats were a special class of coward, eager to claim credit for successful missions they had little to do with and quick to flee from catastrophes that stemmed from their failure to understand how much could be asked of men in the field.

He is under a lot pressure, Garin wrote. *He can only be pushed so far.*

Then he made his demand of Rositske – an aggressive request, more than he needed, but this was the time to ask. Soviet identity documents and passports for GAMBIT, his wife, and his child. Perfect forgeries were needed with the names GAMBIT had provided. Plane tickets – two sets, one for the Finnish border and another for Uzhgorod. Safe passage at the border needed to be arranged. Garin would do what he had failed to do for Zyuganov. And money. He considered Petrov's demand. It was a reasonable sum, in light of the intelligence he was providing and the risks he was taking.

7

THE SECOND MEETING

GARIN FOUND PETROV AT the plywood table, sitting in the
dim winter light that came through the administrative
office's one dirty window. He had an open bottle of vodka and
a half-empty glass. Their eyes met, and Garin knew something
was on Petrov's mind.

'I'm sure you have an excuse for being late. Spare me your
lies.' Petrov pushed a glass across the table. 'The idiots forgot
the *zakuski*. I told them they'd have hell to pay if I didn't get
laid because my drama queen girlfriend refused to warm up
without eating first.'

Petrov made a generous pour in Garin's glass. 'Were the
photographs good?'

'Yes. We had them looked at. They are what we had hoped
they would be.'

Ten days had passed since their first meeting. Contact
between them had settled into a sort of routine. Garin avoided
the neighborhoods he'd walked during his previous Moscow
life, and he altered his route to the postal box. He'd entered
the apartment lobby after seeing a single vertical chalk mark
on the postal box by the tobacco kiosk, and he had retrieved
the exposed film from the envelope wedged behind the steam
radiator. Garin added a horizontal chalk mark to indicate he'd

left a package. His envelope held ginseng root, and then a week later, he'd left a month's supply of clonazepam tablets for the boy's seizures. He also filled Petrov's wife's requests: a portable CD player, jazz recordings, and ABBA's last album. And then Garin had seen two underscored vertical chalk marks – Petrov's signal that it was urgent they meet.

'Then you have competent experts,' Petrov said. 'Weapons of mass destruction have an obvious appeal.'

'How much more is there?'

'A lot. The rest I will bring with me when we cross the border.' He slowly placed his glass on the table. 'Maybe I trust you, but I don't trust the deskmen in Langley.'

Garin felt the man's agitated mood, so he let Petrov do the talking. He saw that he'd been drinking while waiting. One-fifth of the bottle was gone.

'And this too bothers me,' Petrov growled. His eyes suddenly locked on Garin. 'Traitors live in the ninth circle of hell. Traitors are below rapists, below child molesters. I see worry in your eyes, and the way you treat me with condescension to keep me happy and get me to talk. *Shithead*. What do you think? You think it's easy?'

'What's on your mind?'

'Question for question. You wouldn't be so calm if you were sitting in my chair.' He glared. 'I don't even know your name, but here I am, confessing my sins.' Petrov's eyes had drifted off but came back. 'Traitor to what? State? Conscience? Family?' His smile was indignant. 'Don't worry, I'm not backing out. You've got my name. There is a point beyond which there is no return, and as much as your friends in Langley need me, I know I'm expendable if things don't go as they want.' He leaned back, and his expression became wiser. 'Point of no return. Familiar? I wouldn't know to quote it, but in the days of samizdat, Kafka was popular, and someone I know gave me his journals as a joke. Well, now the joke is on me.'

Petrov fingered his empty glass and then poured himself another short shot of vodka, ending the pour at an imaginary line. He raised it, examining the clear alcohol. He threw it back, taking it all at once.

'Here in the Soviet Union,' he said, his voice quieter and more philosophical, 'if you are arrested, for whatever reason, but particularly for state crimes –' He drew a cutting finger across his neck. 'But it could be for any reason, and it's usually a case of simple luck if you survive. You die in interrogation, or you freeze to death in your cell. You die under the fists of the guards. A favorite pastime among the guards at Solovki Prison Camp is forcing naked prisoners to stand at the edge of a steep drop in bitter-cold weather until they lose balance and fall. Prisoners succumb to disease, hunger, despair. Prisoners lose their will to live, and sadistic guards take up their cudgels. But the traitor in this unlucky group – his arrest comes with a certain outcome. And the men who put the pistol to his head are often his colleagues.'

Petrov drew in a breath. 'There are many miserable ways to die if you are arrested, some of them cruel, some absurd, but the man arrested for being a traitor knows how he will go.'

Garin didn't have to wait to hear what was really on Petrov's mind.

'Someone in Directorate A suspects classified documents are being copied. Things are now uncomfortable – maybe even dangerous.'

'How do you know?' Garin asked.

'How! It's obvious.' Petrov slammed his knife blade into the plywood. 'For weeks I took reports from the library on the fifth floor of DOM2, and I would copy them on the machine on the seventh floor of DOM1. Now there are new rules. I must sign out documents. There is always a man who looks at my badge and copies down what I am taking. What's worse is the copier. I had copied the original and returned them, then waited until after work, when no one was around, to film the copies in a closet. Now, every copy I make has to be logged, time stamped, and returned, and if not returned, a written explanation must be given. It's a new security procedure. Someone suspects something.'

Petrov sank in his chair, morose. 'I have gone over and over in my mind why there has been this change. It is highly unusual. There is one logical explanation. Of course, there may be an illogical explanation – it's a matter of chance – but I am a logical man, and I look for the logic in things. The copies on our machines are given a unique signature – time, date, number. If such a copy were sent to your people, because I had photographed it, and if the signature, or even a copy of the copy, found its way back to Lubyanka, KGB security would know to monitor that one copy machine.'

Garin gazed at Petrov, absorbing the implications of Petrov's suspicions. Fading light from the dying sun darkened Petrov's face and made it hard for Garin to gauge the man's worry.

'It's possible,' Petrov said, 'there is a mole in your headquarters?'

'Five people know of you,' Garin said. 'They are all trusted senior men.'

'Yes, but how many experts have seen the documents as part of an evaluation? They would be a different group – military scientists, engineering staff given pieces and asked to verify what I photographed. We both know that is the logical explanation.' Petrov looked at Garin. 'You look surprised, but you shouldn't be. You don't think there is my counterpart inside the CIA? Passing secrets back? We recruited several. Believe me. Now there may be another.'

Petrov placed several film canisters on the table. 'There won't be more of these, for now. I have to be careful. Everything else I have I will bring with me when I cross the border.'

Petrov's grim expression softened, and his voice calmed. 'There may be a way to use this to our advantage.' He looked at the bare table. 'This is when it would be good to eat something. My mind works better on a full stomach. But the shitheads forgot.'

He leaned across the table. 'Here is what I think. You don't know – why would you – Chernenko is dying. He was dying when he was made chairman after Andropov died a year ago, but his end is near. Rivals are at work to position themselves when he goes, and there is a lot of jockeying between the Second and Fifth Chief Directorates. The old guard is getting older, even at the middle level, and we've had our fill of ancient Stalinists. Rival deputies are fighting. The rumor is that the next chairman of the Presidium will be the head of the KGB, like Andropov was. Senior men in the First Chief Directorate are aligning under Deputy Chairman Churgin, head of Directorate S, the illegals program.

'My boss is ambitious. Perhaps you have heard his name – Dmitry Posner. Speaks perfect English and has cultivated his foreign credentials and contacts, and rivals have noticed his dishonesty. He is too intellectual and too well-spoken, and he smokes Marlboros while the rest of them choke on Primas. I don't like him, he doesn't like me, and his rivals have their knives ready.' Petrov smiled his contempt. 'He's not Russian like me.'

Petrov leaned back in his chair. 'I don't know if he suspects me or if it's just that he doesn't like me. Yesterday, he called me into his office and asked why I was making so many copies. He is a careerist, but he's smart, which makes him dangerous.

'He heard my answer, but I could see that he wasn't satisfied. We have never been alike, and he has never shown much interest in my work, but now he wants to see everything I do.

I suspect my name is on a long list of people who are possible suspects. It doesn't look good for him if one of his deputies is on the suspect list, and it makes it even more important for him to be vigilant. His career goes up if he exposes a man under him, but his career sinks if someone in another directorate proves security in Posner's group was lax, and his career crashes if *he* comes under suspicion. Hundreds of people are suspects at this point. Hundreds of people use that copier. Posner himself has made copies when his assistant was sick – lowering himself to secretarial work. The investigation is tedious, and the process of elimination will be difficult. No one wants to make a mistake, grab the wrong man, and leave the traitor in place. No one wants to find out that their deputy, or the man in the office next door, is the mole.'

'What are you thinking?'

'I think Posner wants to get rid of me.'

'Why do you say that?'

'He's acting strangely. He's worried about something.' Petrov pushed forward an invitation with the embossed seal of the United States of America from Ambassador Thomas Propper and his wife to attend the fiftieth-anniversary gala at Spaso House.

'Posner asked me to go. His boss, Deputy Chairman Churgin, gave him two invitations. What?' Petrov stared. 'Your face went white. You know him?'

'No.' A lie. 'Go on.'

'Posner said, "A big honor." For my good work. I asked, "Why me?" He said because I'm a smart fellow. When he appeals to my vanity, I know he has something in mind. I said, "But I don't know English." He said it doesn't matter. "You've been asked to go. Consider it a privilege."'

Petrov looked at Garin. 'I have no choice but to go. I will be watched. That is why I'm being invited. I assume that you will be there. You must not approach me. You must not look at me. If the KGB suspect something, I'll be taken for questioning. I must be invisible.

'I am putting two things together – the change in security at the copier and the invitation. Someone is tightening the noose on my neck. The best way to protect me is to point a finger at someone else.'

Petrov drew a deep breath. 'My wife is a nervous wreck. Last week, someone in our apartment block was taken. No one says he was arrested, but now no one mentions his name. He's gone, disappeared. The family says he is off visiting relatives, but my wife saw him taken out to a black Volga.' He clenched his hands. 'She won't talk about our escape openly. If we talk at home, it's simple things – how was your day, did you go to the store? Nonsense. When we talk about our plans, it is in our bedroom with the radio playing loudly.

'Why am I telling you this? It's complicated with her. She can't bear the thought of leaving her parents without saying goodbye. I need to give her reasons to believe our son will be safe if we go.'

Petrov turned philosophical. 'If you submit to the state, it gives you what you need, and for me, in my position, we get an annual holiday at the KGB resort on the Black Sea, health care in a special clinic, monthly rations of milk and butter, and a job from which I can't be fired.' He smiled grimly. 'But if you don't submit and you resist, the benefits vanish, the rations stop, medicines become unavailable, your friends look away, and you are watched. There is no privacy, even in your own home. If you persist in your questions, you are considered difficult and the State unleashes its full arsenal of vengeance. You are sent to Serbsky Psychiatric Institute, where you are treated for a condition the KGB calls "lazy schizophrenia" whose only symptom is resistance to the State.'

Petrov stood. 'I tell this to my wife. She knows it, but it's one thing to know this and another to imagine you'll never see your parents again.' He stopped at the door. 'My wife liked the ABBA. Can you get me Queen? And a woman's two-piece lingerie, cup size C. Any color. Look, my wife's unmarried sister's thirtieth birthday is coming up, and my wife wants something to surprise her. It would help me out, okay?'

'Of course.' Garin also stood and tried to appear upbeat in the face of Petrov's grim report and gloomy mood. He handed the newly forged passports to Petrov. The documents had been created by the Technical Services Graphics Department, everything meticulously re-created to appear like originals – paper quality, photographs, embarkation stamps that reflected the wear and tear of years of use. The entry stamps were made to emulate the varied pressure that a busy immigration inspector would use when pressing his rubber stamp, some faint, some bolder, and none of the pages with the obvious crispness of an intentional forgery. Only the names were different.

'Good,' Petrov said, shoving his arms into his coat. 'This will help. Now let's hope no one searches our flat and finds the camera.' Petrov had stepped through the door when he stopped and faced Garin. 'Get Posner off my back.'

'How?'

Petrov's eyes narrowed. 'You're clever. Cleverer than you pretend. You'll find a way.'

8

HELEN WALSH

I HEAR YOU'VE BEEN asking about Dmitry Posner.'

Garin was surprised by Helen Walsh's comment, coming abruptly in the midst of their casual conversation. They were standing together in her crowded living room among guests who talked over one another to make themselves heard as they smoked, drank, and laughed. Her question implied that his few discreet inquiries into Posner had entered the embassy gossip mill.

Helen had a pleasant figure and confident smile, and the slightly flirtatious demeanor of an unmarried career professional in her mid-thirties. Her knowledge of Russian was better than most of the other foreign service professionals, and her long tenure in Moscow came with a two-bedroom apartment with a good view of the Kremlin. She hosted a monthly Friday night salon for embassy staff – particularly the young, single staff, who found it hard to lead normal lives in the closed city – and their French, Italian, and English counterparts. The party's casual atmosphere allowed guests to unwind from a long workweek, free of the watchful eyes of State Security.

Garin had formed his opinion of his supervisor in their first meeting, when she'd stared at him across her desk with

68

a gambler's gaze. As was often the case with his judgments of people, his first impression endured and became a lasting impression, and everything that followed simply confirmed his opinion. She belonged to that class of women who took it upon themselves to be familiar with other people's business – and she knew more than she let on.

Her comment came after she'd described how she made certain that she knew who had arrived to her parties. If she saw someone she didn't recognize, she'd get the person's name and ask what they did and who they came with, and then she'd show them to the bar. That was how she got to know everyone, she'd said.

They were standing by a bookshelf of abundant memorabilia in exotic disarray. 'I'm a hoarder,' she'd said with a laugh when he'd first been struck by the volumes of samizdat first editions and walls crowded with paintings by jailed Soviet artists.

But now she wasn't focused on her collection. Garin saw her eyes fix on him, and he knew that the woman who'd avoided him for weeks had a sudden interest.

'I was told to meet him,' he replied. 'Do you know him?' Garin glanced around, looking for an excuse to escape her company.

'Know Dmitry Posner? Of course. He sold me that painting.' She directed Garin to a canvas of dense black squares set on a background of ivory white. 'He got it off Golukov for nothing when he was arrested and sold it to me for a lot of money. It's a good racket. There's a market for dissident art in London. What's your interest in him?'

'Human rights. Abuses.'

Helen cocked her head. 'A clever answer. Maybe it's even true.'

Garin felt Helen's eyes on him as if she were trying to read his mind. He had turned his head again, looking to get away, and in the moment of distraction he didn't catch her question.

'I'm sorry, I was looking for someone. Anything to say about what?'

'About why Ronnie is motioning toward you,' Helen said. 'Go ahead, she looks eager to talk.' She nodded at Garin's glass. 'Another?'

'Please.' He took the dregs in one swallow and handed her the glass.

'She's talking to Rupert Halsey. He comes from a long line of Cambridge communists from the thirties, when it was fashionable among the English upper class, but I know he works for MI6.'

As he stepped away, he felt her hand on his arm, stopping him.

'What are you drinking?'

'Vodka martini. Straight up. No olives.'

'The bartender makes an excellent Moscow Mule. You should try it. Every Russian should.'

Garin crossed the room to Ronnie, but Helen's comment echoed in the back of his mind. Later, he recorded the incident in his notebook. Her comment was so casual, so out of nowhere, and so notable for its provocative oddity, that it stuck with him. He didn't think it was a random shot, and like her earlier comment and others that had come to his attention, he had begun to think that his cover wasn't as good as he had hoped. Rumors had begun to attach themselves to him like burrs. Garin didn't know how the rumors started, nor did he have a good way to shut them down. And the vagueness of the suspicions was a sort of accelerant – imprecision fueling a wildfire of possibilities that sprung from the dry kindling of the embassy's social confinement. Garin knew he couldn't quash the rumors, so he resolved to get his work done quickly and hoped that the speculation would burn out.

'Helen lives well,' Ronnie said when they were alone by the window, away from the crowd. She coddled a drink and had a large cloth bag on her shoulder. 'Tenure has its perks.' She pointed at the French Empire furniture and the stunning view of the Kremlin. 'She enjoys playing hostess. Everyone wants to come, even the Russians. Look around. Dissidents, poets, physicists, spies. They all want something: a date, to defect, and some want to know who else is in the room.' She sipped her drink. 'Everyone wants something.'

'What did you find on Posner?'

She handed him a two-page document from her bag. 'You're allowed to read this, but you can't take it. Orders.'

'Rositske?'

She shrugged but didn't answer.

Garin scanned the two pages of background: Born October 5, 1938, Moscow. Father a NKVD lieutenant colonel, mother a commercial artist. Attended Moscow Elementary School 130, joined the Young Pioneers at age nine, and transferred to Komsomol at fourteen, becoming head of his high school unit. Entered the Institute of International Relations in 1958. Trained in the KGB institute, School 101, graduating fifth in his class. Served in London, Berlin, and Rome. Spoke fluent English and German.

Garin turned to the assessment section, written in the conversational style of a trained Agency analyst: 'He has a fondness for money and material things, but he hasn't shown a weakness for women, except the casual attention of a diplomat's wife, and he doesn't drink, except the odd glass of wine. He has a harmless, if slightly unusual, streak of vanity. During a posting in London, where his job was to interact with smart City types, he began to imitate their dress, wearing a Savile Row suit with a folded pocket square and a fashionable cravat tied in a Windsor knot. He also adopted a number of English

71

social customs. He arrived at Kensington dinner parties with cut flowers for the hostess and he wrote thank-you notes afterward on monogrammed stationery.'

Garin pondered the profile of an elite KGB officer with Western affectations.

'I'll introduce you,' Ronnie said. 'He's coming to the Spaso House gala next week.'

'What about the other thing?'

She pulled a lingerie box from her bag. 'C cup, as you requested. It arrived in the pouch this morning. Who is it for?'

'Don't reason the need.'

'Maybe it's for you.' She smiled mischievously. 'If that were true, it would put an end to all the other rumors. People have started to take an interest in you.'

Ronnie glanced back at the room of flushed faces engaged in animated conversations, everyone noting who was there and who was not. 'Helen is looking at us,' she said, turning back to Garin. 'Why is there no file on you in Langley?'

Garin never did answer her question. Helen approached and handed him his vodka martini.

Garin recorded the incident in his notebook that night. *Too many people asking too many questions.*

9

SPASO HOUSE

GARIN AND RONNIE STOOD in a long security queue outside Spaso House, the US ambassador's official residence at No. 10 Spasopeskovskaya Square, a graceful stucco building built in the final years of tsarist Russia. It had snowed that afternoon, the first big snow of March, which was an omen for a long winter.

Ronnie slapped her hands together for warmth and leaned into Garin. 'Rositske will meet you in the bathroom when you're inside. He has an answer for you.'

Garin had made Ronnie his drinking partner, and he relied on her to help him navigate the political shoals of embassy life. She nodded at the elegant guests impatiently enduring the cold, some sharing what little they'd been told to expect at the party and what they might actually see.

'A jazz band, seals, birds flying around,' Ronnie said to Garin, shivering. 'I've been told it will be bigger than the party Ambassador Bullitt's wife threw in 1935. Stalin didn't come to that party, but he sent his defense minister, the foreign minister, top generals, and several Communist Party luminaries, including Karl Radek. Emily Propper wants to honor the fiftieth anniversary of that famous event – and outdo it.' Ronnie laughed.

Garin had heard the stories of the 1935 Spaso House party: ice blocks in the Chandelier Room, tame bears, birds landing on people's heads. A German woman in a mink coat in front of Ronnie turned. 'And did you know that the tame bear became drunk when Karl Radek gave it champagne?' she asked. Another guest pointed out the Spanish ambassador. And then a whispered rumor swept the queue: two members of the Presidium were coming.

Ronnie pointed to the front of the queue. 'There's Posner.'

A tall man without a hat wore a scarf tucked into his sable coat, and he allowed himself to be patted down by a marine guard. His salt-and-pepper hair fell back to his shoulders, like a flamboyant orchestra conductor, and his narrow jaw and aquiline nose, red from the cold, gave his angular face a pleasant appearance.

Garin had his eye on Posner when he gave his overcoat to the coat-check girl, who placed it among many others hanging on a wheeled rack. He moved to the Chandelier Room, where a perimeter balcony circled the cathedral ceiling and a glistening glass chandelier hung like a jeweled star. Everywhere, people milled, moved past the tame bear borrowed from the Moscow Zoo, or stared at the barking seal. A large, netted aviary of canaries and sparrows drew awed attention from arriving guests, and others ambled past a stand of white birches set in a meadow of tulips. Somewhere, a gleeful saxophone was paired with a mournful trumpet, accompanied by the nimble fingering of a pianist.

Garin pushed through the ballroom and made his way to the bathroom. He was standing at the urinal when he became aware that a man had entered. Garin moved to the porcelain sink, opening the hot and cold taps, and he felt the man's presence at the next basin.

'What's his name?' Rositske asked.

'He asked me not to share it.'

'You don't work for him.'

'Actually, I do. Until it's done.'

Rositske aggressively splashed water on his face. 'Bullshit. You think he trusts you?'

'He'll trust me more when I deliver the next batch of his son's medicine. Where is it?'

'You'll have it. When does he deliver again?'

Garin stared at Rositske through the mirror. 'He's not a banker. He doesn't work set hours. He'll get me the film when it's safe.'

'Langley is pressuring me.'

Garin grunted. He glanced under the stalls to be certain they were alone. 'The copier he uses is being watched. He thinks there's a breach on our side.'

'We checked on Posner,' Rositske said. 'He's a throwaway. Ronnie will introduce you.' Rositske handed Garin a list of typed questions. 'Langley wants these answered.'

Garin looked. 'GAMBIT is already nervous. These will scare him off.'

'It's not a suggestion. It came from POTUS to the DCI to Mueller to me, and now to you.'

'I don't care who wants it.' Garin crumpled the paper. He dropped his voice. 'He's skittish. I'm not asking for much, just the modest use of good judgment. Wait until he's across the border, then he can answer these, and every other *goddamned* question they've got. Tell Mueller there is a risk he will cut and run.'

Garin thought his caution was brutally obvious. That the acting chief of station did not speak Russian, or read it, was one of Garin's gripes. Nothing had changed since his previous posting. Ambitious men dubiously equipped for sensitive assignments made errors of judgment that put lives at risk.

'I will bring the questions,' Garin said, uncrumpling the page. 'I'll ask how he wants to address them. It would be good if I got the second batch of medicine when I bring up the questions. He might be more inclined to cooperate.'

Garin never did present the questions to GAMBIT.

*

Garin returned to the Chandelier Room and took a spot on the edge of the party, nursing his drink. He was both a lone man observing the room and an amateur actor trying to decide what role he should play. The two things – Garin the man and Garin the actor – did not quite go together. The actor seemed a bit too studied, the man cast as the awkward outsider. And the guests who noticed him didn't know whether to sympathetically approach or to be wary of him. He had the loner's fortitude for privacy and the detachment of a man who found it convenient to withdraw with a tall glass of vodka, which he had taken without olive or vermouth but still called a martini.

'There you are,' Ronnie said, appearing beside him. 'You drifted off. Let me introduce you.'

She took Garin's arm and led him across the ballroom to a pair of Russians standing with an Englishman. The first Russian was shorter, quiet, planted like a bronze statue among a swirl of party guests, and his eyes took in the room. He listened impassively to the taller Russian at his side, who chatted with the Englishman and occasionally leaned down to politely translate. Garin recognized Posner's long, swept-back hair. He wore a bespoke tuxedo, and he had the animated charm of a man in the company of a boss he wanted to impress.

'Comrade Posner,' Ronnie said. 'I'd like to introduce you to someone.'

Posner turned away from his Soviet colleague. 'We were

76

just talking about the speed limit in Moscow,' he said. 'It's still sixty kilometers per hour, but it was never respected and never enforced, and now the new radar detectors are a big headache. Three convictions and you lose your license. Everyone has the same question. What can we do about it?' He leaned forward to Garin. 'I didn't catch the name.'

'Aleksander Garin.'

Comrade Posner bent slightly at the waist and presented his hand. 'Garin, you said? A Russian name!' He looked at Garin, taking a measure of the man. 'A Russian name with a rich significance. Erast Garin was one of our great stage actors. Nikolai Garin-Mikhailovsky wrote popular novels. And there is the protagonist in Chekhov's story, "Ward 6." Dr Ragin, a perfect anagram of Garin. Welcome to the Soviet Union, Mr Garin.'

Posner turned to his colleague. 'Let me introduce Deputy Chairman Churgin.'

Churgin nodded once, but he scowled as if irritated at being in the room, and he made no effort to be pleasant. His hand stayed at his side as he gazed at Garin.

The next head of the KGB, Garin thought. He stared back.

Posner intervened. 'What have you found so far? Does our winter appeal to you?'

'Appeal?' Garin smiled. 'Endure.' He used the Russian word.

Posner's eyebrow raised. 'Your accent is unusual. Perhaps you're an émigré. I've met children of émigré Russians who come looking for their grandparents' villages, which they left to escape the Bolsheviks. Are you one?'

'I was told you could help me.'

'I can't fix traffic tickets.'

'I want to interview a vocal critic. Someone fed up with the Party.' He stirred his drink with his finger and met Deputy Chairman Churgin's eyes. Garin had encountered Churgin years before in a different context, in a different country, with a different problem, but he saw the same smug hostility on his face. 'A dissident.'

Garin gave a casual critique of the Soviet Union's human rights abuses, putting on the careless show of a man eager to prove his importance. His cheeks had blushed from alcohol, and his voice deepened. In the space of two drinks he had been able to put on the convincing act of a dissolute drinker with dangerous opinions. He raised his empty glass. 'To free expression. I want to meet an artist who proves the exception to the rule of censorship.' He looked at Deputy Chairman Churgin. 'If such a person exists.'

Churgin turned to Posner. 'Send him to Golukov.'

'Good choice,' Posner said. 'A painter. He lives two hours from Moscow. You need a special permit to drive there, but you can join me. My colleague will drive us. She is familiar with the roads.'

Posner called to a tall woman nearby who was watching the jazz pianist play an up-tempo Dixieland tune. She wore a black strapless gown and silver earrings that swung as she turned her head. Her scarlet lips parted with an audible gasp when she faced Garin.

'Do you know each other?' Posner asked. He looked between Garin and his colleague. 'Is that possible?'

'Anything's possible,' she said. 'Natalya Alexieva.'

Natalya's eyes on Garin were severe, as if forgetting her manners, but then she put forward her hand to meet Garin's, which she shook once, forcefully.

'Alek Garin,' he said.

'He looks at you with surprise,' Posner said.

'Tolerant surprise,' she said, 'to your ridiculous suggestion.' She spoke to Posner, but all the while she looked at Garin, speaking about him as if he wasn't there. Then she addressed him, judging him like a new dress she wasn't certain she wanted to try on. 'Very nice to meet you, Mr Garin. May you have great success in our country.'

She stopped a passing waiter with an upraised tray of champagne flutes and plucked one. 'You are behaving badly, Mr Garin,' she said. 'You are staring at me. Maybe you think we *have* met.'

Garin's surprise was gone, but his memory was alive. Her raven hair was the same, dark eyes the same, and her rudeness identical. All that was different was the flute of champagne she held where she had once held a white rose.

'Perhaps you think we've met because you saw me onstage. In London, perhaps,' she went on. 'I've had men come up to me and claim they know me, but of course, it's impossible. Do you enjoy the ballet, Mr Garin?'

'No.'

She raised an offended eyebrow. 'That shows only that you haven't seen the right ballet. Ballet has something for everyone, even someone who says it is not to their taste. It was my life.' She presented her Ace-bandaged ankle. 'And now it is not.'

Garin snagged a flute of champagne. 'I'm sorry.'

'That's a stupid thing to say,' she said. 'Something an Englishman would say.' Having raised the topic of England, she continued on, aware of the English ambassador nearby. 'I lived in England as a child. English food and manners were not to my taste. I found that English people wanted to turn me into a suffering victim of a totalitarian regime.' She laughed. 'It made them feel good about themselves when I described life in Moscow, and they would commiserate. *How sad. How terrible.* And then they would suggest that I defect. My father was in the embassy, so the suggestion was ridiculous – me, a young girl, defect. When I returned to London as a ballerina they said, *Now, Natalya, you're an adult.*' She looked at Garin with a tolerant smile. 'I don't dance anymore, and they no longer ask.'

'What does a ballerina who no longer dances do?'

'I work with Comrade Posner, the Cultural ministry. And you? What do you do?'

'Human rights.'

She smiled. 'In the Soviet Union, we have human rights and human writers. Sometimes they are the same, and sometimes they are different. Some of our writers go to jail. The longer their sentence, the larger their public. It's different in America. Your popular writers count for nothing. They're not regarded as dangerous, and no one pays attention, except to be entertained. They are free but irrelevant.' She looked at Garin. 'Which is the better life? Free and irrelevant, or influential and in jail?'

'You talk like a writer.'

'I talk the way I think.' She smiled. 'Doesn't everyone?' Comrade Posner intervened. 'You should know, Mr Garin, the KGB could destroy samizdat in two days, but they don't. And why? It can be useful to let the mice play.' Posner held a cocktail cigarette holder and knocked the long ash from his Marlboro into his palm. He turned to Natalya. 'Golukov would make a good interview.'

Still holding ash in his palm, Posner turned back to Garin. 'He is outspoken, but he is a good portrait artist, so the Party elite sit for him. We will go together.'

The others drifted to the bar or to another conversation, and suddenly Garin found himself alone with Natalya. They glanced at each other, but their eyes drifted, and neither spoke. She looked for an excuse to leave, but then abruptly faced him.

'You were rude in the cemetery, and you are still rude. We should forget that we met. It is best for both of us,' she said brusquely. 'I will drive you to Golukov. When is a good time? Tomorrow? Noon?'

'And Posner?'

'He is available tomorrow at noon.'

Later, when he remembered the conversation, he recorded his surprise in his notebook. *Nothing is ever that easy.*

*

The chandelier's lights grew brighter, the jazz band played loud jitterbug music, and an opera of voices tried heroically to keep up conversation. The laughter got boozy, and minute by minute the party's conviviality grew higher in pitch. Groups formed and dissolved, swelling again as new arrivals from the cold warmed to the room's blazing excitement. Birds chirped in the aviary, and the seal on its melting ice block became languid in the deafening noise, like an intimidated guest. All around, single men wandered, looking morose, and confident girls in long dresses had men following them, offering compliments.

It was just then that Garin heard his name called. He'd taken a position behind the pianist so that he could look out at the room without appearing to observe the crowd. He turned at the sound of his name and saw Ronnie approaching with two flutes of champagne, and being offered one, he accepted it and drank it at once.

'I understand that you successfully managed to annoy the next head of the KGB,' she said. 'Congratulations. You've got balls.'

'I've encountered him before.'

'You've met him?' She didn't hide her surprise.

'Encountered him. He wouldn't remember.'

A suburban Virginia cul-de-sac in late 1953. Another time, another world. The stranger's face in a car parked across the street. His mother weeping in the window.

'Years ago,' he said, 'but we didn't meet.'

Ronnie's smile vanished, and she changed the subject. 'I

understand your trip to Golukov is arranged.' She raised her flute. 'To success.'

Garin tapped a waiter passing with a tray and discharged his empty flute. 'Yes, all arranged. Did you have a hand in it?'

'Is that a compliment?'

'It's not an insult.'

'I'll take it. Everyone is curious who else is here.' Her eyes were on him. 'I'm curious about you. The solitary man always on the sidelines, scheming.'

He nodded but said nothing.

Ronnie's eyes drifted across the room. 'The KGB are here if you know how to spot them.' She pointed at Churgin, who was chatting with Posner. 'He doesn't have wide lapels, thick shoes, cuffed pants, or an ugly tie. That's the stereotype. But the man who doesn't look the part is the one you don't suspect, and he's the one to watch.'

Garin contemplated Deputy Chairman Churgin, who he had never expected to see again. Velvet anger slowly filled a cold hollow in his chest and he felt the surreal drama of being in the same room with a man he had sworn to kill. His palms moistened at the memory of his oath, but his mind stayed clear. He considered how dangerous an adversary the man might be.

Garin turned back to Ronnie, but she had seized a lime-colored cocktail from the raised tray of a passing waiter, downed it for courage, and stepped onto the dance floor. Her hands moved from her head to her knees, seductively traveling down her swaying hips. Heads turned to look, and the band leader instructed the clarinetist to vary his rhythm following her moves. There was a burst of applause when she completed her passionate tango.

10

DACHA

THE NEXT DAY, SHORTLY before two in the afternoon, under a sky darkened with a slow-moving storm, Natalya and Garin stood outside the bright red door of a dacha made of finely fitted logs caulked with mortar. Except for the wisp of smoke rising straight into the air from a stone chimney, the two visitors had no sign anyone was home. Natalya's three loud raps on the brass knocker had gone unanswered except for a dog's tyrannical barking, and she was about to strike a fourth time when a voice inside called out.

'Yes, yes. I am here. Don't wake the grandchildren.'

The door was thrown open, and an older man, shrunken with age, stood on the threshold, startled and briefly suspicious. He wore coarse wool pants tied at the waist with a cord, a bulky sweater, and sandals with socks. His thinning hair was gray and long, and what he'd lost on his balding head erupted from his ears, giving him the appearance of a hobbit. His eyes widened and his cranky voice hissed, and as he spoke he motioned his visitors forward.

'Natasha, darling. Come in. Come in. The whole winter is entering while you stand there.' He nodded at her feet. 'And you didn't wear boots. You must think you're still in Moscow. Hurry. Hurry. What a surprise.'

'I called. I left a message with the housekeeper.'

'I got it, but I was in the studio. I forget everything when I'm in the studio. Come in.'

The two-story dacha was penetrated by small windows set deeply in the walls. They kept out the cold and the light. Garin followed Natalya and found himself in a small foyer crowded with boots, coats, hats, and scarves, and passing through, they came to the kitchen. A blue ceramic-tile oven hugged one wall and dominated the room. A short, stocky woman with flushed cheeks vigorously wiped her hands on a cloth apron.

'My housekeeper,' the man said. Having been introduced, the woman smiled self-consciously, revealing a missing tooth.

They passed from the kitchen to the living room, where a monstrous stone fireplace rose two stories and held glowing coals of a dying fire. It was a tall room full of mismatched furniture – a ponderous, claw-footed French Empire sofa faced two rustic wooden chairs, and everywhere the fastidious disorder of a forgetful man. Framed family photographs were propped on an antique breakfront, old copper-plated daguerreotypes of ancient relatives next to snapshots of children.

'This is Vladmir Golukov,' Natalya said, prompting their host to turn.

Golukov looked at Garin, as if for the first time. 'And who are you?'

'Aleksander Garin.'

Golukov nodded judgmentally, taking a measure of Garin. 'Posner said you want a portrait.' To Natalya, 'Why didn't Posner come?'

'There was a problem,' she replied. 'We aren't here to buy a painting.'

'Then why did you come?'

'To talk.'

'Talk? Sure, I have time for that. Let's have some slivovitz. Talking is better if we drink.' He added, 'You picked a bad day to visit.'

'What's wrong with today?'

'A big storm is coming. But that won't bother you. You're young and foolish. I am old and wise.' He smiled. 'And forgetful sometimes. But I'm not too old to enjoy the company of my Natasha.' He winked at Garin. 'Beautiful, isn't she? A gift to the eye.'

'Then you've gone blind,' Natalya said. 'You spend too much time with your nose on the canvas.'

Golukov whispered confidentially to Garin, 'I have several portraits of Stalin you can have for a good price. No one buys him anymore. Lenin, yes. Brezhnev, not so much.' He nodded at Natalya, who had moved ahead. 'She scolds me that I go on like an old man, but I tell her I *am* an old man.'

Golukov led them into a large studio with a stone floor, two skylights, and a woodstove with black piping that penetrated the roof. A large wooden table held tin cans overflowing with brushes, a field of misshapen, partly squeezed tubes of paint, and an ashtray filled with butts. A single easel stood in a rectangle of sunlight. It held an unfinished portrait of a young ballerina seated in a chair, knees apart, elbows on thighs, in a confident pose. Her black hair was tightly wound in a bun, her face was chalk white, and her eyes stared with an insolent expression.

'It's not finished,' Golukov said, pointing with his walking stick. 'She won't sit for the one hour I need. The eyes don't work. Look at her.' He pointed at Natalya, who tolerated his attention. 'The way she looks at me now. I need to paint that. Her tolerant irritation.'

'Enough,' she said.

'Don't make her angry. She is a snake if provoked.'

They had just arrived, but already Garin had the impression that Natalya wanted to leave. She kept looking at her watch and glanced out the window at the darkening sky. Garin thought she would have already grabbed him and departed if Golukov hadn't been an insistent host. He prattled on with the determined garrulousness of a lonely man happy to have company, and he ignored Natalya's impatience.

'I am a painter,' Golukov said. 'You would think that was obvious, but I had an East German here once, an educated man, who looked at the portraits on the wall and asked how I had come to collect so many. He didn't believe there were painters in the Soviet Union who weren't in prison.'

Golukov pointed at the walls of the studio, where there were portraits of grim Soviet Party bosses in dark suits and haughty, overweight, middle-aged women in military uniforms.

'These clients didn't like what they saw and refused to pay. They are my gallery of unhappy vanities. You know,' Golukov said mischievously, 'everyone thinks they are more handsome than they are. Everyone wants to look younger or thinner, or more important, or to be shown without the mole on the chin. That is my challenge – not to change the painting, which I would never do, but to convince the client that the painting is an improvement. Sometimes they agree, and sometimes they cry or rage. It's a trick to get them to look honestly. Who looks in the mirror and says, "How lovely my mole is"?' He nodded at Natalya. 'She is an exception. She is perfect, don't you think?'

'Stop it,' she scoffed. 'You'll embarrass me. Now, it's time for us to go.'

'You just got here. Here's the food. Sit. Eat.'

The housekeeper, who'd entered the room, put down a tray of sausage, black bread, cheese, pickled beets, and strong tea.

'Why didn't Posner come?' Golukov asked, his lazy eye judging Garin.

Before Garin could answer, a child no more than seven years old ran into the room, but she stopped suddenly when she saw the guests.

'Come here, child,' Golukov said. 'Meet an American; touch him, if you like. They have skin like us, eyes like us, they bleed like us, and they eat the food we eat. Yes, they are like us.'

Garin took his granddaughter in his lap and kissed her cheek, making her squirm. When he released the startled child, she fled the room.

'In school,' he said, 'they are taught scandalous things. Americans have fangs. They eat children. Everyone is on heroin. Milka has never seen an American. I am sure she is in her bedroom exclaiming to her brother that she's seen you and, "My God, he has no fangs."'

Golukov chuckled, then looked at Garin. 'Did they tell you I'm a dissident?' The old man led them to another room off the studio. The light overhead illuminated a windowless, cramped space, with many oil paintings hanging on the walls. Each canvas was a washed field of white dotted with dense, black squares that differed in size, number, and position from canvas to canvas but were otherwise identical. 'My decadent art,' Golukov said proudly. 'I am like artists everywhere. I paint for myself, I paint for friends, and I paint for money.'

He looked at Natalya, who had become nervous at his long-windedness. He pumped his hands for her to calm herself. 'The drive is two hours. It's the same time if you leave now or in ten minutes.'

'The storm is coming.'

He shook his head and looked at Garin. 'I got in trouble when a French critic saw these. His review said that I had drawn an impassable line between old and new, between God and his devil, between life and death. The word "God" got the KGB's attention. Three of them showed up. Smart men, but obviously

87

literal and dull, and uneducated in art. I had to explain that the French critic was making things up. I pointed at the paintings. I said, "What do you see? God? Life and death?" "No," I said. "Look. Black squares on a white canvas. That's all."' After sharing a glass of vodka, they became convinced.'

Natalya tapped her temple. 'It makes for a good story. If only it were true. It's time to go.'

'I hope you got what you came for,' he said. 'Stay for dinner. The road to the E109 is dangerous in a storm.'

*

Later, falling snow laid a false peace on the two-lane road. Garin had seen a black Volga follow them from Moscow, but it was gone when they started back. They were twenty minutes into their journey, and Natalya was driving slowly on a back road that she claimed was a shortcut. He'd seen her glance ahead nervously when she turned off the main highway.

'That is Golukov,' she said. 'He spent ten years in a psychiatric clinic diagnosed with schizophrenia before he became a sought-after portrait artist. Now he is cantankerously prosperous.'

They drove in silence. The snow was falling heavily, but Garin saw the fresh tracks of a car that had preceded them. Garin heard the hypnotic rhythm of the wipers, and from time to time he glanced at her, judging her driving and the worry on her face. She clutched the steering wheel tightly. Garin glanced behind to see if they were being followed.

'We will be fine,' she said bravely. 'Did you get what you wanted?'

'What I wanted? No. I wanted to talk with Posner.'

'He's a busy man.'

'What does he do?'

She frowned, her eyes ahead, and didn't answer.

'Who does he work for?' Garin asked.

'His boss.'

He saw that her abrupt manner and vague answers were the limit of her pleasantness. 'I don't trust Posner.'

She glanced at him again. 'We have something in common. He knew this would be a long drive. If he'd come, Golukov would have pressed him for money.'

The car hit a pothole, and Garin was thrown against her. The physical contact startled them both. Garin sat back in his seat, and there was a moment of quiet as they composed themselves. Their shoulders had touched, and they'd been close enough to smell each other's breath. Her face was blanched with embarrassment.

It was an unpaved section of road, and the car bounced again. When it came down, his thigh brushed hers. And then it happened a third time. He scooted over and held the door handle, but the road didn't improve, and he kept falling against her. He did his best to ignore the contact, and then the road improved. He closed his eyes to shut out the tedium.

They traveled that way for some time. Garin was lulled by the wipers moving across the windshield and the mechanical hum of the car's engine. He found a spot for his head against the cold window, and his eyes closed while looking at the dense darkness of the passing forest. It was then, in the twilight of sleep, that he felt her fingers on his hand. Her gentle touch was warm, and when he turned to look, she had withdrawn her hand to the steering wheel.

Garin turned away and looked out the window, speechless. The silence between them became intolerable, and his mind fretted what she had been thinking, until he could stand the quiet no longer. 'What was it like?' he asked, making conversation. 'The life of a ballerina.'

She glanced at him nervously and then peered out the

windshield, her knuckles white on the steering wheel. 'My injury was a gift. I left with my dream intact. I wasn't the best, but I was good enough.' She grew more contemplative. 'I don't regret leaving ballet. The daily regimen, the scrutiny, the vicious jealousies. I enjoyed the stage, and it was fun to perform in London and Paris and to be prima ballerina, even if only briefly. That was special. But I have that memory. Now, I have a new life.' She looked at him kindly. 'Why do you ask? You have no interest in ballet.'

'Ballet doesn't interest me. But you do.'

'There is nothing interesting about me. But ballet *is* interesting. I will take you, and you will change your mind. *Swan Lake* is at the Bolshoi. You must come with me.' She smiled. 'I was lucky. There is nothing so sad as a prima ballerina who is too old for the stage and too vain to see she's an ordinary person. She shits like us, and she'll die like us.' Again, she looked at him and held her gaze there for a moment, before turning back to the windshield. 'And what about you? What's your talent? Everyone has one thing they do well.'

'What am I good at?' He threw out an answer. 'I know people.'

She scoffed. 'Really?'

'People show themselves in ways they aren't aware – impatience, anger, nervousness.'

'What do you know about me?'

'I make you nervous.'

She smiled confidently. 'I don't think so. Maybe it's the other way around.'

'You were nervous in the cemetery. You're nervous now.'

She shot him a glance.

They were approaching a narrow bridge that crossed a deep ravine. Far ahead, beyond the bridge, in the darkness of the winter storm, he saw a Volga and two UAZ military vehicles blocking the road.

'I've made a mistake,' she whispered to herself. Gray apprehension washed her face, and she moved to stop the car.

Later, Garin remembered the moment vividly. The radio had been playing something vaguely like music – mostly static, but calming in the storm for its connection to the world. Then her comment to herself, odd at the time, which drew his attention, and he saw her try to pull over. He felt the brakes lock, and the car entered a sideways skid, turning in gentle rotation, and then came the deafening bang and jolting force of the collision. A sudden explosion of sound that hours later still echoed in his ears.

Their conversation had distracted him, but a premonition came to him as they drove that this was the night he would die. Death would come for him on the remote road she'd taken for no good reason. Fear gripped him, but then the idea settled in an old song. That was when his head hit the windshield.

*

The first sensation was an excruciating pain in his neck, which traveled the length of his arm until his fingers tingled from numbness. He willed movement in his fingers, slowly clenching and unclenching a fist, working the hand to prove he could use it. He felt an old fear trying to get his attention, and he felt death lurking nearby, angry and cheated.

The car had slammed into a guardrail and was tipped forward. Beyond the bridge he saw the three parked vehicles, headlights illuminating the forest.

Natalya was slumped over the steering wheel, unconscious. Her head had struck the windshield, cracking it, and she bled from her lip. His first thought was that she was dead. He placed two fingers on her carotid artery and found a weak pulse. He was suddenly alert. The car's engine was stopped and the wipers were frozen, but one wheel spun freely. His door was badly sprung, but he forced it open with his shoulder, exciting a screech in the metal. He circled the car, and when he came to the driver's side, he saw that one front wheel hung over the embankment, rotating slowly. It was a long drop to the frozen river below. Snow was falling heavily, and river water breathed out cold in the narrow channel cut into the pack ice. Gentle snowflakes softened the violence of the moment. He listened for more danger, but there was only gurgling water. He looked again at the Volga and military vehicles. They seemed unaware of the accident. Garin considered running to them for help, but instinct told him to stay where he was.

'Natalya.' He looked at her face. Nothing. 'Natalya!'

She needed medical help. He got her to the passenger seat with some careful lifting and sliding over the stick shift. He was close to her face, and he felt her weak cooperation, but her eyes remained closed. When she was seated, he wiped blood from her split lip.

The Lada started on the third turn of the key. He kept the headlights off, rehearsing gear movements in the dark, until he found reverse. The engine warmed up, and then he eased his foot onto the gas pedal. It surprised him that the wheels didn't spin. He applied more power and eventually coaxed the car backward until he felt the front wheel top the embankment. He stopped the car when he was off the edge. The immediate danger was gone.

For several minutes, he drove without headlights, leaning his head out the window to discern the road. Their earlier tire tracks were already disappearing in the falling snow. When he was certain they were beyond view of the parked vehicles, he turned on the headlights and increased their speed, following the tunneling beams through the dark night. He understood that everything that day, and the day before, had been arranged. *Stupid*, he thought. *Foolish*.

While he was trying to make sense of things, Natalya stirred, her eyes opening. She seemed confused and tried to speak.

'Don't talk.'

'Are you okay?' she whispered.

'Me? You're the one who's hurt.'

She touched her mouth and saw blood on her hand. He gave her his handkerchief.

'What happened?' she asked.

'You braked. We skidded. The car hit a guardrail.'

She clutched his arm and sat up. 'I remember.' But he knew that she didn't.

'Your head hit the windshield.' He pointed to the cracked windshield. 'Dizzy?'

'No.'

They had arrived at the intersection where she'd turned off the main road. 'Which way do I turn?' he asked.

'It will take hours to reach Moscow in this storm. We must return to the village. I'll drive.'

'You'll kill both of us. Which way do I turn?'

They were the only car on the road during the hour-long drive. The crash, her injuries, the entombing storm, and a near-death experience shattered all pretense of formality between them. Her head lay on his shoulder in a fragile truce, and they settled into a quiet that stretched on with the distance they traveled.

After a long stretch, Garin looked over and saw that she had slumped forward, blood leaking from her nose. He called her name and got no response. There would be trouble if the car was stopped and they found a dead woman. Questions would be asked, and his cover would combust. How could this happen, his life transformed by events that he failed to foresee? He slammed the steering wheel with his palm. *Shit.*

Garin put two fingers on her carotid artery and found a pulse. It crossed his mind to leave her in the snow, but his heartlessness didn't extend to murder. He drove faster and took the turns recklessly.

The village of Koltsovo appeared first as a faint glow through the curtain of snow, but then there were houses on either side, and he found himself moving through unplowed streets. Garin roused Golukov, who came to the front door in a long robe and cotton nightcap with a candle. The two men helped Natalya to a bedroom off the kitchen that had been hastily prepared. Garin waited at her side, angry and resentful, as the housekeeper buzzed about excitedly. Water was boiled for aromatic potions made from herbs, and black tea was brewed. The housekeeper was sent into the storm to fetch the doctor, who had gone to attend a pregnant neighbor.

Through all of this, Natalya lay on the bed under a deep comforter, her pale skin jaundiced by the flickering candle. Electricity had been knocked out by the storm.

*

Garin heard a cock trumpeting dawn outside. Then he opened his eyes to sunlight that pierced the treetops and streamed in the window, blinding him. Bit by bit, he became aware that he was slumped in a hard, wooden chair and in the moment of waking his unpleasant dream took wing and vanished. He sat up.

The room smelled of woodsmoke. For a moment, he didn't know where he was. He saw the Lada parked outside and remembered the drama of the storm.

'So, you are alive.' Natalya sat on the large bed, gingerly

holding a hot cup of tea. She sipped. 'You've been restless. I called your name twice, but there was no response.'

Garin was cold, and his breath fogged. He was still dressed in his clothes from the day before, and an old blanket lay across his legs. He heard voices outside the room, and then he turned his attention to Natalya. There was a small bandage on her lip and her forehead had purpled, but her eyes were fixed on him.

'You look better,' he said.

'I'm fine. It was nothing.'

'Nothing?'

'Nothing.' She tapped her head. 'A bump.' She saw his skepticism. 'Would I be drinking tea if I was hurt? Would I be making jokes? Do you notice any difference?'

'Same voice. Same ingratitude.' He saw her mouth open, aghast. 'Remember what happened?'

'I stopped the car.'

'You crashed the car. I drove us here. Golukov found a doctor who stitched your lip and examined your head. He said you were lucky.' He looked at her. 'Maybe the blow knocked some sense into you.'

'Insults!' She threw off the covers.

He pointed out her clothing, which lay folded on a dresser. 'The housekeeper put you in a nightgown.'

Natalya had begun to undress, but she stopped and shot him an angry look, nodding at the door. 'If you don't mind.' She added, 'We should return to Moscow. People will be asking questions.'

'Who?'

'We have been gone overnight. Questions will be asked.'

'Who?'

'People,' she snapped. 'There are people whose job it is to ask questions.' Her hand swept the room. 'This will interest them. Are you naïve?'

95

Garin gazed at her for a moment. 'There were two Soviet Army jeeps parked across the bridge.'

Silence. 'I saw them,' she said. 'I recognized the Volga. We need a story for what happened. It is better if we have the same story.' She touched her forehead. 'We should say that a tree had fallen across the road. I didn't see it in the storm. The car skidded, and we drove here.'

'Is that to protect me or you?' Her eyes flared. 'Does it matter?'

Garin agreed the details with her without asking for further explanation. It was easy for him to be complicit. The story was believable. In substance, it was true. Natalya's stitched lip was real, the bruise on her head was visible, her worry was evident. All that was false was the tree and the omission of the vehicles.

The morning was still young when they left Koltsovo. Diamond-bright sunlight sparkled on the freshly fallen snow, and the clear sky burned pale blue. Plows had cleaned the road, and the warming sun was melting snow from the pine branches.

'Who were in the vehicles at the bridge?' Garin asked.

'Shitheads. Second Chief Directorate. They are looking for Afghan war deserters. Pashtun and Uzbek conscripts who don't want to fight.'

They were coming up to the intersection where she had turned off. He glanced down the unmarked back road, remembering. The sudden turn and her excuse for a shortcut.

He looked at her. He knew. Posner's absence. The turnoff. Her hand on his. Her lies. He played out the puzzle pieces in his mind, trying to make sense of what she wanted of him. She was young and inexperienced, and he had seen those qualities before, but there was something else he saw in her amateur performance.

11

MOSCOW STATION

S HE'S KGB.'
Garin offered his judgment the next day to Rositske in
Moscow Station. Mueller had joined the conversation by secure
telephone link from Langley. Garin waited a day to make his
report. He wanted to let his suspicions settle overnight, hoping
he'd make sense of what had happened, but the opposite
occurred when he shaped his thoughts in his notebook. The
incident made no sense unless he saw everything through the
lens of entrapment. Her invitation to the Bolshoi. Her insistence
that they have a story to cover up her mistake. But entrapment
didn't explain the vehicles waiting across the bridge.

Garin waited for Rositske's response. He couldn't gauge
Mueller's reaction except by the silence on the phone, but he
saw Rositske's neck redden and his fist clench.

'Your cover is blown. She's a sparrow,' Rositske said.

The door opened, and Ronnie Moffat walked in. 'Sorry I'm
late.'

Garin was startled to see her.

'She works here,' Rositske said. 'She knows what's going on.'
He motioned for Ronnie to sit. 'He thinks the woman is KGB.'

Garin looked from Ronnie to Rositske and felt suspicion
begin to corrupt his thinking. But paranoia was the real enemy,

so he moved on. He spoke carefully, measuring his words. 'Nothing fits together. Why was the Volga there to meet us?'

'It makes sense if your cover is blown,' Mueller said, his voice tinny through the speaker.

'George, hold on,' Rositske said. 'It was dark. How do you know it was a Volga?'

'Three vehicles,' Garin said. 'Their headlights illuminated each other. There were four men inside. A Volga with radio antenna and two UAZs.' He met Rositske's eyes. 'I could be wrong, but the danger of being right outweighs the risk of being wrong.'

There was crackling static on the telephone. 'George?' Garin said. 'Are you still there?'

'Yes.'

'What do you make of this?' Garin asked.

'I don't know. What's your guess?'

Garin had folded his hands on the table, and his face was gray. 'Something is off. She seems too untrained. Too indecisive. Too naïve. She may be a sparrow, or a sparrow in training. They may be using her to see what she can do.'

'Your cover is blown,' Rositske repeated.

'I don't think so. Something doesn't make sense.'

'What, then? Coincidence?'

'Maybe.'

'A coincidence?' Ronnie didn't try to hide her skepticism. 'You tried to get close to Posner, and you found yourself alone with her.'

Garin met her challenge. 'If they doubted my cover, I'd have surveillance on me when I leave the embassy. I don't. No one follows me. I'm clean when I meet GAMBIT. Something is off, but I don't think my cover is blown. They've targeted me for another reason.'

'What's next?'

'Go dark,' Mueller said.

Garin looked at the others. 'Why would a temporary, non-diplomatic employee suddenly withdraw and go dark? That would attract attention. We still need a way to protect GAMBIT from Posner.'

'Do nothing,' Rositske said. 'Take the risk. Business as usual.'

'She's invited me to the Bolshoi. Do I ignore her? Call it off?' His question was met with silence. 'I saved her life. Now I don't talk to her? Let's play this out,' Garin went on. 'There is a greater risk in changing how I operate. Their people will take an interest in the hard-drinking fuck-off who has suddenly changed his spots.' Garin addressed the speakerphone. 'What's the worst thing that could happen, George?'

'They try to recruit you,' Ronnie interjected. Her remark was made in jest, but when the laughter faded, a long silence followed and the idea settled in like the missing piece of a puzzle.

The audacity of the suggestion, its symmetry, and the power of its appeal silenced them. Could it work? Let Garin be turned? A CIA asset working for the KGB, playing both sides.

'It's ridiculous,' Garin said. He'd played that game before. He knew what to expect. 'Ridiculous and dangerous.'

'That's why it might work,' Ronnie said. 'If she isn't KGB, nothing happens. If she is, Alek's cover improves, we feed them misinformation, and we buy time until May 28.'

Garin kept his thoughts to himself as the others debated the idea, tested it, considered its implications, its dangers, and its possibilities. Mueller was asked what he thought.

'Let's assume the worst,' he said. 'They suspect you. Then, by our own rules, we should play this out. If surveillance has seen you, keep going and stay with your cover. That's the rule.'

Mueller queried the group: Rositske?… Garin?… Ronnie?… Garin?

'He's thinking,' Ronnie said.

'I don't like it.'

Rositske's brusque voice cut off the conversation. 'I want to speak with George alone.'

The room emptied. It was late. The meeting had been convened at an hour when it was safe to bring Garin to the off-limits seventh floor.

Rositske moved closer to the speakerphone. 'I'm alone.'

'What's on your mind?' Mueller asked.

'I didn't like him when he showed up, and I have seen nothing to make me comfortable. He is not one of us. Who knows where his loyalties sit. Do you trust him?'

'Up to a point,' Mueller said. 'He has issues with us, but he has contempt for them. It doesn't matter. We don't have a choice. GAMBIT requested him.'

'How do you know he's stopped working for the KGB? I got the file. *Jesus fucking Christ*. He was never cleared. There were questions. Some people thought he was responsible for the loss of General Zyuganov.'

'It was never proved.'

'He was forced out.'

'He quit.'

'He had to leave. There were questions and no good answers. He took what he was offered.'

'What do you suggest?' Mueller grunted. 'Think about it. GAMBIT is out there. He requested Garin. If we remove Garin, who would you slot in?' There was a beat of silence. 'We are where we are.' He added, 'Send Garin back in. I want to speak with him. Alone.'

Garin stepped into the Bubble and moved toward the speakerphone's red light. He glanced out into the hallway at the two people staring at him. He sat down and placed one hand on the other, and his voice, when he spoke, was matter-of-fact.

'George, you want to speak with me?'

'Are you alone?'

'Yes, except for the ones standing outside the Bubble staring at me with their lime-shriveled, pucker-faced expressions. What did Rositske want?'

'He doesn't trust you.'

'I don't trust him. You didn't say what you thought of the plan.'

'I said I didn't like it. Have you been recognized for the work you did here six years ago?'

'No one knows about that.'

'GAMBIT knows. Talinov knows. Their side knows. Are you being targeted?'

Garin lifted his eyes to the people in the hallway, and he felt anger stir and with it a desire for a drink.

'What happened with General Zyuganov?' Mueller asked.

'We made a mistake.'

'You made a mistake.'

'A mistake was made,' Garin shot back. 'They knew he was meeting me at the boat in Vyborg.'

'Have you been compromised?'

'Here?'

'Yes. Do they know you're back?'

'No one has connected me. But how would I know? Wouldn't it be stupid of them to say, "Oh, Alek, welcome back"?'

'Where is their interest coming from?'

'Who the fuck knows? George, don't go there. It's a tunnel without light. It was six years ago. My body was never found. They were led to believe that I was at the bottom of the Baltic. Or dead on the tundra.'

'What happened that night?'

'Read the file.'

'I want to hear it from you.'

Garin knew how his version of the incident differed from the conclusions of the official inquiry. He had no need to defend himself. Their judgment had been made and punishment rendered, his reputation tarnished, his life altered. 'How much time do you have?' he asked.

'Go ahead.'

Garin delved into the part of his memory that contained the willfully forgotten. 'It was a Friday,' he began. He described how General Zyuganov had made his way to Vyborg, near the Finnish border, with a plan to meet a small fishing trawler that would make its way to the Finnish coast under the cover of night. The plan required heavy fog, so the exact date of the exfiltration was not fixed. Then the right conditions arrived and the boat docked in the harbor by the old castle. The trip was sixty kilometers and would take eight or nine hours in normal seas. The plan had been to reach a specific drop-off on the coast by dawn, where the CIA pickup team waited. Garin paused. 'Tell me if you already know this.'

'Go ahead.'

Garin shook his head at a private thought. 'So,' he went on, 'maybe this is the part that you haven't heard. The inquiry was eager to assign blame, and no one wanted to admit it was a bad plan. The idea that a senior KGB officer would make his way alone to Vyborg without raising suspicions in Moscow Center. Langley was convinced of the plan, and no one wanted to hear that it was radically flawed. One man. Visible. Recognizable. Traveling with false documents by Aeroflot. Brilliantly stupid. But no one wanted to listen, so we went forward.'

Garin paused. 'Or maybe this is the part you don't know. It was spring and cold fronts were unpredictable, but frequent dense fogs covered the coastline when cool air followed a warm day. Zyuganov needed a safe place to hide in Vyborg until the weather turned and made the crossing safe from Soviet shore patrols. Zyuganov knew he had to hide until conditions were right, but being unfamiliar with Vyborg and unwilling to risk going to a hotel where he might attract suspicion, he had someone arrange a hiding place. He had help from a trusted person. A Russian. That's what I heard. Another man, or maybe a woman, and I heard both versions of the story afterward. One version had the woman being a girlfriend, but that was the fevered imagination of a man who knew less than I knew, and he was happy to embellish his story. It had to be another KGB officer. That's what I believe. Someone Zyuganov trusted, who had access to false documents – or someone whose trust he bought.'

Garin stared at the blinking red light. 'He never made it to the boat. A dense fog was moving into the harbor, and the time to leave was approaching. The trawler's captain was the first to hear footsteps on the cobblestones, and then I heard a man moving quickly across the dark plaza, staying in the shadows of buildings. A second man emerged from a parked car, and a third followed. There was a brief chase, but then the square filled with cars. Bright headlights revealed Zyuganov, and his fate was sealed. He was brought to his knees by a blow to his head.

'A stranger can disappear for a few days even in a small town like Vyborg, but the KGB knew where to wait. I could hear that from the boat. Five Volgas converged at the same time in a coordinated operation. He wasn't betrayed by a suspicious neighbor or a curious hotel clerk. They were waiting for him.

'The fog was rolling in, but the cars' beams were bright and the square was not far away. I could see some of what was happening, and what I didn't see, I heard. Zyuganov was beaten. They were interrogating him. The operation was blown, and we had very little time before the KGB found the boat. We had paid the captain well, but he refused to leave his trawler, and he paid dearly for his mistake. I left on foot and avoided roadblocks over several days as I made my way to the Finnish border. The KGB was embarrassed by the whole episode. They invented stories about my death that excused the sloppiness that allowed me to escape. In one version, I tried to swim away and drowned in the frigid water. I prefer the version that had me walking across the rocky terrain camouflaged with branches and leaves, carrying a stinking, dead possum to throw off their tracking dogs. The terrain was rough, my body was never found, and they believed I was dead.

'Langley was also astonished that I survived. No one could believe that I got through ten cold days and nights without food wearing only my light parka. So, those skeptical minds assumed that I had been allowed to escape because I had collaborated with the KGB. They had made up their minds. A few were uncertain, but unproven suspicion is the end of trust – and the end of trust is the death of an intelligence officer's career.'

Garin concluded, 'And here I am again. Rositske doesn't trust me. Maybe you shouldn't either. But I'm here. What do you want me to do?'

'Find out what they want from you.'

'And risk GAMBIT?'

'Let them play their hand. You're here. You won't get out of the Soviet Union unless it's with GAMBIT.'

Garin heard the threat. He lifted his eyes to the curious faces outside, then turned back to the speakerphone when Mueller spoke again.

'GAMBIT's copier is being watched because we have a leak in Moscow Station that's compromising this mission. Let's square the circle. Exfil GAMBIT and plug the leak. We'll give them corrupted information to lead them away from GAMBIT. Both of you will get out at the same time.'

Garin stared at the red light. 'I'm the bait?'

There was a long silence. Garin felt the muscles in his neck constrict. He saw Ronnie, still staring at him through the Plexiglas. 'It's easy for you to make the call,' he said. 'You're in Washington. I'm the one who is being asked to climb out of the trench and into the line of fire. Well, I didn't sign on for that. I don't want to find myself in Lubyanka with a pistol to my head.'

'Calm down, Alek. It's a simple entrapment that we're turning against them. If it gets uncomfortable, we'll bring you back inside.'

Silence lingered. Mueller spoke again. 'The White House is asking for updates.'

'Make something up,' Garin snarled. 'Tell them everything is fine. Lie to them, George. Use your talents.'

'I'll make sure you get the credit when it's over. It will clear your record.'

'I don't give a fuck about my record.' Garin slammed his hand onto the red button, disconnecting the call.

*

Garin drew a frigid bath when he got to his apartment. The prostitute had been outside again, and he had been tempted to use her to relax, but instincts warned him off. Shockingly cold water surrounded him when he slipped into the tub, and his breath quickened, but he tolerated the temperature. It bothered him to think of himself caught between Agency bureaucrats, who reduced his life to a few debriefing remarks between sips of coffee, and the diligent KGB. He felt used and angry. He never wanted to find himself at risk in Moscow again. He felt old contempt for Agency puppeteers moving his arms and legs in a flippantly pedestrian production of espionage commedia dell'arte.

Garin pondered his bad choices. He remembered Rositske's and Ronnie's startled faces when he'd walked out of the Bubble, and he enjoyed thinking they were mad with worry that he was abandoning the operation. He put his lips to a newly opened bottle and coughed at the metallic taste. *Tainted vodka.* He emptied the solvent alcohol into the toilet.

A thought struck him when he slipped back into the frigid water. Not all missions succeeded. He should get out now. He had lived the world of two lives – one open, seen, and known to all who cared, and the other running its course in secret, unknown to all except his KGB handlers. And then he'd been compromised, turned, and everything had changed, wearing a mask over his mask. The lies had been harder to keep up, and he'd struggled to keep the layers of deception straight, knowing that a single mistake could be fatal.

He contemplated the steady torture that would come from suspecting every stranger's gaze, the caution of what to say, what to avoid, hoarding his words, living every moment with his old fear of being hunted. If things got unbearable, he could cut and run.

But could he? His old contacts in the Ukrainian mafia would happily accept hard currency to arrange safe passage on a freighter out of Kiev, but he knew them, their corruption. Taking his cash, turning on him.

There was only one way forward.

12

BOLSHOI THEATER

GARIN DID HIS BEST to keep his mind on the performance. He sat in an aisle seat a few rows back from the orchestra pit with a good view of the stage. Tchaikovsky's glorious music and the ballerinas' graceful movements helped unwind his wariness and put him in a pleasant mood. There came a time when he ceased to be aware of Comrade Posner, who sat in the adjacent seat, and Natalya, who was farthest from the aisle.

The curtain came down at intermission and the house lights came up, bringing the audience to its feet with applause. Light from the overhead chandelier deepened the scarlet velvet seats and brightened the packed house.

'Do you like it so far?' Posner asked.

'I wanted to like it,' Garin said. He had seen many worse productions in New York and London, but they didn't know he was fond of ballet. 'I didn't expect to like it.'

'Well, then, success.' Natalya leaned across Comrade Posner toward Garin. 'Every night, they perform to this same standard of perfection. That is why they are the world's best. Every night, they transport the audience to an imaginary place and we all forget our lives for a moment.'

She rose from her chair, and as she did, her willowy figure wrapped in its colorful shawl drew the gaze of lumpish men standing nearby. She tossed the shawl over her shoulder, covering her white silk blouse, which made her look as if she belonged onstage. Lightly brushed pancake makeup on her forehead covered her remnant bruise.

They joined intermission's exodus to the lobby. Natalya wasn't the only fashionably dressed woman, but her lustrous hair, glistening pearls, and scarlet lipstick made her the most striking. Her confident walk and contemptuous smile gave her seductive charm.

Posner nodded at a Soviet Army general with a chest full of medals, and without turning his head, he whispered to Garin, 'He is the deputy director, GRU. He nodded at me, but he noticed you. No one is invisible here. This is one of the few places where it is appropriate to be seen. I am sure someone is already asking who you are.' He abruptly changed the subject. 'Natalya's debut performance in this ballet brought her great attention.' He looked at Natalya. 'Do you mind if I tell the story?'

'It's stupid,' she said.

'But worth telling, Natasha.' He turned to Garin. 'She was magnificent throughout, but her brilliance came in the fourth act, when Odette is distraught. You'll see it when intermission is over. It's the scene when the swan maidens try to comfort her, and Siegfried returns to make a passionate apology. Rather than remain a swan forever, Odette chooses to die, and Siegfried chooses to go with her, forever united in love.'

'You're spoiling everything for him,' Natalya said. 'He doesn't know the story.'

Posner raised a hand. 'It is beautifully tragic, and she performed it perfectly. The audience was mesmerized. When the curtain came down, the audience leapt to its feet in wild applause. She won over the skeptics – of which there were many – and then the next week, having performed so brilliantly and earned high praise, she also became the object of vicious jealousy.'

Natalya swatted Posner's hand when he pointed to her ankle with its flesh-colored wrap. 'You would exaggerate the time of day if you could,' she said, and turned to Garin. 'Don't ever let him see your weakness. He will never forget it.'

A trio of blinking lights signaled the end of intermission. An usher approached Posner, handing him an envelope. After reading it, he looked at his companions with grave eyes.

'There is an emergency. An editor in London is still at his desk and asks to speak to me. An Englishman without a life now has a claim on mine.'

Garin and Natalya returned to the hall. She passed Posner's empty seat on the way to her own, but seeing it empty, she changed her mind and sat next to Garin.

'He won't be returning,' she whispered, placing her hand on his arm.

After a moment, he withdrew his arm to his lap, slumped in his chair, and fixed his eyes on the stage. He tried to ignore her.

'I think he planned it this way,' she whispered.

Garin made sure to look surprised.

*

The Metropol Hotel was a short walk from the Bolshoi Theater, but Natalya and Garin were shivering when they spun through the hotel's revolving doors on their way to the Metropol restaurant. The maître d' stood at his station, a thin, short man with graying hair swept back and dark eyes. His severe face softened when he saw Natalya.

'Good to see you again, Natalya Seergeevna,' he said. 'I have a nice table for you. Will Comrade Posner be joining you tonight?'

'No. Just us,' she said.

The maître d' led them to a corner table set for three, and he crossed the knife at the third setting, signaling the change for the waiter. Silverware was perfectly aligned, and the linen napkins were folded to reveal the hotel's embroidered insignia.

'Is this to your liking?' the maître d' said.

'Yes. Perfect. Thank you.'

'You come here often?' Garin asked when the maître d' left and she was unfolding her napkin.

'Not anymore. It's too expensive. We would come after a performance to drink, and if someone managed to entice a patron to join, we got a meal out of him.' She nodded at the maître d'. 'He sees everything but keeps his mouth shut. There – look.' She discreetly pointed across the room to a woman in a beaded silver dress who possessed unambiguous celebrity, collecting polite sideward glances from other diners. 'She is Brodskey's favorite now. A good dancer, ambitious, clever with her compliments, and very cold. An ice queen.' Natalya pointed to her ankle. 'It was her boyfriend, but he wore a mask, and it was never confirmed.'

Two flutes of champagne arrived at the table on a silver tray. 'Compliments of the maître d',' the waiter announced.

Natalya started to sip but hesitated, and then raised her glass. '*Na zdorovye*. To your health.'

Garin threw back his drink and grabbed the escaping waiter's arm. 'And one vodka martini, straight up, no olives.'

'Two,' she said.

Dinner was ordered, wine selected, and the prompt arrival of the appetizers followed by entrées put them in a pleasant mood. She chose a red Burgundy from a good vintage that she knew was in the cellar, and they had taken the chef's suggestions – he had the cranberry-braised goose with a tower of aromatic rice, and she had taken the steak pommes frites, eating the frites one at a time.

'You would wait hours for this beef in a store, but this is the
Metropol. Posner has his sources, and he lets his palm be filled.'

With the food and the wine, their conversation turned from
dull topics of war and corruption to lively gossip, and then to
the differences between men and women – and specifically
their different tastes in literature.

'I didn't know you read novels,' she said, shocked. She was
a fan of *Wuthering Heights*, which she'd read in London and
loved for its audacity and Heathcliff's cruelty. And then, in a
flirtatious way, she said that men only liked books by other
men – Hemingway, or Tolstoy, or the Englishman, le Carré. 'In
their books, young men never die of broken hearts. They die
from knives and bullets. Which do you prefer?'

'Broken heart or bullets?'

'No!' She laughed. 'Which authors?' She looked over her
lipstick-smudged wineglass. Without waiting for an answer,
she added, 'Your question may be the better one. I can see
from your hesitation you aren't familiar with those authors. I
guess you are the type who would prefer a bullet.' Her eyes had
averted, but they settled on him. 'I prefer the tragedy of love.'

'You're a romantic,' he said. He swigged the dregs and licked
the wineglass. 'Drowning is low on my list of preferred ways
to die.'

The check came in a red leather portfolio. She made no effort
to pick it up. He let it sit between them, thinking that Posner
would have paid, but now it was his to pay. He put cash from
his wallet inside the portfolio.

'Thank you,' she said brusquely.

*

Light snow had been falling earlier, but it had stopped when
they stepped into the night. A brisk wind swept the boulevard

111

and park across from the Metropol. They found themselves standing under the Karl Marx monument, a looming figure who commanded the square. A few Russians were out at that late hour, and a few foreigners from the hotel took advantage of the fresh snow to make snowballs, which they threw at each other playfully, laughing.

'What now?' she asked. 'Have you had enough of me?' She formed a snowball in her hand.

'It's late,' he said.

She threw it at him, striking his shoulder. 'I know the time. You don't have to tell. It makes you sound dull.'

He batted away a second snowball. He looked at her playfully mocking face and tried to look inside her mind.

'Maybe you prefer men?' she chided.

Garin's eyes had drifted to the dark edges of the park, and to the night's stillness, as he looked for surveillance. 'Do I look reluctant?'

'Yes. Or disinterested.' Her third snowball hit him in the face, powdering his eyes. 'You should be cautious. You're an American in Moscow. It is past midnight. You might encounter a woman who wants to take you home.'

Garin saw an energy and vitality that were different from the abrupt, scolding woman he had come to know. 'Yes, I might meet such a person.'

He balled snow and returned her volley, and an energetic snow fight ensued, each approaching the other, seeking playful advantage. They scooped handfuls of snow, hefting it at each other at close range, and she called him endearing obscenities, until they found themselves face-to-face. Their eyebrows were white, cheeks flushed, lips wet from melting snow, and she planted a kiss on his mouth.

She pulled away, slightly embarrassed. He stared at her, uncertain what to make of the advance. He remembered to smile, and then she leaned forward and put her lips on his again, indulging a moment of nervous excitement. They remained kissing in the open snow, and the surprise of the intimacy caught the attention of several hotel guests, who clapped like an audience.

Snow had begun to fall again, laying a false peace on their romance.

*

Garin hopped off the No. 39 tram. He followed a few steps behind Natalya until she put her arm into his and pulled him forward along the quiet, tree-lined street of prewar apartment buildings. She dug for her keys at the entrance to a five-story building with a Beaux Arts façade. In the distance, he heard the tram's bell clang. She inserted a key in the front door, and they passed through a small vestibule to a circular staircase that wound up toward a dark skylight.

'Shhh,' she whispered, finger on her lips. 'Neighbors.'

They walked up the wide, curving marble steps, passing a baby stroller outside the second-floor apartment. His hand slid along the ornamental cast-iron railing, and his eyes took in the terracotta fresco, wooden moldings, and ornate wall sconces that dimly illuminated their way.

'You live here?'

'What do you think?'

'How long?'

'So many questions.'

Garin glanced back down the staircase and looked for an escape route, if needed. Instinct and experience made him cautious. She walked ahead in darkness, like a ghost.

Natalya hit the vestibule wall switch inside her third-floor apartment, and the living room filled with dim light from a

Venetian chandelier above a mahogany dining table. He was struck by the apartment's size and grandeur. A worn Chinese rug lay on the parquet floor, and set against one wall was a claw-foot sofa of worn crimson velvet. Against the opposite wall was a French Empire breakfront with crystal glasses and stacked dishes.

Garin tried to make sense of the objets d'art obviously collected over a lifetime. He lifted a porcelain vase of exceptional craftsmanship, and when he looked closer, he saw the glue lines where it had been poorly repaired. When his first impression passed, he saw everywhere the hints of a place that had fallen on hard times. The wall paint was yellowed with age and flaked in spots, parquet squares were loose, and the beveled wall mirror was cracked. Several dark wall sconces were empty of replacement lightbulbs. Twined newspapers were stacked in one corner beside empty glass jars saved for the occasion when a use presented itself. He noticed the duality of the apartment – the richness of a time capsule that helped make its present poverty less visible.

'This was my grandfather's flat. He got that vase in Germany.' She placed her shearling coat on a closet hanger and invited him to do the same. 'Drink?'

'Vodka.'

'I have port wine. I'll bring two glasses. We'll drink a little, talk a little. You can tell me why you are in Moscow.'

She returned in a moment from a hidden room, holding two glasses and a decanter. He was standing at a wall of framed photographs. A young Soviet Army officer in uniform was standing in the turret of a T-62 tank among a group of shirtless enlisted men with ammunition bandoliers draping their necks and beer in their hands, mugging. He was tall, dark-haired, with fierce, commanding eyes.

'My brother,' Natalya said, seeing Garin's interest. She

poured modest portions of port. '*Zdorovye*.'

Garin nodded at the photograph. 'Does he live here?'

'He's dead. Last year, in the mountains outside Kabul. A mujahideen rocket hit his tank.'

He turned and looked at her.

'We were close.' She abruptly turned away. The room was cold, but she'd lit a kerosene heater when she entered, and it put out meager warmth. She stood by it. 'It's warmer here. The heat goes off before midnight. Do you like the apartment?'

'No one lives like this in Moscow.'

'My father had a good position, and he kept it when Grandfather died. We were three generations. Now it is only me.' She nodded at the photograph. 'He was a brave soldier and a stupid patriot.' She looked at Garin. 'And you? Tell me something that will surprise me.'

Garin sniffed the port.

'It's local. Not good, but not poison. So,' she said. She didn't finish her thought and suddenly went to the sofa, relaxing into the cushions and stretching her long legs onto a Turkish hassock. She patted the sofa. 'Sit. My father collected things on his foreign postings. He collected the Meissen porcelain in Dresden after the war. And you,' she said, 'where did you learn Russian?'

He sat beside her. 'As a child.'

'An émigré? That makes sense.' She sat up, dropping her legs from the hassock, and took the glass he had placed on the coffee table. 'May I?' She took the amber liquor in two quick swallows and looked at him with curiosity. 'You speak Russian, but you're not a real Russian. You're difficult. I don't understand you.'

She snuggled against him. 'It's cold. Put your arm around me.'

He did, and they sat together in silence for a moment. Then

she pulled away and looked at him. She began to undo the top button of her silk blouse, and her eyes dropped to the second button, which she also undid. Her fingers fumbled nervously.

'I want to do this,' she said, her eyes averted. 'Everything else will go away. You will leave. But we will have this evening.'

He saw her nervous excitement, her defiance, and her fear. She had rehearsed well, he thought. He felt her hand on his, taking it gently and placing it on her neck. He knew she was acting. *Acting, but not acting?*

They moved to the bedroom, and in letting her guide him forward, he looked for the silvered smokiness of a two-way mirror or a hidden microphone. His ears were alert for the soft click of the front door closing.

She had stepped out of her black skirt and removed her stockings, which she placed carefully over the back of a chair. She leaned forward, reaching behind to undo her bra, and laid it by the dress. She stood before him naked – alive with apprehension. Her fingers worked to undo his belt buckle, her eyes meeting his, and he struggled out of his shirt, working an uncooperative button. She admonished him with a whisper: 'Slowly.'

Her body was as pale as milk and thin, but with the sinewy strength of a dancer. He found her performance amateurish, which was attractive in its own way, and she seemed ignorant of how to help him along. He saw sullen urgency in her movement, and he admired her willingness to take a risk. For one frightening moment, he felt a terrible attraction.

Her hand was on his arm, slowly moving along the scar on his neck, feeling its contours. She kissed his lips with a passion he was returning, and she continued until she coaxed his ardor and he relaxed the vigilance that was a reliable companion when he sensed danger nearby. Her eyes closed, and her body moved with the frothy passion of an inexperienced lover. In the back of his mind, he heard someone enter the apartment.

'You would be more beautiful without your fear,' he said.

'A stupid, romantic thing to say,' she whispered in his ear. 'I'm not a romantic.'

Two men burst into the bedroom, bringing a confusing kaleidoscope of sensations. Bright overhead light washed everything in harsh illumination; shouted instructions came fast, and he smelled violence on the men who took him. He was naked, and his arms were pinned behind his back. In the midst of the drama, he struggled to look shocked and embarrassed. His cheeks purpled with anger, and he stared indignantly into the beefy, thick-necked faces of two KGB.

Garin caught a glimpse of Natalya. She had hurriedly wrapped herself in a bedsheet and was rushing from the room. Garin twisted his head toward the two men holding him. They were professionals who knew how to immobilize without leaving marks on his body.

'Shitheads,' he grunted.

Both men stepped aside, and Garin saw a third man standing in the doorway. What struck Garin first was the man's nonchalance, and then Garin noticed the unpleasant way he had of looking at Garin with predatory interest.

'Don't struggle,' Comrade Posner said. He drew on his cocktail cigarette holder and released smoke from the corner of his mouth. 'You might bruise yourself.'

Garin felt the man's gaze like a fashion designer evaluating a model on a runway.

'You won't look good bruised. Someone will ask what happened, and you'd have to come up with a believable story. You are better unmarked.' He threw Garin's clothes at him. 'Get dressed.'

Garin shoved his legs into pants and his arms in his sleeves, buttoned his shirt, and sat on the bed to put on his socks. He

PAUL VIDICH

focused on his clothes, but his mind calibrated what would come next and how he could use his jeopardy to his advantage. Nothing so far had surprised him. Then Posner added the predictable details: a microphone in the lamp, the record of the encounter, the hidden camera with a lens that looked through a small dark hole in a black-and-white oil canvas on the wall. 'It's one of Golukov's,' Posner said. 'We had to damage the painting, but you are worth the cost.'

Garin finished tying his shoes but didn't respond.

'How clever you've been, thinking you could enter the country, do what you are up to, and be gone before we found you,' Posner said. 'I have diligent staff who matched your visa to our old photos. A young woman saw the visa's forgery, and that started our investigation. The glasses threw us off, and the graying hair, but the girl noticed the scar. You've changed your name, shaved the moustache, gotten rid of the mutton chops, but the scar is the same, and the face, too.'

'What do you want?'

Comrade Posner stood in the middle of the room, and having the upper hand, he wasn't to be rushed. He held the cigarette holder delicately and nodded at the door Natalya had fled through. 'She has suffered. Her father's execution, her brother's death, and then the ankle. So much pain for such a young woman. What does an ex-ballerina do?

'I knew her father. He was high up in the First Chief Directorate. I was able to protect her. A handsome young woman, even an orphan, attracts supporters. Her brother's death was a terrible blow. After her father's execution they were close and now... well, she works for me.'

Posner held his cigarette at arm's length, observing it. His eyes dropped to Garin again. 'This doesn't have to be hard for you.'

'What do you want?'

118

Posner motioned for the shorter KGB agent to bring two glasses and the bottle of port. Posner filled both. 'Chernenko is dead. The news will be in tomorrow's papers.' He drank the ersatz liqueur and put down the glass. 'Local shit,' he said. He looked at Garin. 'Why am I telling you this? I will get to that. Patience, Alek Garin – or whatever your name is. Patience in a spy is a useful thing. Though I am not sure you are patient. Excitable? Cautious? But I haven't seen your patience. Maybe you will surprise me.'

Posner brought the glass to his lips but stopped. 'Americans don't understand what is happening in the Soviet Union. You are still fighting the Cold War of ten years ago, but the Soviet Union of Brezhnev and Khrushchev is dead. Chernenko was the last Bolshevik – elderly, dull, uninspiring, the personification of decay. He has been sick for years. The surprise is not that he is dead but that it took him so long to die.

'He could barely stand at the podium to read his eulogy of Andropov last year, and when he finished, two bodyguards helped him from the stage. He was a chain smoker and a drunk, and he suffered from cirrhosis and heart disease, and who knows what else. He was a stumbling example of the Soviet Union. Now he is dead. His death will be announced on page two of tomorrow's *Pravda*. Gorbachev's ascension will be on the front page. He will be making changes.'

Posner looked at Garin, making a judgment. 'Excitable, but also stupid,' he declared. 'Deputy Chairman Churgin found your performance at Spaso House insulting. He was livid when he was told his thugs didn't get to rough you up on your way back from Golukov. Maybe he's forgotten about you, and maybe he hasn't.' Posner took a measure of Garin. 'Do you know Lieutenant Colonel Talinov?'

Garin considered which answer to give. There was a risk to any answer, but only one answer preserved his cover, but that was also the answer that shut down the conversation and left him clueless of Posner's intentions.

'Yes.'

'How?'

'He's KGB. Ambitious. Ruthless. Plays the piano.'

Posner tapped cigarette ash into his palm. 'So you do know him.' He smiled. 'I too am KGB, First CD, but you probably already knew that, or suspected it. I don't try to hide myself. How do you know Talinov?'

'I don't.'

'You said you did.'

'I know *of* him. I've heard the name. What do you want from me?'

'Cooperation.'

'For what?'

'Zyuganov.' Posner rose and closed the bedroom door, revealing on the back of the door a photograph of a younger General Zyuganov with his wife and two young children on a picnic blanket spread on a lush green meadow in front of a Scottish castle. 'He was thirty-six when this was taken. He'd just been promoted and summoned to headquarters from London. Perhaps you recognize his daughter, Natalya. She is eight years old in the photograph, but you can already see her defiance.'

Garin felt the long arm of coincidence at work. Nothing surprised him that night, but later he would write in his diary that he'd been startled to discover that Natalya was General Zyuganov's daughter.

Garin leaned forward to look at the photograph and then settled back in his chair. He had admitted too much. His memories of Zyuganov returned like bad dreams. There was no room for attachment in his work, but he had been younger, and he'd made that mistake. Their conversations along Moscow River had surprised him. He had come to respect the man, if he was honest with himself, but that wasn't something he put in his reports. Wise, troubled, and eloquent in five languages. He had admired the man's humanity and came to know his fears.

Posner said, 'We have surveillance photos of the two of you sitting on a bench by the river. Two spies sharing a friendly conversation.'

'I reported my contacts,' Garin said with a grunt. 'I'm sure he did as well. That was the protocol. It was our job to probe each other. It was our job to meet.' He glared at Posner. 'And I'll report this meeting.'

'We'll see how you feel about that when we're done. Why did you meet Zyuganov?'

'He asked me to defect.'

Posner was skeptical. 'What's your real name?'

'Aleksander Garin.'

Posner drained his glass and poured himself another. Almost as an afterthought, he raised his glass, offering Garin one, but Garin shook his head.

'It will be a long night,' Posner said. 'Why did you come back?'

'Human rights work,' Garin said.

'Stupid answers.' Comrade Posner's demeanor hardened and his eyes narrowed. 'You are in a small box. This evening, the photographs we took, your history. I have enough to expel you. You will be gone in forty-eight hours, and I will get a big commendation. And you will have to explain yourself to Langley.'

Posner's expression was fastidiously unpleasant. 'That would suit me, but it wouldn't satisfy me. I need more than that. I need your cooperation. I see I have your attention.' Comrade Posner paused. 'The CIA and the KGB have men who abuse their positions, corrupt men who are promoted because they tear colleagues down. I am sure you know men like this.

Perhaps you are one. Our politics may be different, but our sins are all human.'

Posner lifted his silver cigarette holder and gazed at the lengthening ash, which he knocked into his palm, adding more to what he already held. 'Each day, we wake up devising ways to defeat each other. But we have a common adversary: corruption.'

Posner stepped forward and stood over Garin, his lips pressed, eyes narrow. 'I want Talinov.' He spoke the name like a curse. 'Chernenko is dead. Things will change. The KGB will rid itself of corrupt men, and Talinov is on the list. He must be discredited to the deputy chairman for wrongly executing Zyuganov. I want your cooperation.'

'Why this?' Garin nodded at the bed.

'Jeopardy, to focus the mind.' Posner leaned forward. 'I will tell you something, but only because I want your cooperation. We are enemies, yes, but there can be cooperation between enemies if it serves a common purpose. Talinov is such a purpose. He betrayed General Zyuganov and has incriminated colleagues to advance himself, and if needed, he would put a gun to your head. A corrupt and evil man. He likes to say he plays Chopin, as if that absolves him. Our side is better off without him. You will also benefit. What I need is evidence of his crimes – evidence only you can provide.'

'I don't have evidence.'

'You may not know what you have. If you were the dissolute, hard-drinking embassy employee you claim, you'd be sweating by now, or screaming innocence, but look at you. So calm, so guilty. So well trained. Your cleverness incriminates you. I had my doubts, but Natalya was certain. I see she is right. You are CIA.' Posner's head shifted side to side like a viper. 'Why are you in Moscow?'

Garin didn't respond.

'Your presence will be of interest to my colleagues, but that's not why I have you here.' Posner looked around the bedroom before his eyes settled again on Garin. 'Talinov is Second CD and I am First CD. The famous KGB compartmentalization keeps us ignorant of each other's work, but I hear gossip, or have drinks with a mutual colleague who lets something slip, or see documents I'm not supposed to see. I have heard Talinov thinks the embassy is running an asset inside the GRU or the KGB, a senior military specialist. There is a list of men who use a particular copier that is going around. I am not on the list, but men who work for me are.' Posner stared at Garin. 'Are you his handler? Is that why you're here?'

Garin raised an eyebrow. 'If I were, would I be so stupid to let myself fall into this trap?'

Posner went for his drink but found the glass empty. He paced the room nervously, like a caged zoo lion. 'I don't think you're stupid.'

Garin saw in Comrade Posner the brooding anxiety of a man on death row. Posner's tired eyes and the beads of sweat on his upper lip helped Garin believe what he was hearing, that he was being recruited by one side against the other in a power struggle among rival KGB factions. He tried to imagine the contention and distrust that had prompted this extraordinary circumstance. Garin possessed a tenacious mind, and once he heard something that he didn't fully understand, he didn't banish the problem to forget it. He kept the mystery alive, knowing that unless he had a satisfactory answer, he was in danger of being drawn deeper into a labyrinth of deceit. Suddenly, he had the uncomfortable sense that he had lived this moment before. A similar room. Friendly blandishments from a clever interrogator. Garin looked at Comrade Posner. He saw an erudite, self-important Russian with nervous eyes.

Garin shrugged. 'What else?'

'A common interest.'

'We have no common interests.'

Posner nodded at the bedroom door. 'She is a common interest.'

It was later, when he reflected on Posner's comment, that he understood Posner's affectionate reference was a threat.

'It is in your interest – the CIA's interest – to discredit Talinov,' Posner said. 'If it could be proved that Zyuganov was falsely accused and wrongly executed, Talinov would be exposed, tried, and punished.' He watched Garin. 'I see you are skeptical of my motives. And you should be. It's an unusual request. The only way you could surprise me is to say that General Zyuganov wasn't a traitor.'

'A traitor to what?' Garin asked. 'Family? Russia? The Party? Maybe he *was* a CIA asset.' Garin smiled at the confusion he saw on Posner's face. Lying had always come naturally to Garin. Falsehoods had been his childhood protection from a Russian mother who lied to her American husband. Lies, he had discovered, were more helpful and sometimes more satisfying. They gave him power. Lies kept people from being able to plunder his truths. As a consequence, he had developed a taste for secrecy and a facility for lying. And he knew that the *appearance* of a lie could sometimes be more effective than the lie itself.

'I don't believe it,' Posner said flatly. 'But if it was true, and you would know, there is still reason you would want Talinov discredited.'

The two men looked at each other, and a communion of interests was understood. It was a rare moment of agreement that had nothing to do with trust and everything to do with self-interest.

'I need evidence,' Posner said. 'The men who made your visa can forge the incriminating documents I need.'

'Are we done here?'

'No.'

Garin was already moving to the door. 'What else?'

'You are getting a bargain. If Talinov is removed, your asset is protected. I am told he is an important person.'

'You think this puts you in a position to make requests?' Garin's hand swept the room.

'Yes, I believe it does.'

'What do you need?'

'Money.'

'For what?'

'For me.'

Garin scoffed. 'You should be paying me.' Then he cocked his head. 'Who do you work for?'

'Myself.'

Garin heard in his abrupt answer, carelessly thrown out like a boast, a truth. Greed. It didn't surprise Garin. There was never enough money for the man with an appetite. 'How much?'

Posner threw out a number.

Garin laughed.

'How important is he to the CIA?' Posner asked.

'Half.'

Posner shook his head. 'I'm paid no better than you. I can't live on my shitty pension.'

Garin was silent, giving the impression it was a hard bargain.

'How much is on you?' Posner asked.

Garin produced a bundle of US currency he was carrying for GAMBIT. 'A down payment,' he said, handing over the envelope and watching Posner count. 'Don't contact me,' he added. 'I will communicate through her, and she will pass along everything: account number, wire instructions, evidence against Talinov. Everything through her.'

Garin slipped out of the building and stayed in shadow,

away from the streetlight, a precaution until he was certain no one was waiting to follow. His breath plumed in the night air. He regretted leaving home without his gloves and wondered what else he'd forgotten. He went down the list of things he hadn't foreseen, all of which had changed the game. This had been his life too long. He darted into the street and hopped on an empty, brightly lit tram.

Later, he drafted a summary of the meeting for Mueller, adding at the end: *I've been away six years, but nothing has changed. Personal survival among KGB rivals is still a blood sport. Middle-aged intelligence officers look forward to becoming pensioners with a dacha and a small vegetable garden and maybe, if they're lucky, a nest egg of hard currency.*

13

METKA

Two DAYS LATER, GARIN received an urgent note from Mueller instructing him to contact Ronnie, who would give him after-hours access to the Bubble's secure telephone.

Garin stood alone in the dark conference room. Waiting. The phone rang almost exactly at the time arranged. He lifted the black handset on the second ring, but there was no one on the line. Static. He hung up. It was then that he saw an office light on at the end of the hall. Someone in Moscow Station was working late. The telephone rang again.

'Hello?'

'Alek, it's me.'

Garin took his eyes off the office light. He had rehearsed how he would explain what had happened, and he'd decided what he could say and what he would avoid. 'You got my list of his requests?' he asked.

His note had been explicit. He wanted a classified internal KGB memo that sat in CIA archives altered to implicate Talinov in General Zyuganov's treason; he asked that Technical Services falsify coded transcripts that rewrote the history of General Zyuganov's defection; he'd specified dates, paper stock, and the exact Soviet stamp.

'What's going on?' Mueller demanded.

'Posner wants to discredit Talinov. There's a power struggle inside the KGB. Who knows what's really going on, but they're rivals and it is unstable, and I have been sucked in. Understand? What Posner doesn't know is that the documents I want Technical Services to create will do the opposite of what he wants. They will implicate him.'

'In what?'

'Does it matter? It will buy time. A few weeks, maybe more. And there is something else. He wants two hundred fifty thousand dollars wired to a Swiss bank account.' Garin waited for a response. 'George, you're quiet. You've never been this quiet.'

'What's the money for?'

'Him.'

'*Christ.* That's crazy.'

'He's corrupt. What choice do we have? He matched my visa to old photos in their files. He knows I'm CIA, but he doesn't know why I'm here, and he hasn't connected me to my earlier work. We're buying his silence.'

'GAMBIT?'

'He's heard rumors. He suspects something.'

'What?'

'It doesn't matter. Posner wants to make it look like he's recruited me, but it's a cover to explain his contact. He's blackmailing me, putting me at risk. Play it out. Whose idea was it? Nothing happens by chance. You were set up, blown, expelled. I am being set up.'

There was silence on the other end of the line.

'Get me the documents,' Garin said. 'Wire the money. It will buy time.'

'How much?'

'We can't wait for Border Guard Day. We need to move up exfiltration. You're quiet again. Do you hear me?'

'Loud and clear. *Shit.*' A beat. 'You have to go dark,' Mueller said.

'And the plane tickets to Leningrad?'

'You'll leave by train. Finland is what they'll expect. You'll travel to Uzhgorod, and we'll pick you up on the Czech side.'

'And just walk across the border?'

'We've used a smuggler before. He'll drive you across.'

'When?'

Mueller threw out a date. 'If you can't make that date, I'll be there the next night. Same procedure. Same time. We'll be there every night for a week until you show up. The Czech driver will pick you up at the train station. He'll have a false trunk that will hide GAMBIT. You'll ride up front with the wife. Understand? You have to get out of Moscow.'

'How will I know him?'

'We'll get you what you need.'

'How?'

'Ronnie. She'll be your contact.'

'You trust her?'

'Only her. Understand?'

'Yes.'

Mueller paused. 'This is the last time we talk until we meet at the border. Is there a drop point she can use?'

Garin went down the list of places he was familiar with in Moscow. He considered the postal box by the metro station, but it was too public. It was suitable for messages, but there was no place to leave documents. He rejected the radiator in the apartment lobby where GAMBIT left film canisters. He couldn't risk a mix-up.

'There is a small church at 25 Mayakovsky Street,' Garin said. 'Below a Madonna and child icon, there is a gap between the wall and a cabinet. Tickets and documents go there. I've used it before. It's safe.'

In the silence that followed Garin knew Mueller was writing.

'Leave your apartment tonight,' Mueller said. 'Stay someplace they won't look. Tell GAMBIT there has been a change of plans. Do you hear me? Go dark.'

Garin felt fear settle in like an old friend who'd come to visit. Things were not happening the way he had foreseen, but he'd been here before. Since early the previous week, many unexpected dangers had required an extraordinary faith in himself. That greedy wretch Posner, making his sudden demand and turning his job upside down. He had arrived in Moscow knowing he might be recognized, but he'd thought it a remote possibility. He had never expected chance to triumph over a reasonable plan.

'Go dark with what?' Garin demanded. 'Where? What money?'

'There is a wall safe in my old office. I doubt Rositske changed the combination. You'll find what you need there.' Mueller was emphatic. 'Stay away from the embassy. Wait for Ronnie to make the drop, and then get GAMBIT to the Czech border. Understand? You're not safe.'

When he stepped out of the Bubble, Garin saw the office light at the end of the hallway go out. Garin turned the doorknob of Mueller's office and pulled the door shut, closing it softly. A muted click. He stood absolutely still in the darkness, his ears a tuning fork for danger. The alto clap of a woman's heels approached down the hallway, passed the door, and then faded on their way to the air-lock entrance.

Garin went to work quickly. His butane lighter illuminated the combination safe on the wall, and Mueller had been correct about Rositske's laziness. Garin emptied the emergency pouch on the desk and sorted the contents. He took the envelope of cash, a dozen krugerrands, and the list of emergency Moscow contacts, safe houses that wouldn't be safe now. He considered the Colt pistol. He knew that if it came to the point where he needed to defend himself, he was probably already a dead man and a casual interrogation that uncovered the pistol would doom him. But there was comfort in knowing he was armed. He stuffed the pistol under his belt and put an extra magazine in his pocket. He pondered the cyanide capsule. He had known one compromised Russian spy who'd opted for suicide over torture, but he was not that brave.

*

Garin's luck had been on a good run, but everyone's luck runs out – the car that careens around the corner as you step off the curb, the aircraft engine that fails on your flight home. How many times had death been his companion in a dream, his corpse in a body bag at a remote border crossing? Long ago he had tried and failed to banish those images. He reminded himself that his work in Moscow wasn't his most dangerous. His work in Hungary during Prague Spring had been more daunting; his work in Beirut had been more terrifying. But every job had its moment of truth, when the unexpected met the unforgiving, forcing him to improvise.

It happened to him as he passed through the air lock and waited for the elevator, having impatiently pushed the button twice. At the sound of the arriving elevator, he patted his chest, a tic, to confirm that the things he'd taken were safely hidden. The elevator doors opened to reveal Helen Walsh, standing in the back. It would be hard to say who was more startled and equally hard to say who did a better job of hiding that surprise.

'I thought I was the last one on the floor,' she said.

Garin knew that he had only to muddy her judgment, not change it. 'I had to call Langley.'

131

'How did you get up here? I'll have to report this, Alek. Give me a reason why I shouldn't. A legitimate reason.'

He gazed at her. 'I'm authorized.'

'Oh, come on. You've been an odd duck since you arrived.'

Garin saw her eyes, alert, her mind working. A fragrant scent came to him in bright purples and pale lavender. He experienced the colors like a hallucination and under the elevator's fluorescent light, he saw a phosphorescent glow on his hands. Purple tint like a faint inkblot. Dizziness, the smell. His mild case of synesthesia was accompanied by a pulsating headache.

He stared at his glowing palms. *METKA. What did I touch? The doorknob?* The light in the elevator became intense, and he fumbled for a stick of chewing gum, popping the peppermint stick in his mouth.

'It's nothing,' he said, watching her stare. 'Elevators make me nauseous.'

Blue latex gloves poked from her handbag, and seeing him spot them, she tucked them out of sight. 'Do you need a doctor?'

'No. Gum equalizes pressure in my ears.'

The elevator made a slow, rattling descent, and they stood side by side against the elevator's back wall, watching the floor-indicator light mark their descent. Garin was taller by three inches, and he had the advantage of strength, but weight and height weren't of use to him in a situation that called for him to think clearly. He rubbed his temple to focus his blurring eyes.

He heard her question and saw her hand reach for his jacket, and he reacted badly, brusquely pushing her away. Then an apology. 'Let's talk tomorrow. I'll explain when I'm feeling better.'

*

Ten minutes later, Garin was walking along Tchaikovsky Street when a car pulled up alongside. Through the lowered window, he saw Helen Walsh.

'Get in,' she said. 'I would have offered you a ride if I had known you were walking.' When he hesitated, she added, 'You'll freeze.'

He sat in the front seat.

'Where do you live?'

'Kutuzovsky Prospekt.'

'It's on my way.'

She sped up for a block and suddenly braked into a U-turn, confirming that the KGB surveillance car following them was lost. 'You'll get the hang of things in another month or so,' she said. 'Some day when there's world peace, we'll sit down with our KGB counterparts and have a good laugh about the games we play.' She glanced at him nervously. 'How long is your posting?'

'Two years.'

'That long?' She raised an eyebrow. 'I heard less. Special assignment. Where are you from?'

'Nowhere, really. Moved around a lot.' Garin looked over his shoulder.

'I lost them two turns back. The car behind us is a civilian Lada. No antenna.'

They arrived at Garin's apartment block, empty of traffic at that hour, but there was no parking, so Helen let him out on the street. He had the uncomfortable sensation that she was staring at him when he opened the door.

'Feel better.'

Metallic light from the full moon came through skeletal trees and cast shadows on Garin as he walked toward the lobby. He saw that the twenty-four-hour security guard was gone, but the local prostitute smoked a cigarette by a parked car, blowing

PAUL VIDICH

kisses. The lobby's bright light was a beacon ahead, and then he heard a car door open.

'You forgot this.'

Helen Walsh walked quickly toward him, gripping an object. At first, he thought it was a pen, and he reached into his pocket to confirm his Montblanc was missing. Then he saw her raised arm. He had been momentarily distracted, but when his eyes came off his jacket pocket, he saw that she had closed the distance in a sprint. Moonlight reflected off the syringe in her raised fist. She was upon him when he saw her fierce eyes and determined intent – and the glinting needle coming at his neck.

He had raised his hand to block her attack, but a figure emerged from the shadows and tackled Walsh. There was a violent scuffle and muffled grunts that became a deep-throated scream. The person had blunted the force of Helen's attack and reversed it. The needle had plunged into Helen's neck, sending a squirt of blood onto Garin's cheek.

Helen was momentarily stunned. The syringe hung limply from her neck as she stumbled backward, pulling at it. The drug was weakening her as her eyes dilated and her body struggled to resist the poison. She collapsed on the sidewalk, gasping repeatedly. Her effort to breathe ended, and she lay on the ground, her legs bent at a terrible angle, her hands still clutching her throat. Her eyes were wide and fixed.

'That could have been you.' Garin turned to his defender – Natalya – who stood a short distance away. Her hair was unkempt from the struggle, her hat thrown to the ground, her jacket torn, and she had a scratch on her cheek. She removed the syringe from Helen's neck and wiped away blood from the puncture wound, erasing evidence of the needle's entry. She arranged the fallen woman so her hands were at her side, not at her throat, and she faced Garin.

'We have to leave. KGB are on their way. I heard the radio transmissions.' Natalya searched Helen's pockets and tossed the car keys at Garin. 'Take these.'

'What are you doing?'

'She has to be moved.'

He stood over the dead woman. *Think*. 'You're crazy.'

She took the legs and motioned for him to take the shoulders. 'It stopped her heart. When she's found, it will appear to be a heart attack. A new KGB tool.' She looked at him. 'She is Second Chief Directorate.'

Garin finished getting the body in Helen's car, and he sat behind the wheel, working the unfamiliar ignition. He heard a hissed pop, like a soda can being opened, followed by a startled cry. The prostitute stood in shadow just beyond the apartment lobby's light. Her arms were extended, her feet planted, and she sighted along the barrel of a silenced pistol. A second pop went off, accompanied by a dim muzzle flash. Garin saw Natalya on her knees, keeping behind the cover of a parked car. He was suddenly alert. It crossed his mind to leave the scene of the murder, but he knew that was a bad choice. He took his Colt from his belt and quietly slipped out of the car, dropping to one knee in a crouch by the front wheel. His first shot dropped the girl. He had aimed at the chest, and the bullet entered the pale skin above her low-cut blouse, sending her violently backward.

He went to the fallen girl. So young. Dead. He didn't linger on the sight. He knew that even a brief glance would haunt him. He found it hard to expunge the faces of his dead.

'She is KGB,' Natalya said breathlessly. Her eyes darted, looking for more danger.

'She was going to kill you,' he said.

'Was it easy for you?'

'It's never easy,' he said.

Apartment lights above them had gone on one by one, and one curious resident had thrown open her window and stared at the dark street.

'We have no time,' Natalya said. 'Get in her car. Follow me. Police will arrive soon.'

Garin drove behind Natalya through the narrow, twisting streets of central Moscow for fifteen minutes and pulled up behind her when she suddenly stopped in front of an apartment block. He opened his window for Natalya when she approached.

'Put her behind the steering wheel.'

Garin did as instructed. They lifted the corpse into the driver's seat, placing the head so it slumped forward. Garin managed to jam Helen's booted foot on the accelerator, and they watched as the car lurched forward, jumping the curb and hitting a tree. The hood popped, the engine continued to run, and steam drifted up from a burst radiator.

Garin joined Natalya in her car. 'She lives nearby,' Natalya said. 'She will be found shortly. It is in everyone's interest to keep this quiet.' She turned to him. 'The prostitute saw everything. They know who you are. You will be linked to the prostitute's death, sought for questioning, interrogated, and expelled. Or shot.'

She pumped the gas pedal twice, struggling to start the Lada, and then, on the third try, the engine turned over. She looked behind and around and confirmed there was no witness. She saw Garin staring. 'What?'

'Why are you doing this?'

'You are no help to me dead or expelled.' She glared. 'I want to defect.'

They drove in silence for several minutes, but then she pulled to the side of the street, breathing hard. She looked straight ahead in a great effort to avoid meeting his eyes. A great gulf opened between them. He could feel it, and he knew she did, too. A line crossed. 'Surprise' was not a big enough word to describe his understanding of what they'd done. He would do anything, give up anything, to be free of the consequences that had begun to settle in like an approaching storm.

Natalya started laughing, horrible, nervous laughter, full of fear. When she quieted, she turned to Garin, her eyes defiant and contemptuous. 'You don't know me. You only know what I've allowed you to see.' She took a deep breath and said, 'This is something that I've planned for a long time.'

Her body began to tremble. Garin touched her cheek. It was burning.

'I am fine,' she muttered. 'We will be safe. You can stay in my flat a few days. A week. We'll make a plan.'

137

14

ARBAT DISTRICT

H<small>E WOKE UP THE</small> next morning in Natalya's apartment. His headache had passed, as it always did, but the disorientation of a chemical hangover lingered. He had suffered these episodes before, mostly when he came in contact with a certain type of scented shampoo or cleaning product, and he had recognized METKA's staining phosphorescence in the elevator's fluorescent light.

'You slept for fourteen hours,' she said when he emerged from the bedroom. 'You look terrible. There is a towel in the bathroom if you want to shower. I will make coffee. Then we can talk.'

He lingered under the shower's meager stream of cold water. He soaped up and found a way to ignore the cold. The chill helped clear his grogginess. Moscow hadn't changed. Intermittent electricity made hot water a game of chance. He toweled quickly. He used the safety razor she had put out on the sink, and he also found neatly folded socks and men's boxer underwear.

'So,' she said, sitting opposite him at the dining table. She had prepared toast with peach jam, which she pushed toward him. He added four sugars to the intense dark Turkish coffee she'd served, and he stirred slowly counterclockwise, giving himself time to consider his circumstance. He sipped and then took the drink all at once.

'I ate hours ago,' she said, watching him.

He took several bites of toast while she refilled his cup, and he repeated his routine, stirring the sugars slowly in one direction, thinking. He kept his eyes on her but said nothing.

'You're lucky,' she said.

'That you were there.'

'That wasn't luck. I was doing my job. Lucky that she was an amateur. A trained assassin would have killed you. She must have thought you were a danger. You suspected her?'

He lifted his palms. 'METKA.'

'That explains her attack.' Natalya looked at Garin as he stirred his coffee. 'My father was like that, a patient stirrer. I always wondered why he stirred his coffee so slowly. He liked his coffee sweet as well.'

'I stir, and I think.'

She slid a photograph of General Zyuganov across the table toward Garin. 'You knew my father. That is why you were in Vvedenskoye Cemetery.'

He looked at the black-and-white photograph of a middle-aged man on a London street, posing by Big Ben. There was a smile on his face, a man in front of a tourist attraction, but the photograph didn't open up, and it gave no hint of who took it or what was on Zyuganov's mind.

Garin saw a likeness between father and daughter. She wore a long-sleeve blouse, open at the neck, and her hair was pulled back in a bun. It surprised him how many different appearances she was able to assume. He recognized her concerned expression. It was similar to Zyuganov's – intense, but almost sad. All hint of her capacity for violence was gone.

'Yes, I knew him.'

'Did you know him well?'

'What he allowed me to see. A decent man. A good officer. You're a little like him.'

She leaned back and folded her arms on her chest. 'He never mentioned your name. I knew he was planning to take us out of the Soviet Union, and he said not to worry, which of course made me worry. He said he trusted someone, and if things went as planned, I would meet him.' She looked at Garin. 'You must be that man. He said you were a Russian, and I assumed he meant a *real* Russian.'

Garin smiled at the thought that there was something false about his birth.

'He's been gone six years,' she said, 'but I still remember that week. You must remember it, too.'

'I do.'

She waited for him to say more, but when he did not, she leaned forward in her chair and gazed at the photograph. 'A young girl doesn't know her father. Only later, when you're grown, do you begin to appreciate your parents. You see them as people.' She paused. 'He was a typical father. Kind. Distant. Funny. A stubborn man, yes, but with a big heart and firm principles. He hated what Russia had become.'

Natalya sat back abruptly, her arms again folded tightly over her chest, and looked directly at Garin. Her voice was matter-of-fact. 'He was taken to Lefortovo Prison. I later read the report, which I had Comrade Posner request. They interrogated him for two days but got nothing. Then he was taken to a basement cell. He was executed this way.' Her finger pointed to the back of her neck. 'It's a technique the Cheka developed called *Genickschuss*. A shot to the nape of the neck that causes minimal blood loss and instant death. That is how he died. His head was bent forward, and Talinov fired slightly downward at point-blank range. I don't dream of that horrible moment anymore, but for a long time, I was sorry I had read the report. Some images stay with you.' She exhaled to expunge the thought. 'He never gave up the name of the man who betrayed him. That is who my father was.'

Natalya's face was a cocktail of emotion – sad, fierce, angry, and forgiving. The living daughter remembering her dead father. She wiped a tear with her finger.

She stood abruptly and went to the window, where she looked onto the empty street, lost in thought. She turned back and faced him. 'What happened to him?'

'We were in Vyborg. He had come by airplane with false documents. He was to meet us at the dock when the fog was thick. Border guards and KGB knew he would be there.'

'Who betrayed him?'

'I don't know.'

'Posner thinks it was you.'

'He is mistaken. I was working for the Americans.'

'And the KGB.'

'Who told you that?'

'Posner says it was you.'

'But you don't believe him.'

'Why do you say that?'

'If you believed him, you wouldn't have saved my life.'

She scoffed. 'I have my reasons.' She gazed at him across the table. 'You visited his grave with a flower. That isn't the act of an enemy, even an enemy with remorse. That is what I believe. And there is one more thing – I will find that man with your help. And then you will take me out of the Soviet Union.'

Natalya collected cups and plates from the table. 'How will you get me out?'

'It's dangerous.'

'Staying is dangerous. By now, two bodies have been found. No one will admit she was KGB inside the embassy, but suspicions will lead to you. In time, that will lead to me. The

Americans will demand her body; the KGB will keep it until the autopsy is complete. You will need to move quickly.'

The room was quiet except for the tyrannical ticking of the wall clock. Garin spoke at last. 'A dozen things need to happen,' he said. 'You need travel documents. Tickets. We will leave by train to the Finland Station. It will look better if you are traveling as a party of two. I will buy train tickets to Uzhgorod as well.'

'What day?'

'I will know tomorrow.'

She disappeared into a bedroom. After a moment, she returned with a men's two-piece suit. 'Wear this. You are my brother's size. They will be looking for a foreigner. This will make you look Russian.'

Garin accepted that chance occasionally worked in his favor and sometimes did not. He had fought against the tyranny of chance when he was a new intelligence officer working his case load, but after several failures and a few successes, he understood that it was easier – and safer – to accept the unpredictable outcomes of chance and turn them to his advantage. He put on the suit and became a Russian again.

15

SOKOLNIKI AMUSEMENT PARK

Garin entered Yugo-Zapadnaya Metro Station. He pushed through the afternoon crowd of commuters and came to a group of Komsomol youth in uniform holding basketballs. He got on the first train that arrived and took a seat at one end of the car, lowering his hat and absorbing himself in a newspaper.

Twenty minutes later, he arrived at Kropotkinskaya Station. The doors opened, and a few people got off. Garin looked up from his newspaper at the sound of the car's pneumatic doors closing, startled to see where he was, and jumped up, mumbling, 'Damn it. Kropotkinskaya,' and he squeezed through the closing doors. On the platform he confirmed no one had come off the train after him.

Garin boarded the next train. He got off several stops later, stepped onto the crowded platform, and headed for the stairs. When he got to the mezzanine, he slipped behind one of the fluted columns. He waited half a minute while the flow of riders went through the arched space, and then he continued to walk in the same direction. He emerged on the street and set out on foot for his rendezvous.

*

General Zyuganov. Deputy Chairman Churgin. Lieutenant Colonel Talinov. Comrade Posner. Garin felt the world around him shape and reshape as men played out their roles, but he'd found enough connecting threads to bridge the gaps in his understanding. His suspicions began to settle inside the dark labyrinth. Garin didn't share any of his worries with Petrov when they met. It was a short and uncomfortable meeting.

'It's rude to eat before your guest arrives,' Petrov said.

Garin had entered Sokolniki Amusement Park's administrative cabin and found Petrov with his elbows on the plywood table, cutting sausage. The bottle of vodka was open, two glasses were set out, and the brown paper wrapping was open.

'But I'm starved.' He threw a glance at Garin. 'And now you're a Russian playboy. Fuck me.' He laughed. 'Did you trade a carton of Marlboros for those clothes?'

Petrov placed two slices of sausage on a brown bread and bit into the sandwich. He poured Garin a tall glass. 'I know I won't be wasting this on you. What happened? You look terrible.'

Garin drank, said nothing.

'Quiet. Like usual. I saw your signal. I was here yesterday, too. What's so urgent?'

'We have to move up the date.' Garin saw a grim response on the man's face.

'*Yob tvoyu.*' Fuck. 'I assumed something was wrong.' He looked steadily at Garin. 'I heard an American woman died. Rumors are everywhere in Lubyanka. What I know is that so many rumors carry a lot of falsehoods, but just the fact of the rumors is enough. Talinov is livid. For an implacable man, he is loud. His office is down one floor, but I pass it on my way in. She must have been his asset. I heard him screaming into his telephone. There is a search on.'

Petrov cut a slice of cured meat and moved it to his mouth with his blade.

'We are crossing the border at Uzhgorod,' Garin said.

'Not Finland?' Petrov gazed at Garin. 'It's better. They would expect Finland. It's better to do what they don't expect.' He looked up from the meat, cautiously suspicious. 'You are now a risk. If they look for you, there is a chance that they will find me. What do I tell my wife?'

'We won't be seen together. You will travel together with your son in first class. I will be in third class. You have your documents. You only need to buy train tickets. Buy four round trips to Leningrad and four to Uzhgorod. If they look through the reservations, they'll be looking for a party of three.'

'When?'

'In nine days. A week from Friday. You will board the train after work.'

Petrov poured another glass of vodka. 'Have you written my obituary?' With a butcher's eye he patiently cut a thin strip of fat from the meat. 'Beyond a certain point, there is no return. Perhaps we have arrived there. Or perhaps we arrived there when I gave you my name. I will miss these little meetings of ours. It's pleasant to speak with you.' He threw back his vodka and slammed his glass on the table. 'Okay.'

Petrov stood. 'Let's take a walk. I think better when I walk.' He laughed grimly. 'The point of no return.'

It was an unusually warm and sunny afternoon. They walked along the narrow path, using the occasion of the mild weather to escape the administrative office's claustrophobia. Bright white clouds flitted across the pale blue sky, and birds were a chorus in the budding flower beds. It was already spring and the implacable thaw of Moscow's winter had turned the path into mud.

Petrov dismissed Garin's concern that they'd stand out walking in a park that had not opened to the public. This was Petrov's danger, Garin thought – a man who took unnecessary risks on a whim.

*

They met once more the next day. Garin came at noon with arguments to address the reluctance he expected to hear from Petrov. The big, hulking Russian glided over the path, almost weightless with an uplifting enthusiasm, and when he was seated, he pulled out a cloth bag of film canisters. Garin reached for them, but Petrov kept them.

'When we cross the border,' he said. 'And there will be more. It will help in trusting you if I keep these.' Petrov stared at Garin. 'The papers you had me put on Talinov's secretary's desk have stirred a hornet's nest in Lubyanka. There are meetings, rumors, speculation, and violent apprehension about who will be pulled from his office. So, the process starts. It is a good time to leave.'

Again, the weather was nice, so they walked, and Garin provided the new details of the exfiltration, using information that he had found in the envelope Ronnie had left at the agreed drop-off. A Mercedes with a specially fitted compartment would meet them to cross the border. His wife would be up front and he and his son would be hidden inside.

When Garin was done, they continued in silence for a time, and then Petrov pointed to the park's aging attraction.

'They planned the Ferris wheel originally as a replica of the seventy-one-meter-tall ride in Prater Park in Vienna – the Wiener Riesenrad. Have you seen it? No? Well, it's stunning. This one was supposed to be like that, but funds were short, and it kept being shrunk until it is what you see, a plaything for children. It's like the Soviet State. Big ambitions, the beautiful idea of worker equality. But there was no will to build that world. It was easier to execute the ones who saw the hypocrisy. Billboards declared prosperity on collective farms while children starved. It was miserable under the tsar, and my family starved then too, but there was no hypocrisy.'

Petrov sat on a bench and patted it, signaling Garin to join him. He lifted his face to the warming sun and enjoyed the spring moment's little pleasure. Then he leaned forward, elbows on his knees, lost in thought. It was ten o'clock in the morning.

'I have discussed a plan with Olga. We can't just be seen going off to the train station with suitcases. Neighbors will take note. The guard in our lobby will report something. So, we have arranged to visit her parents for the weekend in their village, where we go frequently, but we will never arrive. We will make it look like we have died, but no bodies will be found. We will leave word with her parents and our friends that we are stopping on our way at a lake. I will make sure the boat is missing. It will appear as if we capsized. It will be days before the alarm sounds, and then a few more days before the KGB piece together their interviews with neighbors, relatives, and co-workers, and from all this they will only know that we arranged everything for a weekend visit to her folks. They will first think we were murdered. By the time they suspect I am alive, we will be across the border.'

Petrov suddenly turned glum.

'We found a listening device in our apartment. It's not unusual, but still, when you find it in your own home, it's upsetting. Posner may have planted it himself. Son of a bitch. Olga is beside herself. Now, when we talk about the plans, we walk along the river. At home, everything is "How was your day?" "Did you go to the store?" Stupid domestic stuff.'

'We are handling Posner. Be careful.'

'I am fully aware of the danger,' Petrov said. 'I know the long list of the KGB's counterintelligence successes, but there has never been the case of a man caught talking to his wife. Caught in a dead drop, yes. Caught in a brush pass, yes. Caught operating a clandestine radio, sure. Those are dangerous things, but there is no case of the KGB arresting a man because he happened to be strolling with his wife.' Petrov spat his opinion to the sidewalk.

He glared at Garin. 'Our preparations are complete. Everything we own will stay in the apartment. Clothes, photographs, old letters, jewelry, money. Everything. It must look like we left for the weekend and planned to come back. When we are reported missing, the KGB will come. They will examine everything, even the dust. As you requested, Olga has bought four first-class tickets to both cities.

'We have set out clothing so we can change our appearance. We will leave the apartment in track suits. In the metro station bathroom, she will change into a dress, high heels, and a blond wig. You will know me when we get to the station because I will be wearing wire-rim glasses, a German suit, and paisley tie. Our appearance will match the identity documents. They are very good. Olga was impressed. They made her feel better.'

'Have you told your son?'

'He is five years old. We only have a chance if he genuinely doesn't know.'

'He has a new name.'

'Olga has a pretend name game we will play. But he will also be sedated. He will sleep on the train and again when we cross the border. He will be asleep at my side inside the compartment.'

'What haven't you thought of?'

Petrov spat. 'What haven't *you* thought of? We will play our part. It's up to you now.' He paused. 'The story I heard was that Zyuganov made it to the border, and he was crossing alone.'

'I will be in the car with you. What about your wife? Has she agreed?'

'It depends on the day. She is worried about the boy. The sedatives will calm her, too.' Petrov looked at Garin for a moment. 'If I am arrested, I want you to look after my son. He is smart, clever, and he should have a full life, even if I am not there. He's a good kid.'

'Nothing will happen.'

'Something always happens,' he snapped. 'I want to hear you say it.'

'He'll be safe. You have my word.'

'Good. It might be your first decent act.' Petrov was silent again. 'How do I know you won't make the same mistake with me that you made with Zyuganov?'

'I may make a mistake, but it won't be the same mistake.'

Petrov laughed. 'Some sense of humor you have. The saddest men have the best jokes.' He looked at Garin. 'I don't know what you're thinking. I don't even know your name. *Sukin syn.*' Son of a bitch.

Petrov raised his face to the warming sun again. 'This you don't know,' he said. 'I will be bringing with me a technical report that will be of great interest to your Pentagon. We have built an ingenious weapon that can destroy your early-warning satellites, making you vulnerable to a nuclear first strike.' He smiled. 'It's why we win chess tournaments but can't run a factory. A special type of concentrated intelligence.

'You look interested. I too was interested when I first read it. Space is different. A world without gravity, and conventional explosives don't do well, and then there is the problem of objects approaching each other at very high angular speeds. Pursuit curves are either the dog's pursuit, where the dog chases its prey by running straight at it, or the wolf's, where the wolf aims at a point in front of its moving prey. Neither works for the entire flight of an attack missile. Too much fuel is required, and it is impossible to be exactly accurate over the great distances the missile must travel.

'I am an engineer by training. For an engineer, solving a

big problem is very special. And the way we solved this crazy problem, well, the best way to solve a crazy problem is with a crazy solution.' He looked at Garin. 'How did we do it? Huge filament nets studded with ball bearings, which hit the satellite at a speed of nine hundred meters per second. You won't know we've launched a nuclear attack until it is too late.'

Petrov stood. 'And just to be certain I have the CIA's full attention, and its best thinking on my escape, I will carry the film with me when I cross the border.'

He started to walk along the muddy path, but arriving at a gate a few yards away, he happened to turn. The instinct of a man who knew he was being watched. Two militia stood on a bridge across the swollen creek.

'A woman!' he shouted, nodding to Garin, who had slumped on the bench. He flicked his cigarette into the mud, adding, 'Always a woman.' He opened the gate and was gone.

Garin waited until the two militia had made their way back to the Ferris wheel. Then he too passed through the gate and walked in the opposite direction to Petrov.

16

DINNER PARTY

GARIN LEFT THE APARTMENT and set out to arrange the final details of the exfiltration. He had his shoes shined inside the entrance to the metro station, and when he was done and ready to pay, he asked the boy if he could buy one tin of black boot polish. When the boy hesitated, Garin added twenty more kopeks to his offer. Next, he found a secondhand shop that sold eyeglasses. After trying on several, he chose a wire-rim pair that pinched the bridge of his nose – the careless choice of a *tekhnikum* instructor. He added to his teacher's appearance with an old coat he convinced a pensioner to sell.

He made his last purchase at the train station. He paid cash for two pairs of round-trip tickets for travel on successive nights from Moscow to Uzhgorod. For identification, he presented the Soviet passport Technical Services had created under another name. When he left the station, he made sure not to hurry. He knew he was being hunted. He settled into the persona of a Muscovite minding his own business, making his way home in the bustling street. He ignored sounds that made pedestrians around him jump, and he was careful not to look at the militia who watched him.

There was one more errand. The Russian Orthodox church at 25 Mayakovsky Street was small and rose-colored, with a sad, cracked bell tower. It sat between taller, more robust buildings on a quiet side street, lost in time and neglected. He entered through the wooden door and found himself facing a dark nave with a single flickering candle. Cold dampness filled the unheated space. The shadows of evening added their depressing tone to the unused sanctuary – and to the dismal problems of his challenge. No one had ever been successfully exfiltrated from the Soviet Union. Below an icon of Madonna and child, in the gap between the wall and the cabinet that General Zyuganov had used for his dead drops, he found Ronnie's envelope.

Garin inspected the paper of the document. One edge was torn, the ink was faded to give the appearance of age, and the surface was worn as if repeatedly handled. He verified the Russian paper stock. A perfect forgery, unless you knew what to look for. He looked in the envelope for the second document, but it was missing. He looked behind the cabinet and on the floor but found nothing. *Shit.* He wrote a note for Ronnie and placed it where he knew she'd find it.

He turned to leave but stopped briefly and placed his fingers on the icon's delicate silver frame, submitting to his urge to test the relic's powers. Then he stopped. She would come, or she wouldn't. No prayer would change that fact.

*

Garin stood at Natalya's third-floor apartment, raising his hand to knock, when suddenly the door opened and Natalya stood before him, horrified.

'You're late,' she scolded. Her black hair fell to her shoulders as if each strand was weighted. She wore scarlet lipstick, and her chartreuse blouse revealed a pearl necklace that curved to her cleavage. 'Did you not remember? I had friends who were coming for dinner. They arrived an hour ago.'

'I didn't forget.' A lie. 'Something came up.'

'You're rude.' She stared at him. 'Come in. We just sat down. Let me introduce you.' She double locked the door and led him toward the dining room, where lively laughter made a festive atmosphere. She presented him to the three people who sat at the dining table, which was set with crystal wineglasses, mismatched china, and serving bowls of stewed meats and vegetables. She pulled him forward.

'He's been found,' she said to the table. Then to Garin, 'We couldn't wait. They were threatening to leave.' She whispered in Garin's ear, 'For a man who obsesses over time, you are remarkably late.'

Garin sat between two flamboyantly dressed ballerinas with wild scarves over their shoulders and unkempt hair that they swept back self-consciously or pushed from their sullen faces. They stared. Natalya sat across from Garin, beside a man in his forties with long, graying hair, a decade older than the women, who ignored Garin. He tossed pieces of torn bread into his mouth and entertained Natalya with flirtatious whispers. They all seemed to know one another and, being familiar, they interrupted one another in the course of yelling. Garin slipped into his seat, happy to be ignored and, for a moment, he thought, unnoticed, but Natalya looked up.

'This is Bogdan,' she said, swatting the man's hand from hers. 'An old friend. And they are Anna and Galina. Serve yourself.'

Garin was quiet most of the dinner. He observed the others, listened without appearing to listen, and smiled when something clever was said or if one happened to look at him for his reaction. Anna and Galina were confident and haughty, stealing glances, and they talked about the ups and downs inside the Bolshoi company, offering their view of the artistic director's new favorite. With each sip of wine, they opened up more and said funny or insulting things. Surly Bogdan popped bread in his mouth and kept looking at Garin until at last he couldn't contain his curiosity.

'Who is he?' he asked Natalya, looking straight at Garin, as though he were a rival. 'He sits there like a turtle with his head in his shell.' Bogdan leaned toward Garin. 'Tell us a little about yourself. You haven't opened your mouth all night, except to fill it. We all know Natasha's friends, but you are a new face.' The man poured himself a generous glass of wine. 'We are all friends here. Writers, dancers, and Natasha – who knows what she does. Honor us with a few words of biography.'

Garin met Bogdan's boozy presumptuousness with a flat expression. He saw Natalya redden. There was a long silence around the table.

'I am a translator,' Garin said.

'Who do you translate?'

Garin threw out a few writers, still current enough for the purpose of the conversation, and books he'd read so he could speak knowledgeably, if needed.

'Anti-Soviet writers like Bulgakov?' Bogdan asked. 'He was at the famous Spaso House party.' There was a startled silence. Bogdan leaned forward and looked directly at Garin. 'Do you believe in God?' He pushed away Natalya's hand. 'Let him answer.'

Garin paused. 'No one has ever asked me that.'

Bogdan laughed. 'You know, God doesn't exist in the Soviet Union. He's been exiled. Anyone who has seen him walking like a beggar, or disguised as a child, is quickly reeducated.' Bogdan looked at Garin like a cat who had cornered a mouse. 'You speak Russian well. Old phrasings, unusual accent, but a native speaker. Do you translate Russian into English or English into Russian?'

'Both. Sometimes Russian into Russian.'

Bogdan smiled. 'We used to risk our lives to share samizdat

manuscripts of dubious quality, made precious because they were forbidden. But those days are gone. They died with Brezhnev. Things are better now.'

The two dancers laughed. The dark-haired girl with cherry lipstick and a long olive neck mocked Bogdan. 'Don't be a toad. You don't have to show off your stupid Party allegiance.' She looked at Garin. 'This man is being polite. You should learn from him instead of trying to seduce Natalya with your secret whispers – which are obvious to all of us, by the way.'

The second dancer had flaxen hair, thin black lips, and scolding eyes. 'Maybe you'd like to invite both of us to bed to show off your Party affections.'

Anna and Galina were giddy with laughter.

'Fine,' Bogdan said. 'No more insults. There's always something to look forward to. Always a tunnel at the end of the light.'

Bogdan leaned toward Garin. 'I was once a samizdat publisher, and for that I was called a traitor – but not enough of a traitor to go to jail. I applied unsuccessfully for an émigré visa right after I lost my job as a civil engineer and shortly before I took a job on the night shift at the botanical garden, joining the pool of the marginally employed. It was essential for a Soviet citizen like me, a Jew and a writer, to keep a low profile, and no one has as low a profile as a night-shift guard at the botanical garden that closes at dusk.

'That is who I am,' Bogdan concluded, nodding at Garin. 'Tell me about yourself.'

Natalya stood and began to gather the plates. 'Enough of politics. It's boring. I have a walnut *rogaliki* for dessert. It is all I could find.' She handed a large serving dish to Bogdan. 'Help me clear.'

Garin never did say anything about himself. After-dinner aperitifs were poured, and with them conversation moved from one topic to the next, avoiding politics. The evening began to wind down, and inevitably the conversation returned to politics.

Bogdan lifted his glass of wine. 'Chernenko *est mort*.'

'Why in French?' Galina asked.

'It sounds more civilized to say death in French. The French seem to die gracefully in bed.'

*

Natalya called down the circular staircase to the lobby, reminding her departing guests to secure the front door on their way out. She turned to Garin, who stood behind, glass in hand.

'Well, those are my friends,' she said. 'You succeeded in drawing attention to yourself by saying almost nothing.'

'I should have kept my mouth shut.'

'He was baiting you. He is jealous of men with faith.' She gazed at him as if trying to look into his mind. 'Something I see under your mask.' She raised an eyebrow. 'Now, when I meet Bogdan again, which may be never, he will remember you. But he is a dissident, and he will have no desire to draw attention to himself by reporting you to the KGB. He is a good writer, but he writes about his crummy dissident life, so nothing will ever get published. He didn't like you, but you are safe.' She looked at him. 'Are you adventurous?'

'About what?'

'Let's walk to the roof. I will show you a different Moscow.'

*

The night sky was a pincushion of stars that dimly illuminated the dark, suffering city. The closest stars of the Milky Way were visible as distinct points of light, which made the constellation seem close and tangible, as if one could reach up and touch it. Natalya remarked on the clarity of the sky and how she rarely saw stars like this anymore.

They stood at the edge of the stone parapet and were cold, having left the apartment without coats, and without thinking she put her arm in his. Suddenly realizing what she'd done, she withdrew and wrapped her arms around herself.

'I come here on summer nights,' she said. 'I look out and wonder what Moscow was like in Tolstoy's time. I think of the people then, their lives, their struggles, and the smells of that city. All gone. And this too, what we are looking at, will be gone. But gone in a different way. I miss what it never was.' She looked at Garin. 'Do you understand?'

He didn't respond.

'I'm talking nonsense,' she said, laughing to herself. 'I was brought up here as a child by my father, who told me stories about his father, and he pointed to the landmarks. Then I would come up by myself and look at St. Basil's, the Kremlin, and Moscow River. I was an unhappy child, but I was content here. I wished I had lived in Tolstoy's Moscow. I thought it would have been a better time to be alive. As if I had a choice.'

She raised her arm toward the red star on the Spasskaya Tower inside the Kremlin wall. 'Now there is only the State and the Party. Our Evil Empire.' She mocked the words. 'It is a stupid phrase. We are not evil, and we are not an empire. Your politicians denounce us to feel good about themselves. This is Russia. We are only people. Yes, we have Party apparatchiks like the ones who pulled Maria Yudina from her bed to perform. They were frightened of Stalin. Fear rules here.'

She studied his face. She straightened her back. 'I am a little frightened. Frightened of you.'

'Why me?'

'Because I am fond of you.'

They were standing close to each other, not touching, but their eyes met. Neither said anything for a long moment.

'Come,' she said. 'It's cold.'

'It's cold!' he shouted into the night.

'What are you doing?'

'It's cold!' he shouted again.

'You're crazy. Neighbors will hear you. They'll call the militia.'

'This is the Moscow I remember,' he said, resisting as she pulled him toward the roof door. He pointed at the sheltering sky and the grim beauty of the sad city. He howled.

'Come,' she said, laughing. 'We'll freeze to death, and then all the food in the refrigerator will go to waste.'

They descended four flights down the winding marble staircase to her apartment.

'You will sleep in my brother's room.' She pointed to the small room at the end of the hall where he'd slept for two nights. 'You know where the bathroom is.'

The bedroom had a frilly dressing table and a satiny bedcover she had neatly turned down. He slid under the covers. A full moon had risen and washed the room in silver light. There was a fight in his heart that kept him awake. He went over their conversation, and even as he pushed aside thoughts of her, Natalya kept invading his imagination, until finally he forced himself to concentrate on Petrov's escape. He considered the plan and tested its parts to understand where it was weak and where it could fail. The repetition of detail had a sedative effect. He clung to his drowsy worry like a drunk coddling his empty bottle, until the numbing patterns put him to sleep.

At one point, he thought he heard a sound outside. He went to the window, closed the curtain, and pulled back one corner, making sure that he couldn't be seen from the street. There was only a three-legged dog loping in the shadows. Garin looked in both directions, certain that he had heard the sharp click of a car door closing. The quiet street was dark and empty. He dropped the curtain. Before slipping under the bedcovers, he happened to glance down the hall and confirmed that Natalya's bedroom light was off.

*

Garin woke with a start. Bright morning light bled through the edge of the closed curtain. For a moment, he didn't know where he was or even what part of his life he was in. He sat up quickly and recognized his shoes, clothes, and then the bedroom. He remembered.

Garin was on the bed tying his shoes when he noticed his wallet on the dressing table was open. He went through it and confirmed its contents: cash, false identification, several old photographs, and two random receipts. He unfolded one. The trick was simple. He kept a strand of hair in the fold, where it would be imperceptible to any person who went through his wallet. If it was missing, he knew his wallet had been searched. The hair was gone.

Garin considered her deceit. There was nothing in his wallet that compromised him, but she had been looking for something.

17

ON THE RUN

'COMING, COMING.'

Garin had knocked three times when he heard Natalya call from inside the apartment. When the door opened, he presented a cloth bag with eggs, a loaf of black bread, and a duck he had bought on the black market in his old neighborhood. The toothless old woman had recognized him when she took his money but said nothing.

'Thank you.' Natalya wiped her hands vigorously on her apron. Under the apron she wore a long skirt, a black silk blouse, and her pearls. She pulled him into the apartment and glanced nervously down the stairwell. 'You're late, but you weren't followed. An American businessman was arrested this afternoon.' She took the cloth bag. 'I made my mother's favorite recipe. She had only one, so it was her favorite. *Kotlety*. I will also cook the duck. We will have the eggs for breakfast.'

She looked at him, her head cocked slightly. 'Your disguise is terrible.' She straightened his glasses on his nose. 'I expected you hours ago. I thought you might have been detained. Thank God you weren't. I hate to eat alone.' She removed the envelope from the bag. 'What's this?'

Garin had made a second visit to the Russian Orthodox church. 'It's for Posner. He's expecting it.' Garin removed his shoes in the vestibule, as he'd been instructed. 'Smells good.'

'We'll see. I don't cook often. There is always someone who asks me to dinner.'

She had set the dining table and placed a vase in the middle with a single red rose. 'White is for cemeteries. Red goes with the wine I got from a friend.'

Garin washed his hands. He was aware that she'd straightened up. A pair of beige hosiery hung on the shower rod, and the overpowering lavender fragrance of a cleaning product came to him as violent red.

'Comrade Posner was questioned today,' she called out from the other room.

Garin emerged and pretended surprise. 'For what?'

'I don't know. We had a meeting in his office, but he didn't come. I asked where he was. Everyone was quiet. His secretary was almost in tears. Everyone knew something, but no one said anything. This is the way it happens.' Her brow wrinkled, and her voice deepened. 'He protected me, and for that I am grateful, but everyone in his department will be under suspicion.'

So it had begun. Garin tried to look worried. 'Get him the envelope tomorrow. It's important.'

Wine and nervousness made Natalya garrulous at dinner. He asked about the apartment, and she said that it had belonged to her maternal grandfather, a prosperous criminal defense lawyer, who had once defended Lenin in St. Petersburg. After the Revolution, he'd had the privilege of joining the Party and keeping his bourgeois lifestyle. 'He gave it to my mother, and now I have it,' she said. 'With all its ghosts.'

'Is that her?' Garin said, pointing to a photograph.

'No, my father removed her pictures. He didn't want to be reminded.' She drank her wine and was quiet. 'She was a typical Russian Jew. She decided the best thing for me was to become a ballerina, and I thought, well, that's a good idea, but then I realized that she wanted me to accomplish what she had dreamed for herself as a child. All her frustrated ambitions landed on me. And then she died.'

She shrugged. 'My father saw her suffer, and the needless inefficiency of the clinic made him angry. She died from their carelessness. It was the turning point in a series of difficult transitions, if you can think of tragedy as transition.'

'What happened?'

'Enough! I don't want to talk about myself.'

His silence undermined her resolve, and then slowly she was telling the whole story of her parents, as if she had been waiting a long time for an audience. 'My father was not the same man after her death,' she said. 'Moody, angry, blaming her doctors, and he drank. He began to resent the Party. I never knew a man could love a woman so much. All I remembered was their shouting, but in death she became a saint. Who knows what goes through a man's mind? He put all his attention on me after her death. She had encouraged me to dance, and he took up that cause. It was like I had two parents pushing me. He knew men who put in a good word for me at the Bolshoi School. I was good enough to get in, but you only discover how bad you are when you compete against talented girls – and all the time I was thinking I should dance for my mother. I was fourteen years old. What did I know?

'I never would have had a long career. My injury was a godsend. It protected me from public failure.' She refilled her wineglass and his. 'You drink a lot. I know about heavy drinkers.' She stared at him. 'My father was executed when I was twenty. That was the second transition. I am now on my third tragedy. What doesn't kill you makes you stronger.'

She laughed sadly. 'They said no child should bear the sins of her father. Dmitry Posner took responsibility for me, giving me the privileges I would have had if my father had lived. He helped my career at the Bolshoi, and he protected this flat from a bureaucracy that wanted to evict me. And when I was injured, he helped me find employment in State Security. My brother and I took a new last name after Father was executed. We were told that if we had the surname Zyuganov, we'd be connected to the traitor Zyuganov – and we would suffer.'

She pointed to the photograph of her brother on the T-62 tank. 'Luca was the talented one. Three years younger. Stupidly patriotic, but a clever boy. So eager to erase his father's stigma with his own heroics. He volunteered for the front. And do you know the worst part? They used him against me.'

Garin had been picking at the duck when she made her claim, and he lifted his eyes.

'Posner. Talinov. All my father's colleagues said, "Don't dig up the past, Nastia. Don't ask questions."' They made it clear that Luca would suffer if I tried to find out why my father was executed so quickly.' She put a pistol finger to the nape of her neck. 'I know how he died. I know where he died, and I know why. What I don't know is who. Talinov pulled the trigger, but I don't know who betrayed him.'

Natalya carefully placed her knife on the table, aligning the blade vertically, and she raised her fierce eyes to Garin. 'Was it you?'

Garin didn't respond.

'Or maybe you just failed him,' she said. 'Guilt doesn't become you. For a quiet man, you have a hard face.' Her voice had turned angry.

'He was compromised,' Garin said calmly, his eyes on hers. 'Compromised from the inside. Someone knew he would be crossing that night. Yes, I visited his grave. Yes, I regret the failure. Could I have done more? Probably. I often ask myself what we did wrong. But in time, I have come to understand the problem was inside the KGB.'

PAUL VIDICH

Natalya leaned back and pondered Garin. She tapped her palm with the knife. 'They made it clear. "Don't ask questions. Don't do anything stupid, Natasha. Luca has a good career. You will hurt him if you are too curious."' Natalya slowly leaned forward again and took her wineglass, coddling it. 'I was quiet for years. Then Luca was killed. My third transition.' Her expression became a sad, careless smile. 'Now, I am free to ask questions, free to leave, free to avenge him.' She patiently tapped the knife on the table. 'A prisoner of all my freedoms.'

She was silent for a long moment, then said, 'We have a joke. We like jokes. There is a billboard near Red Square that proclaims capitalism is rotting away. A diplomat returns from his two years in London and a friend asks, "Well, is it true? Is it rotting?" The diplomat says, "Yes, of course, but the smell of decay is quite pleasant."'

Natalya smiled. 'A stupid joke, but soon I will again smell the bouquet of decay.' She noticed that Garin had been looking at her pearls. 'Maybe you're a thief,' she said, laughing, her fingers at her neck as she touched her pearls. 'I don't dress like this often. I want to feel better about myself. Does that happen to you? Do you dress up to feel better about your life?'

Natalya suddenly looked at him. 'There is a woman's photo in your wallet. Of course I looked. Who is she?'

'My wife.'

'Where is she?'

'I don't know.'

She was skeptical.

'Ex-wife,' he said.

'You left her?'

'She left me.'

'Did you love her?'

'I don't know.'

Natalya scoffed. 'If you say you don't know, then you don't

164

admit it. Men don't know what they feel for women. They get confused by affection.' She paused. 'I never wanted that responsibility – marriage. It was easy for me, as a Bolshoi dancer. Everyone wanted to sleep with me.' She shrugged. 'Some men were nice, most were clumsy. I was with Bogdan a year ago. He still thinks I owe him some emotional privileges because I once took him into my life and read his shitty novels.'

Garin listened to her casual insults tossed out like discarded cigarettes. He heard a hint of regret in her easy toughness.

'Were you ever happy?' she asked.

'A stupid question. Only an unhappy person would ask that question.'

'Maybe not. What do you know?'

'I know what you've told me. This apartment. Your childhood memories. Your brother, father, mother. So much pain for one life.'

'I'm Russian,' she snapped.

'So am I.'

She laughed her answer. 'A strange Russian with an odd accent who thinks you can be happy. Where is your suffering? You, a Russian American mongrel.'

Garin felt the first stirrings of anger. The wine, which had begun to pleasantly numb him, and her rudeness combined to irritate him. He was glad neither of them was good at flirting. It was a kind of game, a deception, but at that moment he knew that they were not acting.

'Speak,' she said. 'Tell me your suffering.'

'Your father knew.'

'Well, perhaps you should tell me, since he never shared it. Where were you born? Who was your mother?'

'It doesn't matter,' he grunted. 'I don't talk about myself. It's not safe.'

She laughed. 'As if everything else you do keeps you from an early grave.'

He surrendered. 'It doesn't matter what my mother's name was. Let's call her Yelena, for the purpose of this conversation. There was a woman, and maybe she had a son. Is that satisfactory?'

Natalya nodded.

'She was a Russian translator working in Moscow for the Americans who'd come here during the war to manage the lend-lease logistics for tanks supplied to the Red Army. She was a widow with a five-year-old son. Russian men were all at the front. She worked for an American captain, and they had an affair. When he was sent back to Washington, he took her and her son. The boy grew up there. She spoke Russian to him at home, but he was raised as an American.'

'You speak about yourself as if it weren't you.'

'I didn't say it was me, okay?' He paused. 'So, this boy spoke Russian at home and English at school. He had a Russian mother who, he discovered years later, happened to be an illegal working for Directorate S, and an American father who traveled, drank, cheated, and never caught on that his wife reported to Moscow. Can you imagine the boy's surprise when one day his mother sat down her son and said, "Now, this is who your mother is, and you will be sent to Moscow to visit your grandparents, and while you're there, a nice man from the KGB will talk to you about your responsibilities to the Soviet Union"? The boy was twelve. What did he know?'

Garin looked at Natalya. 'Say something.'

'You're KGB?'

'I was. Then I was CIA. Now, I work alone.'

'Who was your real father?'

'I never knew him. He was a doctor in Moscow arrested for something, maybe for practicing medicine. He was taken to

Solovetski Detention Center on the White Sea. Two months after his wife's second conjugal visit, he was among a dozen prisoners selected for punishment in reprisal for a prison escape. They were made to walk outside the walls and stand before five soldiers in a firing squad. They were ordered to kneel, and all except my father did. He kneeled for no man, or so the story goes, and the commander promptly shot his leg, bringing him to his knees. The prisoners were shot, but the soldiers were drunk and their aim was not good. The fallen prisoners were thrown in a mass grave they'd been made to dig. But some were not dead. The next morning, the commander came out and shot his pistol into the moving earth until the ground was still.'

Garin looked at Natalya. 'This is the story that the boy's grandmother told when he visited his father's village. Is it true? Who knows? The boy believed it. Everyone believes what they want to believe about themselves. And the boy never knew who reported his father to State Security.'

'You told this to my father?'

Garin smiled. 'It makes for a good story. Is it possible such a thing could happen to a small boy? It is a dangerous world for children. You aren't the only one who can cry crocodile tears in bed.'

She slapped his face.

Garin touched his cheek, still hot from the sting. He saw in her anger a kind of empathy. 'So we both have dead fathers,' he said. 'It happens to everyone.'

Garin set his wineglass on the doily and carefully centered the base, turning it bit by bit until it was perfectly placed. He saw her staring at him.

'Who are you?' she asked.

He tore a piece of bread from the loaf. 'I am the man eating with you.'

167

'Fine. You don't have to tell me. You are Aleksander Garin. That's enough.'

She stood and began to clear the table, stacking serving dishes and dinner plates and topping them with cutlery. She started for the kitchen but stopped at the door and turned. 'I'm glad we've met.'

She did not return immediately from the kitchen, and he thought something was wrong. He found her at the sink, head leaned forward, struggling to breathe, chest heaving.

He startled her. She turned to him. Her face was pale, though her cheeks were flushed, and her eyes were red and tearing.

'Yes, I cry.' She composed herself and wiped a tear with her knuckle. 'I don't mean to be emotional. I should never have met you. This is all wrong.'

'What's wrong? Have you told them I'm here?'

She grimaced through her tears and laughed. 'You don't know, do you?' She looked at him. She took his head in her hands and pulled him forward, kissing his lips. She relaxed into her sudden, startling passion, and then she pulled away. 'No one is coming.'

She stepped back and held herself, suddenly cautious and embarrassed. 'Do you remember the night here in the bedroom?' She breathed quickly. 'I looked at you, knowing how Posner was there behind the wall watching, and I was scared you would see my fear.'

Garin's eyes drifted to the walls around.

'There is no one.' She laughed.

Garin's eyes returned to her, and he felt terrified. He saw that she struggled to keep her distance, and he saw that she too was terrified by what was happening. Neither of them moved. Silence and a brittle formality separated them.

She took his hand and placed it on the smooth skin of her neck and held it there.

Garin saw fierce yearning in her eyes and felt her loneliness, and he was aware of the danger that attached to intimacy. He knew that he had come face-to-face with a person as lonely as he was. A terrible caution held him back. But what was he afraid of?

'You're quiet,' she said. 'Thinking too much.'

She kissed his lips with feeling. Her eyes signaled the bedroom's open door.

She was under the bed's comforter when he entered. Her clothes were draped over a chair, and she had pulled the comforter to her neck so only her head poked out. She watched him undress, stepping out of one pant leg and then the other, and he pulled off his shirt, laying it casually over the chair. He removed his socks last.

He slipped under the comforter beside her and felt the pleasant warmth of her body. Her nose was cold, but her legs and arms were warm. He touched the silken smoothness of her skin.

Suddenly, she rose up on her elbow and looked down at him. Her finger traced the raised scar that went ear to throat, investigating the old wound. 'How did you get this?'

Their bodies were close, and they looked warily into each other's eyes, waiting on the question: two people shedding distrust; two people looking to escape loneliness; two souls coveting the pleasure that was theirs to pluck.

She lay down beside him. A finger of moonlight entered the curtain and drew a line across the comforter and hit her dress on the chair and her brassiere, which had fallen to the floor. Two figures lay side by side on the large bed.

'We don't have to do anything,' she said. 'Hug me.'

He did. As he rolled over, her dancer's body folded on him and she wrapped her arms over his chest to complete their innocent embrace.

*

She was still awake. All was quiet, and he was asleep. His dark hair was wild on the cushioning pillow, and his cheek was warmed in the silver moonlight that shone through the window. His restlessness had kept her from sleep. She sat up and looked at him for a long moment, gazing at his face. Even in sleep, he had a determination so strong that the bitter disquiet of pain was visible. Beaded perspiration unmasked his struggle with an unseen adversary in the wild dominion of his dreams. She gently placed a hand on his forehead and said something to comfort him. She wished that she could provide him as much solace as his loneliness deserved. Then she kissed his cheek and lay down beside him, drawing close.

18

INTERLUDE

MORNING LIGHT WOKE GARIN. He saw that the comforter had been kicked off and she was cuddled against him, her arm affectionately draped over his chest, her face on his shoulder. He lay there vaguely aware of the sounds outside and glad they had not spoiled the evening with hungry sex. He had known that experience, and he knew what came after.

He was on his back looking up at the ceiling with his palms on his chest, feeling the patient rhythms of his beating heart. He remembered their first encounter in the bedroom – her amateurish, staged seduction and her embarrassed flight, wrapped in a bedsheet. He was glad the new memory replaced the old.

He gazed at her pale body, smooth and porcelain, and her petite breasts. He had been surprised when she suggested they do nothing and pleased because he didn't want to squander the chaste pleasure of getting to know her. He wasn't a young man anymore, and there was something pleasant about not doing what was easy and expected.

He knew that she too was awake. Surprise came over him when her fingers engaged his. Warm yearning in her gentle touch traced the contours of his chest. Part of him wanted to ask her everything about her life, just as she had asked about his scar, and another part of him wanted to know nothing, to keep his distance to protect himself from attachment.

They had begun to explore each other – fingertip to fingertip, hand on hand, the warmth of each other's breath. The patient discovery of a stranger's body. She rolled over and kissed his eyes, then pressed her lips on his with an ardor that he was returning.

'You talk in your sleep,' she said.

'What did I say?'

'It was a bad dream.'

He went to speak, but she stopped his mouth with a kiss. 'No words.' She moved her legs over him and kneaded his chest with her fingers, gazing into his eyes with desire.

Everything they needed to say had been said. Everything they wanted from each other they took.

19

A QUIET WEEKEND

GARIN KNEW THAT EXPERIENCE often repeated itself – at least it did in his relations with women – and he knew that every intimacy was pleasant at first, and perhaps even intoxicating, and made life appear to be an adventure. But in time, the feelings inevitably grew into something ordinary and perhaps unbearable. Each new beginning with an interesting woman held that sad potential, and he hoped that it wouldn't happen with Natalya. He wanted to keep everything between them uncomplicated, if only for the weekend while they lived a pleasant moment, trying to ignore the future.

She had left work early Friday afternoon for the start of the last weekend of Lent. They had spent the day apart, and he felt good being away from her. The idea of too much intimacy had begun to wear on him and crowded out what he knew he must do in his final days in Moscow.

That evening, they found themselves on the roof of her apartment house. The dying sun was an orange seam across the horizon, and threatening clouds had moved their conversation to a dark place without any conscious effort on their part. They seemed to know that whatever pleasures they had enjoyed were behind them. What lay ahead was uncertain.

It was warm out in the spring evening, and windows of the

building across the street were thrown open for air after having been shut tight all winter. They leaned on the stone parapet looking toward the russet dusk. Now and then they looked at each other and smiled, as if surprised to find themselves in each other's company. Intimacy between them was still a new thing being tried out.

Natalya ground her cigarette with her heel, extinguishing it, and without turning her head she asked, 'How do you know Deputy Chairman Churgin?'

Garin didn't know what prompted her question. The wine at dinner? The sight of the luminously illuminated Kremlin? The memory of the meeting in Spaso House?

Natalya turned to him. 'The head of Directorate S is a man who isn't photographed. His name isn't spoken. He is a shadow.'

'He trained me.' Garin addressed the surprise he saw on her face. 'He wouldn't remember. I was twelve. I was in a group at a camp outside Moscow. There were twenty of us receiving training. We were all tan, brown-haired, eager, dressed in the same uniform. The Soviet image of healthy youth. His job was to train illegals to talk, think, and act like regular Americans, even to the point that in our subconscious, we took on a false identity and became a made-up person. It was all very patriotic to be part of the preparation for the day when we'd come out of our holes behind enemy lines and engage rearguard operations against shop clerks, taxi drivers – mothers with strollers.'

Garin laughed at the absurdity of what had been expected of him. Then his face darkened.

'But it wasn't fun and games back in America. If you were seen as unfit or wavering, the punishment was quick and ruthless. You were recalled to Moscow.' He turned to Natalya. 'The woman I spoke of the other night – the one married to the American army captain in Virginia with her son. She was recalled. If you were recalled to Moscow, you didn't return.

The rule was no contact. If a person returned to America and it became known they had been in Moscow, the whole deceit was at risk. So they disappeared. Lost. The woman didn't exist, except as a name taken from a cemetery marker. Probably she was shot and thrown in an unmarked grave, or it's possible she died in a labor camp in the gulag.

'It is always harder for the ones left behind. Death comes as a relief to the condemned, but the living suffer the absurdity and grief. Her crime? Even that was a mystery. Too many complaints against her alcoholic, cheating husband? Too much concern for her son? Too much suspicious behavior? Too few reports? Too many care packages of Easter sausage and *kulich*? Who knows?'

Garin had gone on at length in a quiet voice. The sun had set, and darkness had fallen on them like a shroud. All around, the lights of the city had come on one by one, twinkling. The two of them stood quietly in the deepening gloom of night. Garin had assumed a meditative pose.

'And this too,' he said suddenly, 'has been my life. The mother I resented. What bargain did she make with the devil to believe that the life she chose was worth living?'

Garin's voice was gruff, and he lowered his head, looking at nothing. Then he looked at her. 'You asked how I know Churgin? There were three encounters. I told you about the training camp.

'The summer after that, I saw him parked in front of our home in Virginia.' Garin paused. 'My mother was frightened and pulled me from the window. He never came inside the house, but my mother knew he was unhappy. I saw her fear. She never described the threat, but, like any child, I assumed I had done something wrong. I had failed her in some indescribable way. I would wake up in bed trembling and crawl under my desk, a scared kid thinking it was safe there. Then she left – vanished, actually. I put things together as I got older. Somewhere along the way, I swore I would kill him.

'My third encounter was in Spaso House. I was not surprised he didn't recognize me. But he was a man I would never forget.'

Garin ended the short account of his life. A part of him felt relieved to have a person he could openly talk to about his hoarded emotions and things he'd never shared, and another part of him, the part that managed fear, went along reluctantly. His life too, he said, had been an unforeseen chain of events set in motion a long time ago, and he'd done what he'd needed to carve out a life for himself.

'It sounds terrible,' he said, laughing, 'but it's been fine. I couldn't imagine a desk job in a bank or a dull nine-to-five existence. And I've met you.' He laughed again, but his voice carried a sense of heartbreaking loss. His survival was a peculiar happenstance of luck and skill. He'd fought a Cold War – against the CIA, Langley, the White House; now he was fighting another war against the KGB, Moscow Center, and the Kremlin. They were all the same thing; all the same enemy, he said.

Natalya touched his hand, arranging her palm over his fist. She leaned against him and coddled his shoulder with a gentle embrace. She felt his body tremble, and she pulled away, gazing into his face. 'You're crying.'

'Yes.' He smiled through the tear that had welled in his eye. 'Not a crocodile tear. Just a little one.' He wiped the corner of his eye with his finger. 'Or maybe a speck of dust.' He turned to look at her. 'We're alike, you know.'

'In what way?'

'There are people who want to silence us. A few I suspect want to kill us. And we both want to cheat them.'

*

Every morning that weekend, when the whole of the city beyond the closed shutters of her apartment began to stir, Natalya and Garin were awoken by emergency repairs on a water main. Workmen dug up the street in a leisurely effort to fix the broken pipe, goaded by angry residents who complained they were dragging out the work and disturbing everyone. The crew talked loudly with cigarettes hanging from the corners of their mouths, ignoring the pleas. Then they applied themselves more vigorously with a chorus of clanging shovels, pickaxes, and pounding jackhammers that entered Natalya's darkened bedroom, rising and falling in waves of obscenities that filled the brief silences between the pneumatic pounding.

Garin and Natalya woke reluctantly late that Saturday, and it seemed to them that they awoke at the same time from dreamy sleep, due to the same shrill sound outside. For reasons they could not explain, they were sharing feelings. A mosquito buzzed one and then the other, and they both covered their heads with a pillow. The next morning, Sunday, it was the urgent siren of a passing ambulance that brought them out of bed. She threw open the shutters, letting in blinding sunlight, and went to the bathroom without shutting the door. Still absorbed in a pleasant dream, he rolled over to hold on to the fleeing thought.

When Garin woke, he knew it was late. He lifted his arm and looked at his wristwatch. Noon! How could that be? Then he realized that the street outside was quiet and Natalya was not in the bathroom. He jumped from the bed and walked barefoot to the kitchen, shoving his arms into his shirt sleeves.

'Natalya?'

No answer. He looked in the bathroom, the other bathroom, and then down the circular stairwell. 'Natalya?' He felt an emptiness to the apartment when he was back inside. Her coat was missing. Her purse was not where she usually placed it, and there was an envelope taped to the vestibule door where she knew he would see it. He stared at his name, which she'd written in her precise script. He tore it open.

You were sleeping, the note read. *I decided not to wake you. I left the morning paper. Be careful today. Dinner is at 20:00. If the telephone rings, don't answer it. Two rings followed after a long pause by two more rings means danger. Get out of the flat as fast as possible. Love, Nata.*

He folded the note and placed it back in the envelope. He sat at the table and looked at the envelope for a long while. He felt an odd sense of relief.

He poured himself a glass of vodka, swirling the liquid in the afternoon light. Pouring a drink was an unconscious act, his mind thinking that it would settle his nerves. He glanced at his reflection in the mirror, and he was a little disoriented by his feelings. Without drinking, he pushed the vodka out of reach. He shook his head. The idea that she cared for him. He hated the word 'love,' which had only brought him great disappointment. He gazed out the window, thinking that her tender feelings would complicate things.

20

CONFINEMENT

MUELLER LEARNED WHAT HAPPENED next not from Garin but from his diary, when he reconstructed the events in Moscow and discovered, to his surprise, that Garin was careful, but not in the way that Mueller expected. His dated entries were recklessly contrived summaries of conversations and contained sensitive details that could jeopardize the CIA's efforts, but other entries were the opposite. Facts and opinions were shaded to mislead the casual reader and to provide a smooth wall of deception, hiding the real cracks in the plan. The diary was a serious breach of security protocol, or it was a self-consciously created record to defend his loyalty before a Soviet inquisition. Unfortunately for Mueller – and there would always be moments in his life when he bitterly regretted it – he never got to ask Garin.

*

Garin was two blocks from Natalya's street when he saw a black Volga in front of her building, and in the same moment he heard his name called. He had made a quick trip to the tobacco kiosk outside Novokuznetskaya Metro Station, where he had seen three vertical chalk marks on the postal box – Petrov's signal

179

that he had convinced his wife to proceed. The street was filled with Afghan War mothers who'd lost sons marching with locked arms, yelling fierce slogans. Dozens of tightly bunched *Afgansty* followed with an unfurled banner: *For Our Freedom and Yours*.

Upon hearing his name, Garin joined the motley humanity of loud protesters moving down the center of the boulevard, disrupting traffic. Several protesters were pulled from the group by thuggish plainclothes policemen and detained by militia who lined the boulevard. State Security was there in abundance, and military vehicles with water cannons were parked at regular intervals along the route of the march.

Garin didn't acknowledge the man who called his name, nor could he escape the marchers surrounding him. He kept walking forward until he saw the man emerge from the assembled militia. He was dressed in a long military coat and wore a peaked cap with single red star. He was in front of Garin, blocking his path.

'Aleksander Garin?'

He nodded.

'Come with me.'

'What's this about?'

'We have a few questions. Come this way.' He pointed to a black Volga parked nearby. 'This won't take long.'

The man opened the car's rear door for Garin, who slipped into the back seat and found himself joining a smartly dressed KGB officer. Garin recognized the angular face and vague smile of a churlish man trying his best to be pleasant.

'I am Lieutenant Colonel Viktor Talinov. This won't take long. Papers, please?'

Garin produced his American passport and visa. The driver had started the car, and Garin felt it pull away from the curb. He glanced back and saw protesters being violently set upon by club-wielding plainclothes police.

'Everything is in order,' Talinov said.

'What's this about?'

'Your name has come to our attention. We have a few questions.'

'I work for the American embassy.'

'Yes, we know. An American woman from the embassy was found dead. Perhaps you knew her. Helen Walsh.'

'I met her once, maybe twice. Is this about her?'

'There is an investigation. An autopsy showed that she died of a heart attack. Her body has been released to the American embassy. But my questions aren't about her.'

Garin turned from the scattering protesters and faced Talinov.

Talinov politely offered his hand to Garin. 'Good to meet you. The KGB is a large organization with many branches. I understand that you work for us now.'

Garin raised an eyebrow.

'We paid a sum of money to a Swiss bank account. We noticed the debit from one of our restricted accounts, and we tracked it back to Comrade Posner, who we've questioned. He said he recruited you. You look surprised. Is that not true?'

'We had an arrangement.'

'You both agree on that.' Talinov leaned forward to the driver. 'Lefortovo Annex.'

Congested traffic in central Moscow was bumper-to-bumper at the major intersections, but the Volga's flashing lights opened lanes along their route, and the trip was made quickly. Garin held the door's strap against the driver's swerving ride.

'What do you do for Comrade Posner?' Talinov asked, his polite tone acquiring an interrogator's edge. 'What is worth so much money?'

'Whatever he wants. He put a value on my worth.'

'Maybe you've swindled him.'

Garin smiled. 'Perhaps. You should ask him.'

'We are. We haven't seen you at your apartment for several days. He said we might find you with the woman. You work in the embassy?'

Garin knew Talinov already had his answers and was playing a game. He felt himself being maneuvered. 'Yes, I do. Human rights work.'

'Did you arrive in Moscow on January 5?'

'Yes.'

The Volga entered an underground garage just off the boulevard and followed a narrow tunnel to a drop-off point beyond several parked Chaika limousines. There were two guards – one uniformed KGB security guard with holstered pistol and a Red Army policeman with a Kalashnikov, who presented his weapon in brisk salute when Talinov stepped from the Volga. Talinov led Garin toward an oak door set in an old stone wall. Inside, three plainclothes policemen were waiting. They wore similar gray suits and wide ties, and they had the menacing expressions of policemen everywhere.

'What do you want?' Garin asked, turning to Talinov, who guided him forward.

'Nothing that you can't tell us,' Talinov said. 'These men are from Posner's branch. Counterintelligence. We want to talk about the girl, Natalya Alexieva.'

Garin shrugged. 'Why are the lights in the hallway off?' They had moved through the door into a dank tunnel with mold that made Garin choke, but no sooner had he asked his question than Talinov waved his hand and the motion detector brought up the lights. Overhead bulbs hung at regular intervals down the vaulted underground passageway.

'We've grown too big,' Talinov said. 'The First Directorate now has its own campus at Yasenevo. But Lefortovo still serves us. Crimes change, but we have the same guest rooms. This

Annex was a wine cellar for the old tsarist mansion above us.'

Doors along the corridor had small barred windows, and Garin glanced at several, but saw only confining darkness inside. From somewhere came the steady drip of water.

Garin was led into a small suite of rooms illuminated by dim fluorescent lights. The anteroom had a wooden table, portable electric heater, old sofa, and coffee table, and along one wall, there was a kitchenette with stove and refrigerator. Glossy French pornographic magazines were scattered on the coffee table.

'For boredom,' Talinov said.

There was a second room with a single bed covered with a gray wool blanket and a white pillow, a small writing desk, and a high, barred window through which sunlight entered from the street.

'We will talk here,' Talinov said. 'But first you will wait. There is coffee and biscuits.'

Garin found himself alone. He tried the door, confirming what he suspected. They had locked it from the outside. There was no pretense that he was anything other than a prisoner in the cell. He looked for a camera but saw none. He expected one, because he had fitted rooms like this, and he studied the ceiling molding, where one section had been cut out and replaced, but he found none there, and he didn't find anywhere it was logical to hide a camera lens. But still, he behaved like a man who was aware he was being watched.

How long would it be? What did they know? He had gone through this once before. He knew what to expect, and that made him uncomfortable, but he knew he would have to be released in due course and delivered to the embassy. It was then that he contemplated the alternative. He went down the list of information he could give up to secure his release. Who would he betray?

Two hours passed. Garin's head was slumped on the table when he heard the door open. The tall officer who entered was in his twenties, dressed in an olive uniform with red epaulettes, knotted tie, and a high-crown peaked hat with black plastic visor, which he removed and placed under his arm. He was trim and briskly polite.

'So, you're the CIA guy,' he said in English. 'I am Sergey Nikolayevich Rostov, Special Representative of the Military Collegium of the Supreme Court of the USSR. I am here to ask you questions. I understand that you speak Russian and I won't have to use my rude English.'

'*Da*.'

They proceeded in Russian. Rostov sat opposite Garin at the wooden table, placing his cap on his left and a leather portfolio on his right, promptly removing a white lined notepad. He took a ballpoint pen from his jacket pocket, laying it across the pad. He folded his hands and looked at Garin.

'Where shall we begin?' Rostov asked.

'I'm an American diplomat. Has the embassy been called? When do I get released?'

'I can't answer that.'

'Why am I here? How about that?' Garin scowled. 'Let's start with something simple.' He didn't try to hide his sarcasm.

'You are a witness to an administrative proceeding that is investigating allegations of crimes against the State by Dmitry Posner.' Rostov smiled briskly. 'I am from the prosecutor's office. Let's begin, shall we? When did you meet Comrade Posner?'

'I don't remember.'

'Was it at the American embassy, perhaps?'

'No. He wouldn't be allowed in.'

'Spaso House, perhaps?' Rostov placed a pack of cigarettes on the table. 'Smoke?'

'Yes, Spaso House.'

Garin stared at Rostov, evaluating the man's generous expression, and he wondered if he'd ever distrusted anyone's supposed friendship quite as much as he now doubted Rostov's. He found himself being questioned about an internal Soviet matter, and yet it was obvious they thought he could be helpful, and being locked in the cell was anything but a joke. He sensed an opportunity.

'There was a party,' Garin said. 'We were introduced. He was there, and so was half of the Presidium – and a few of your idiot KGB friends.'

Rostov looked up from his pad. 'Sarcasm won't make this go quicker. Do you understand?'

Garin leaned back. 'I'm not going anywhere.'

'Do you know Natalya Alexieva?'

'She has nothing to do with this,' he said. 'I met her at Spaso House. She was introduced as someone who could help me interview dissidents – anyone with a complaint.'

'Did you know she is Jewish?'

'Half Jewish. And so what?'

'Why were you at her home?'

'She refused to let me leave. She was afraid I would get lost, sleep on a stoop, and freeze to death.' Garin scoffed. 'I don't know what she thought. It was cold that night and I was drunk. I don't trust her. Does she know I'm here?'

'My job is to ask questions, not to answer them.'

'How about one question?'

'Perhaps.'

'How long will I be here? The shorter my stay, the more likely I'll cooperate.'

'I can't answer that. I don't know. Someone else will come later.'

'I am a consular officer held against my will. *Understand?*' Garin shouted this across the table. 'I demand to speak with my embassy.'

185

Rostov glared. 'Yes, Mr Garin, most of us don't like to be questioned like this, and I'm sure someone will contact the embassy.'

Garin considered the flash of anger he'd seen in Rostov's eyes, and he understood that Rostov was a cog, and he found it hard to despise a weak man who was following orders.

There were more questions that Garin answered with a minimum of dissembling in order to keep the interview moving along. He answered truthfully where he could, sometimes obliquely, but never with a lie that could be proved, and in the process, he tried to discern the nature of the investigation from Rostov's questions. Rostov wrote down Garin's answers dutifully in his cramped, precise script, and Garin noted what piqued the prosecutor's interest. When Rostov's questions were too pointed, he replied vaguely and evasively. He wasn't going to sacrifice a piece in the game without a deal in hand. He gave Rostov nothing concrete, but even so he contradicted himself several times, and when Rostov pointed that out, Garin equivocated by saying, 'I can't remember!' After an hour of frustrated questioning, Rostov walked out.

*

'Wake up.'

Garin had fallen asleep in the chair, and his head lay on the table. His leg had gone numb, and he felt the dead appendage's nerve endings waking with the excruciating pain of needles. He rubbed the leg and lifted his head to the man who'd spoken his name.

The man was dressed in civilian clothes, but his expression was military and menacing. He opened the locked second door.

'In here.'

Garin resisted, but the man grabbed his shirt and shoved him belligerently, causing him to stumble. There was no window and one lightbulb on the ceiling. It was an interrogation room. Hooked chains hung from one wall, and metal rods lay on the floor by a foul-smelling, rusted drain. Garin was hit on the thigh by the man's plastic baton, and he crumpled to one knee, screaming in agony.

'Fuckhead,' the man said.

Garin was made to undress and sit on a metal stool. His arms were raised above his head and chained to the ceiling. Then a bucket of cold water was thrown at him. Naked and shivering, he watched the guard circle him, slapping the baton on his hand. He felt the man's cold gaze, like a viper waiting to strike its prey.

The guard unleashed a torrent of abuse. 'Who do you think you are? Scum, bastard, degenerate, shithead, swine.'

He went on for a while, exhausting his list of Russian insults. He paced back and forth and spewed obscenities as he waved his arms, screaming and making violent gestures, demanding that Garin confess. But abruptly, he would pause to light a cigarette and contemplate Garin, drawing on the black tobacco as he evaluated his victim, offering a puff but withdrawing the cigarette and laughing when Garin leaned forward to accept. After his smoke break, he presented a jar of urine, calling it his piss. He threw it in Garin's face, and the monstrous screaming began again.

Garin demanded to speak to the American embassy, but the guard shrugged. Not once did he ask Garin a question. Garin's arms went numb.

This went on for an hour, and then the guard stopped. He sat on a chair opposite Garin.

'Are you done performing?' Garin demanded. 'What do you want from me?'

The guard cocked his head sideways. 'Beating people is my job. I don't want anything. I am paid to do this.'

He stood and slapped Garin on the face, splitting his lip.

'If they ask how I did, tell them you shit your pants,' the man said.

Garin tasted the salty blood. 'Fuckhead.'

The guard smiled. 'I was told Americans don't have a sense of humor. Maybe you're the exception.'

'What do you want?'

'Nothing.'

'I don't believe you.'

'Whatever you want to believe, go ahead. I'm not here to change your mind.'

'How big is this prison?'

'Why do you care?'

'Why not?'

The guard laughed. 'You are the only one who has asked that question. Knowing that fact does nothing for them. No one leaves here. There are three types of prisoners here: ordinary, know-nothing criminals who die of disease, starvation, cold, or too much physical persuasion; dissidents who come in stupid and disappear stupid; and people like you, who know something, don't talk, and then don't exist.' He looked at Garin. 'The graveyard is bigger with more occupants. Scream for me.'

Garin screamed his lungs out.

'There you go. That's what I need to hear.' The guard pounded his baton on the concrete floor. 'See how easy it is?'

The guard whacked Garin's jaw hard with his baton, drawing blood. 'Fuckhead,' he said again. 'What do you do for Posner?'

*

Garin lay on the metal cot in the cell when he was awakened from a fitful sleep. He was in his clothing, which smelled of blood and sweat, and his sockless feet were blue from cold. He shivered terribly. His lip was swollen, and his shoulder ached. He had fallen asleep, thinking there would be another round of insults and abuse. The darkness outside the high casement window told him that it was still night. He glanced at his watch.

Loud, raucous activity in the hall beyond the locked door pulled him from sleep. Then he understood what was happening. An angry voice berated the guard in the hallway for sleeping on his watch.

Garin's eyes adjusted to the light's painful brightness, jolting his numbed brain like an electric prod. He went to turn off the wall switch above his head, but he found it disabled, and his primitive memory recalled the frustration of an earlier effort. He moved his legs off the bed to the floor and cradled his head in his hands. Again his watch. *Twenty hours.*

The yelling outside in the hall stopped, and now there was only a plaintive groan. Down the hall, he heard another voice yell in English that the noise was keeping him awake. Then a sound of metal scraping on concrete, the door opening and closing, and, beyond his cell, an orchestra of uncouth sounds.

Garin sat, head in hand, groggy, unable to focus, for a minute or two. His neck ached and his welted thigh, black and blue from knee to hip, throbbed. His clothes stuck to his body, and he had a terrible thirst.

He became aware of two polished black boots, which had entered the room and now stood before him. He looked up to the fresh face of an unsmiling Lieutenant Colonel Talinov and felt the hot sting of a slap.

'Idiot,' Talinov said. 'You have given us nothing.'

Garin rubbed his cheek and met Talinov's eyes. 'I know what you want.'

21

WASHINGTON, DC

GEORGE MUELLER SAT AT a conference table in a mahogany-paneled conference room in the Russell Senate Office Building. Gauzy light came through the drawn curtains and illuminated the five men who sat across from Mueller – prominent men with grim, skeptical faces.

Coffee cups and bone china dishes sat in front of each man, but only one had bothered to drink, and none had tasted the Danish pastry set out for the early-morning briefing by the new acting head of the CIA's SE Division. Their attention was riveted on Mueller, who had a file open in front of him, which he occasionally consulted in the course of his classified briefing on events in Moscow.

Mueller knew the chairman of the Senate Intelligence Committee, a balding older man with bushy eyebrows, and also a smug lawyer who had never lost his litigator's propensity to appear hostile even when he sought to be accommodating; and he also knew the Director of Central Intelligence, his soon-to-retire boss. He was acquainted with the president's National Security Advisor, a political appointee and toady who saw the world through the lens of public relations; and the Secretary of Defense, a former CEO of a defense contractor who listened with intermittent interest to Mueller's assessment of the value of the intelligence the CIA was collecting from GAMBIT.

'I am a big fan of yours, George, always have been,' the senator said. 'You're quite convincing, but how can you possibly put a billion-dollar price tag on the value of the intelligence you've gotten? I understand you want to make this sound big – and a billion dollars is a large number, and I'll be sure to remember it when you come back to defend your Agency's budget – but where does the number come from? Did someone pull it out of his ass?'

Mueller didn't smile, and he waited for the National Security Advisor to stop whispering in the DCI's ear.

'Mr Chairman, it is a big number,' Mueller said. 'I didn't make up the assessment, and I didn't come up with the number. The Pentagon did. It is based on what we've seen and what we expect to see from our asset.'

Mueller pushed the file to one side, folded his hands on the table, and looked at the senator. He had little tolerance for the gobbledygook that passed for sophisticated thinking on Capitol Hill. He was tired of being a lonely voice.

'We are in an arms race. It isn't a nuclear arms race, but a race to acquire the military technology that is needed for the regional conflicts that are defining our influence in the world. The race requires new weapons systems: look-down radar, drone technology, and compound materials that can make our stealth bombers ghosts on Soviet radar screens. The Soviets, for all their social and economic failures, have dedicated resources to creating weapons technologies that have frustrated the Pentagon's engineers. The billion dollars is an estimate of the R-and-D costs we will save by building only those weapons we need to defend against their arsenal, and it includes what we will save by leapfrogging our failed efforts. How valuable is that? Mr Chairman, does that answer your question?'

It was a long meeting. Mueller was unable to answer many

specific questions, and he was frustrated when the same question was asked again and again. 'Everyone in this room has top security clearance,' he said, 'but this operation is not over. Our asset is still inside the Soviet Union. Our best people are at risk.'

'What *can* you tell us, George?' the senator asked, leaning forward and looking over the top of his reading glasses. 'The room isn't bugged.' The senator put his ear onto the table in an exaggerated show of levity. 'At least I don't think it is.'

'Sir,' Mueller said. 'This is a very delicate situation. Our people are operating in a hostile country. It's a dangerous operation – we have never exfiltrated a senior Soviet intelligence officer from Moscow.'

'How many people?'

'It's one man.'

'One man? Who are you relying on for this billion-dollar coup? I don't need his name. I'm sure it's classified.' The senator looked at Mueller. 'Do you trust him?'

Mueller looked up. 'He'll get the job done.'

'A billion-dollar spy.' The senator smiled. 'Let's hope he is as good as you think he is. I can't imagine one man doing all this, except, maybe, if he were Errol Flynn or John Wayne. That's why I'm sitting here and he's out there.'

The senator sipped his coffee, but it had gone cold, and he set the cup on its saucer, displeased. He looked at the gloomy men around the table. 'I'm the only one asking questions.'

'You're doing a fine job, Senator,' the National Security Advisor said.

'Okay. I'm done,' the senator said. To Mueller, 'Thank you. Very helpful. Good to know we'll save a billion dollars.'

*

Mueller sat beside the DCI in the back of his black Lincoln Town Car, sharing a ride back to Langley. It was not yet 9:00 a.m., and they moved quickly in the opposite direction of the morning commuter traffic coming into downtown Washington.

The DCI had posed a question. Mueller took his eyes off the cars passing on the opposite side of Key Bridge. They had been quiet for several minutes after entering the limousine. Mueller had accepted the DCI's assurance that he'd done a good job, but Mueller knew that the offer of assurance itself meant that he'd done poorly. This was what had always bothered him about Washington – endless bureaucracy, sanctimonious grandstanding, smug dismissals of the Agency's dangerous work, and everyone was expert at putting lipstick gloss on ugly failures.

Mueller was angry. He looked directly at the DCI. 'Those men have no idea of the risks involved. They ask pious questions, make slanderous criticisms, and expect easy answers. They see everything through the lens of expedient politics.' Mueller waved his hand indignantly. 'We achieve what we can with the resources we've got. That's all, goddamnit.'

The DCI nodded. 'I agree, and I sympathize. When I'm gone from this job, you'll still have to work with them.' He turned to Mueller. 'Do you trust Garin?'

'Within limits.'

'How did we end up with him?'

'He was there before. He knows the terrain. We didn't have options.'

'Where is he now?'

There was a long silence. 'He went dark. We know that Moscow Station was compromised, and Counterintelligence is evaluating the damage.'

The DCI's face was fatigued. 'Where is he?'

Mueller had carefully filed Garin's dispatches, and he knew

that things were going off the rails. He could read worry in the vague statements that consciously avoided the obvious dangers, and then the dispatches had suddenly stopped.

'We don't know. He'll show up.' Mueller looked out the car's window at the traffic. He spoke quietly, almost to himself. 'He's resourceful.'

'What's next?'

'I fly to Prague and drive to the border. We have a car fitted with a compartment to hide GAMBIT. The driver will pick up the family at the Uzhgorod train station. I will be at the Czech border with a team to meet the car.'

'Has he got a chance?'

Mueller's eyes settled on the daffodils that had come up in a riot of yellow in the spring weather. *Does he have a chance?* Mueller clenched and unclenched his fist, rubbing his knuckles as he considered the unthinkable. When things started to go wrong, they went very wrong. Events in Moscow had caught the Agency unprepared. Mueller had not known the DCI long, but he had made his judgment quickly – a Washington insider who hopped between senior appointments like a man stepping on hot coals: groomed hair, polished wingtips, perfectly knotted tie, double-breasted suit, and an American flag lapel pin that gave him the gloss of patriotism. He had the relaxed health and bronzed tan of a man who spent weekends socializing on the golf course. He had never known the stress of managing men whose covert work put their lives at risk. He was a non-intelligence professional in charge of intelligence, a man eager for a success that he could share with the Oval Office, and intolerant of failure.

He thought of Aleksander Garin somewhere in Moscow – hiding, frightened, on the run. Even the best spies lived with fear. Would he succeed? Would he become another casualty in a Cold War skirmish? Would he try to save himself?

'Well?' the DCI asked.

'He has a chance.'

'A good chance?'

Mueller turned away from the daffodils and met the DCI's gaze. 'He has a chance. But he's just one ordinary man. Maybe he believes in what he is doing, but I suspect he doesn't.' His eyes narrowed. 'The men in that conference room have no idea the risk we are taking.'

22

MILITARY COLLEGIUM OF THE SUPREME COURT OF THE USSR

GARIN WAS UNSHACKLED, AND he tried to stand. There was a moment when he thought he would make it, but his numb legs had lost feeling, and he fell when he tried to obey the shouted command. Lieutenant Colonel Talinov let him lie on the floor and watched him with a belligerent expression. Garin massaged his muscles to bring his legs back to life.

Talinov nodded at the two guards. 'Lift him. Walk him around. I need him awake. Wash his face. Get the blood off.' He looked at Garin. 'Get up!' he shouted.

Garin waved off the guards' offer of help, and he pushed himself to his knees, using the wall for support. He rose to his full height and stood taller than the others, but wobbly. His shirt was undone at the neck, showing his chest, and he went to button it, but he realized the holes were torn. He smoothed his sleeve and patted his trousers, vaguely aware of his own smells. His socks were across the room, where someone had taken care to stuff them in his shoes. His bare feet were cold on the concrete, and he requested permission to cross the room. He was trembling.

'Clean up,' the younger guard said, handing him a moist, soiled towel and a clean shirt. 'Get dressed. You're leaving.'

'Where?'

'You'll know soon enough.'

*

The courtroom was a dimly lit, high-ceilinged space in a grim Russian baroque building converted into a hall of justice. Fluorescent panels hung on long wires from a dark ceiling and made the courtroom feel cold, and while it was much larger than his cell, the curtained windows and coning light produced a feeling of claustrophobia in Garin when he entered. The prisoner's dock and an administrative table were illuminated, but beyond the perimeter of light, the room was dim. He saw a dozen shadowed faces. He was aware of an echo in the tall space and whispers across the room were audible, as was the shuffling of paper among the two lawyers who sat at a gray desk facing the chairman of the proceeding, a heavyset, middle-aged woman who wore an obvious wig and an olive-green uniform with a white collar. Her deputy was on her right, at the squat administrative table in the front of the courtroom, and two military assessors were on her left. Garin shook off the guards' grip and flexed his wrists. Handcuffs and ankle shackles had been removed before he entered.

After two days of dark confinement, the bright fluorescent lights disoriented him, and he was suddenly pushed into a wooden chair at the witness table. Lime-green plaster walls were bare except for a water stain from a ceiling leak and a large portrait of Lenin. Beside it, there was a ghost aura of darker pastel where dead Chernenko's portrait had once hung, and two limp flags stood on either side of the judge's table. Garin saw Talinov, who sat beside the prosecutor Rostov, and there were five other people that Garin hadn't seen before.

Comrade Posner sat alone in the prisoner's dock wearing a prisoner's gray smock and slippers. He had files open in front of him at the small defendant's table, and he looked up when Garin entered. His flowing gray hair now fell over his ears, and his eyes were shadowed with worry. Garin almost didn't recognize him.

'Is this him?' the judge asked.

'Yes,' Rostov said. 'Aleksander Garin. We are presenting him as a witness against the defendant, who, if I may repeat to the court, is accused of capital offenses under Articles 70 and 72 of the RSFSR Penal Code.'

Garin looked across the faces in the room, and then he settled on the judge. He knew that the proceedings had been going on for hours, possibly for days. The judge had documents piled at her side, nearly blocking the stenciled name plate on the table: *V. Ulrich, Chairman.* Garin submitted himself to the courtroom's proceedings, stating his name, occupation, and nationality.

'Mr Garin,' the chairman said when he was done. 'This is the Military Collegium of the Supreme Court of the USSR. You are here as a fact witness in a sensitive matter. You are obliged to cooperate, and you are required to give truthful answers. Do you understand? Do you need a translator?'

Garin, unrehearsed and unprepared, stood, believing he was required to do so.

'Sit down. Do you understand?'

'Yes. I don't need a translator.'

She nodded at Rostov. 'Proceed.'

Rostov rose from his table, gathered himself, and moved to the center of the room, looking once at Garin. He held files in one hand, which he slapped against his other palm, and stopped suddenly. The prosecutor looked from Posner to Garin and then back at Posner.

'Mr Garin, do you know the defendant, Dmitry Posner?'

Garin hesitated.

Rostov rephrased his question. 'Do you know his name? Have you met him?'

'I know the name.' Garin remembered the prosecutor's nasally voice, his false charm, and the bead of sweat that formed on his upper lip. He remembered his questions from the cell, and he tried to think a chess move ahead, sacrificing a useless fact to test the man's game. He felt the eyes of the room on him. An answer existed, and the outcome that would follow from his answer was his only way to control the room.

'Can you point him out?'

Garin indicated the prisoner in the dock, whose face had drained of color. Posner bore his guilt stiffly.

'It may surprise you that defendant Posner was convicted of bribery and unlawful possession of foreign currency in connection with trade union corruption in a separate case in Zamoskvoretsky District Court. Posner used his privileged position in the KGB to fill his itching palm, and he laundered the money overseas.'

Garin sat morosely and listened to Rostov's plodding accusations, detailing how Posner's knowledge of Swiss banking helped him use shell companies, which he controlled through nephews he appointed as directors, to work around restrictions on a Soviet citizen's possession of foreign currency. 'All this activity,' Rostov said, looking around the courtroom, 'was documented in the Party's anti-corruption campaign, and this man' – he pointed to a subdued Posner – 'was convicted of various crimes, including misuse of office, false statements, and undermining social order. He took cash for favors and used cash to bribe bankers to launder money through overseas accounts. He owns an apartment and an automobile in London. He engaged in malicious anti-Soviet agitation and organized criminal activity prohibited under Articles 70 and 72 of the Penal Code.'

Rostov turned again to Garin. 'This trial stems from evidence found during investigations conducted in the first trial.' Rostov presented Garin with a single printed page from the file he held. 'Have you seen this?'

Garin recognized the name of the bank at the top of the account statement, and he saw one small, dollar-denominated transfer that had been circled. There was no account name on the statement. It was a numbered account.

'This is your account, correct?' Rostov said. 'Account number P12278910Z at Compagnie de Banque et Investissements, located at Rue du Rhone 96-98, Geneva. Can you confirm that?'

Garin guessed that he was being led down a path of forking choices; he couldn't know if his answers would lead to a way out or take him deeper into a labyrinth. Rostov already had his answer, but the process of the trial and its theater required a show. None of this mattered to him, but all of it mattered to his release. He had only to submit himself to the questions to find a way out. His mind saw the room as a two-dimensional maze where to escape he had to do the opposite of what was expected of him.

'Yes, this is my account,' he said. 'These are my funds. Where did you get this?'

'Thank you. And the sum here of nine thousand, nine hundred and fifty US dollars was electronically transferred to your account by Posner?'

Garin said nothing.

'It doesn't matter. I will come back to that. Look at this, please.'

Garin took two schematics of look-down radar designs that were stamped as official court exhibits.

'Let me direct your attention to the very bottom,' Rostov said. 'Do you see the serial number? The underlined sequence of letters and numbers: 207X-1803851820-93. Do you see that?'

'Yes.'

'Can you tell me what it is?'

'I have no idea.'

'I will tell you. The first four digits identify the unique copy machine that was used to make a duplicate of the drawing. The second set of numbers are the date and time the copy was made, and the last two are the number of pages copied. Have you seen this document before?'

'No.'

'Are you sure?'

'Yes.'

'Let me direct your attention to the bottom of the document. Here.' Rostov pointed. 'Do you see the stamped identification – "Top Secret"? In English. You don't have to answer. I will stipulate it is there.' Rostov stepped back. 'Can you tell me, Mr Garin, how a classified Soviet military schematic copied on a KGB photocopier ended up marked "Top Secret" in English?'

Garin tossed the paper back at Rostov, dismissing it. 'This is a cleverly doctored forgery.'

'You work for the Central Intelligence Agency, correct?'

'I am a consular officer who works on human rights.'

'How does a human rights officer obtain a Swiss bank account that receives a deposit from a KGB disbursement account?' Rostov tapped his file slowly and waited for Garin's answer.

Garin had his eyes on the document, staring numbly, while his mind tried to come up with a plausible lie.

'Let me suggest an answer,' Rostov said. 'Defendant Posner has an office on the seventh floor of KGB Headquarters. It is near the copy machine that was used to produce these documents. He made these copies, and he supplied them to you, didn't he?'

'No. And I wouldn't know. I know nothing about any of this, except that your so-called facts are inventions of your imagination.'

Rostov turned to Garin. 'We know there is a traitor inside the KGB who is passing documents to the CIA – camera, film, and a radio transmitter were taken from the CIA chief of station in Red Square. Do you know George Mueller?'

'No. Who is he?'

'You are lying!'

Rostov slapped the documents on the table in front of Garin, punctuating his accusation. The prosecutor's face had reddened, his eyes were fierce, and his anger was palpable. Rostov turned to the judge. 'This man,' he said, pointing to Posner, 'is the man the CIA calls GAMBIT. A morally corrupt traitor to the State who trades military secrets for personal gain.'

The judge examined the documents that Rostov presented and removed her glasses to look at Rostov. 'But why is the money going into the American's account? Shouldn't it be going the other way? The American sending money, not receiving it?'

'Madame Chairman,' Rostov said with a flourish, his voice deepening respectfully, 'the elaborateness of this conspiracy is almost unimaginable. Here is a second numbered Swiss bank account at Compagnie de Banque et Investissements.' He placed the document before the judge with two hands, bending respectfully at the waist as he did.

'The first transfer is from the KGB disbursement account at the Military Institute Commission, which is the only agency allowed to disburse foreign currency,' Rostov explained, 'and when the amount is below ten thousand dollars US, Posner could authorize the transfer, so long as he explained it. And defendant Posner wrote such an explanation, which you can see is the second document. He claims he was paying Garin to be a Soviet double agent.

'Here, however' – Rostov stepped forward and placed his finger on the second numbered account – 'is the real business. Account number Q 45458933A belongs to defendant Posner through his alias account at Coutts Private Bank, London, which has a banking affiliation with Compagnie de Banque et Investissements. May I direct your attention to the sum transferred on the same day as funds went to Garin, but this amount was *from* Garin to Posner, in the amount of two hundred fifty thousand dollars.

'As I said, the cleverness of this conspiracy is almost unimaginable, and the damage to State Security incalculable. We lost a KGB officer inside the embassy. This man Garin has masked his identity, leaving us to speculate who he is beyond who he claims to be. Our military technology shows up in the Pentagon. And the small sum paid to Garin is part of an elaborate subterfuge to give the appearance that Comrade Posner recruited this man Garin as a double agent, when in fact' – Rostov pointed at the prisoner in the dock – 'he is the one who took cash for secrets, just as he took bribes to transfer dissident art into London galleries or secured prohibited alcohol for the Metropol Hotel. His ingenious plan was intended to make it look like he recruited the American Garin, but like the magician, one hand distracts while the other deceives.'

'What does the witness say?' the judge asked.

'He will deny it. He denied it to Comrade Talinov. But I will ask him.'

Rostov and the judge faced Garin. The judge had slightly oval eyes and the matronly face of a grandmother. She leaned forward, looking soberly at Garin, and directed him to answer the question.

Garin watched. He knew that the unreality of Hell didn't mitigate the terror, but it could surprise him in unexpected ways. He heard in Rostov's summary a plausible account, one even he could believe. Justice was outside of time because the crime and the judgment were only connected through facts woven into a reconstruction of the past. But they weren't *the* past, only a version of it, and he preferred Rostov's version.

'That's ludicrous,' Garin said. He waved off the question with the calculated bluster of a poker player holding a bad hand. 'A clever theory. If only it were true.'

Rostov raised his hands. 'See? Nothing can more clearly demonstrate his deception than his denial. Look at his face, listen to his voice. He is trying to protect the man sitting there.'

'Numbered accounts,' Garin said. 'Where is the proof? You would have the court believe you've pierced the confidentiality of Swiss banking.'

Rostov walked to Garin. 'And clever of you too, Mr Garin, thinking we would reveal our methods here in open court.'

23

POSNER'S DEFENSE

THE TRIAL RECONVENED AFTER a two-hour break. The courtroom had no sense of day or night, and the unchanged fluorescent lighting created the illusion that time had stopped.

Garin was escorted into the courtroom by two guards who held his elbows. The handcuffs and ankle shackles were again removed at the door, but he walked in with the slumped posture of an accused man, not a witness. Garin was made to sit to one side, and it was then that he noticed a difference in the room. Defendant Posner stood at the defense table, and Natalya sat alone at the witness table. She wore her gray KGB uniform with its service medal, black leather heels, and a scarlet necktie on a white blouse. Her black hair was tied tightly in a bun, and her pale lips were pressed together in a defiant expression.

Natalya avoided his eyes. She was remote and seemed unnaturally rigid. When their eyes did meet, she did not acknowledge him in any way.

'Madame Chairman,' Posner said, moving from behind the defense table, where he dismissed the restraining hand of his lawyer, a pudgy, short man in a rumpled suit. 'I stand accused of crimes against the State, and if everything I am accused of is true, as the prosecutor alleges, I would be the first to demand your evenhanded judgment. I am speaking now on my own behalf, against the advice of my attorney, but only I know the facts and how they fit together. If I may?'

Posner took his cue from the judge's nod. 'Thank you.' He turned to Rostov with a grim face. 'The charges against me are false, the facts untrue, the allegations malicious, and the accuser Talinov has his own reasons to turn this trial into a mockery. Let me address each point of the charge and you will see that my accuser's motives corrupt the accusations with foul intentions.

'Madame Chairman, I was convicted in a sham trial a few weeks ago of extorting money from trade unionists in exchange for favors. The conviction is being appealed. The vague evidence against me was filled with circumstantial claims, except for one. I was accused of taking bribes to facilitate the import of a prohibited good – specifically French wine – to the Metropol Hotel's restaurant. The principal evidence against me was the confession made by the restaurant's maître d'. What is unconscionable is what happened behind the scenes after the principal witness, A. Y. Vyshinsky, who actually rejected the idea of my guilt, was put in the hands of Directorate Z. Its powerful chief, Viktor Stucka, an ally of Talinov, suddenly took an interest in the case, and the man was transferred to prison where, miraculously, Vyshinsky made a confession. Subsequently, I reviewed the confession, but I had no chance to question the man. He died in prison.

'The idea that I would take a bribe from a hotel employee – it stretches the imagination and impeaches reason. But from this weed they grew a garden of claims that I had extorted millions from art dealers, food wholesalers, and cigarette importers. My conviction was quite convenient for a colleague in the Fifth Chief Directorate who now had no competition for the deputy director's position I was in line for.'

'Comrade Posner,' the judge interrupted. 'We aren't here

to retry your conviction. Speak to the present indictment.'

'Madame Chairman, I will address the charge of treason. I am guilty of many things that, if viewed in the wrong light, as the present circumstances create, support a case against me, and in this I am a victim of my own mistakes. But who among us is perfect? Am I guilty of being complicit in a rush to uncover deceit among my colleagues, and in doing so, have I made errors of judgment that look like I was dishonest? Yes, I am guilty of that crime.

'Madame Chairman, am I guilty of sympathizing with dissident, anti-Soviet individuals who dismiss the false rhetoric of the State and risk their lives to speak out? Yes, I am guilty of that compassionate mistake. But who among us does not see the hypocrisy?

'Madame Chairman, I consider myself responsible for one crime against the Socialist Fatherland and the International Proletariat. It is the crime of ambition. I have advanced myself at the expense of other men, and perhaps I have slandered good men in the hopes the slanders would poison their careers. And who among us has not coveted a promotion?

'But, Madame Chairman, I am not guilty of treason. I have not passed military secrets to foreign agents. I have not provided the CIA with photocopies. And I have not dishonored my loyalty to the State by compromising our national defense. All the evidence against me is circumstantial, except for the one piece of paper – an anonymous, numbered bank account – the meaning of which has been twisted against me. I am supposed to have created a cover for my treason by making it appear that I paid Garin money when, in fact, I was receiving money – again, through an anonymous, numbered account. That is what the prosecutor would have you believe. It is a fabrication, an atrocity. I deny it. Garin denies it. There is no proof of money I received. There is no proof I owned the account. And the claim that I used a copier is unsubstantiated. Tens of dozens of people have access to that copier. To the charge that I provided copies and received payment, there is not one scrap of evidence. Not one. I didn't pass military secrets.'

Posner had shouted his speech. He stood rigid and looked at the judge. Then he pointed at the witness table. 'I have here a woman, a decorated KGB officer, who helped recruit Garin to work for the KGB.'

The judge turned to the witness table. 'What do you have to say?' she asked. 'Speak.'

Natalya rose from her chair, tall, poised, and dignified in her uniform. She commanded the attention of the room. Her hands were at her side when she turned to the judge. She gave her name, her rank, and her responsibilities in the KGB. She was subdued as she spoke, and her description of the events necessarily involved describing Garin.

'He was a target,' she said. 'We knew he was vulnerable. There was intelligence from within the embassy that his work on human rights was a cover. We suspected that he worked for the CIA.'

Natalya did not look at Garin as she spoke. Her voice remained flat, almost hostile, when she described the events of the evening at the Bolshoi Theater and then dinner afterward. 'He was cautious but drank too much. I brought him to the designated house where, by previous arrangement, KGB officers were stationed, and this man was compromised. Of course, he was surprised, and he became angry. It was clear that he was upset, and he had no interest in cooperating with Comrade Posner.'

The judge leaned forward. 'What did you expect to learn from him?'

'We wanted to recruit him,' Posner interrupted. He had moved away from the defense table and stood between the judge and his witness. 'He was an important target.'

'Go on,' the judge said to Natalya.

'We knew he had information on the death of General Viktor Zyuganov, and that case remains unsolved.' Natalya stopped. 'It was settled, but questions remain. Garin was an important target to turn, but his value was also in what he knew about General Zyuganov.'

She looked at Talinov. Her eyes were dark embers, fixed and accusing, but her voice was calm. 'That man,' she said, 'Lieutenant Colonel Talinov, executed General Zyuganov. Zyuganov was a patriot who uncovered evidence of corruption in the KGB, and he was falsely accused of sedition. He was executed by that man before he could make a defense.'

Natalya paused. 'Forgive my emotion,' she said. 'I have known Comrade Dmitry Posner since I was a young girl. I have the highest admiration for him. We recruited the American Garin in an authorized operation to develop him as a source inside the CIA. I conclude my testimony.'

'Did Garin mention Lieutenant Colonel Talinov?' the judge asked.

'No.'

'Who authorized the action against Garin?'

'I don't know. Someone higher up.'

'But you don't know?'

'No. It wasn't required that I know.'

'But did you ask?'

'No.'

'So, you don't know if it was authorized?'

Natalya turned to Posner, her eyes searching.

The judge prodded, 'You don't know if it was authorized?' Natalya turned to the judge. 'No, I did not know that.'

'Thank you. You may sit down.'

An agitated Rostov popped up, like a jack-in-the-box. 'It

wasn't authorized, Madame Chairman!' he shouted. 'Defendant Posner misled her, as he is trying to mislead this court.'

Rostov lifted several stapled pages and waved them theatrically over his head. 'To exonerate himself he would have us believe he is the target of a corrupt rival who has slandered him. He has submitted evidence to this court, which I hold here. This document from KGB archives suggests that General Zyuganov was not working for the CIA – and we must then conclude that he was wrongly accused of treason by Lieutenant Colonel Talinov. Defendant Posner would have us believe that he too has been wrongfully accused by Comrade Talinov. This document claims that General Zyuganov was sent to Vyborg to meet an English MI6 agent who Zyuganov had recruited during his two-year posting in London. General Zyuganov was not defecting; he was secretly recruiting a senior MI6 officer. But there is a problem,' he said, his voice rising.

'This six-year-old document is a forgery. Long-lived cotton-fiber paper used by the KGB for classified reports contains an almost invisible date-code watermark to protect the integrity of the document from fraud. The date-code on this document is March 27 of this year. How does a six-year-old document come to have last month's date-code?' Rostov looked around the courtroom and let his question hang in the air. He waved the document.

'It is a counterfeit. A well-done counterfeit. Three men know it is a forgery. The alert KGB technician who spotted the incriminating mistake, the American forger who created this evidence, and defendant Posner. An ingenious forgery, yes, but the mistake usurps its ingenuity.'

Garin gazed at Posner, feeling no compassion.

Rostov continued: 'This document is final proof of defendant Posner's treason. A forgery created for him by the CIA. He would have you believe he is an ordinary victim of human failings when, in fact, he is working for the CIA. Duty, honor, country. Hollow words from his foul mouth. He has betrayed the State just as he betrayed General Zyuganov.'

Natalya's face was ashen, and she looked stricken, as if day had become night. She stood at the witness table until a guard took her arm and escorted her from the courtroom. She stared at Posner in disbelief. She continued to look at him as she was hustled out of the room.

*

Talinov was summoned to the witness table. 'Our first suspicion that Posner worked against the State came in 1979,' he said. 'We discovered that Zyuganov conspired to pass classified material to the Americans. Posner alerted us to his friend's crime, and only later did we suspect that Posner knew Zyuganov was to be arrested and turned against him. Later, we discovered that Posner owned a townhouse in London and traveled frequently. We can see a pattern in his clever arrangements. Posner is the man the CIA call GAMBIT.'

Garin gazed at Posner and saw a man who understood the ghastly snare that he had stepped on. The pallid face of a dead man. His crime was wrong, the evidence against him false, but justice had found Posner.

211

24

ESCAPE

GARIN HEARD THE GUARD's loud voice through the cell door's grated window: 'Hey, you in there. Wake up.' He had been returned to his basement cell in Lefortovo Annex before the end of the proceeding and told nothing. He had been unshackled and thrown onto the floor of his cell. He had spent some time looking for a way out. There was a weakness in every prison, and he had made a concerted effort to find it in his cell. He had tried the bedroom's grated window, testing the iron anchors in the crumpling mortar, but he found that no amount of force dislodged them. He spun around to look for a tool, but the cabinets were empty. The kitchenette, the sofa, and the small bedroom all added to the appearance of a voluntary confinement, but the outside door was firmly locked. He was a prisoner of the State, and he knew from experience, and from the way the Soviet bureaucracy worked, that the full lens of State Security would focus on him until the magnification caused him to combust. To escape, he had to get past the guard, which seemed like an impossible challenge, but he knew that his most dangerous enemy was his feeling of helplessness.

His plan was terrible, but it kept his mind from the numbing fear that he didn't exist to the outside world – and would cease to exist, with a bullet to the nape of his neck, buried in an unmarked grave. The mortal void angered him. As he had done all his life, even as a child, he put his fear into the service of crazy ingenuity. He screamed and then was quiet. Again, he screamed, pounded the door with his fists, and screamed. This went on for several minutes, and then he listened through the door. He had counted the minutes that the guard took to reach the end of the hallway in his rounds, inspecting each of the hallway's cells, and he timed his activity to the guard's schedule. He loosened one leg of a three-legged stool and tested its strength, proving to himself that it was an adequate weapon. He hid it under his belt.

Garin lifted his head from the table, where he pretended to rest, and looked at the guard's face through the grated window. 'Fuckhead,' Garin growled. 'Look at me. So quiet.'

'Come to the door,' the guard said. 'Snap to it.'

Garin heard the door bolt slide free, and his hand went to the club. *A quick blow to the head, drag the man inside.* Garin had mentally mapped the turns he'd taken in the old mansion's basement tunnel when he'd been returned to this cell, so he could reverse them.

The door opened with a great, aching screech of hinges, and the guard pushed against the rusted resistance until it was fully open. 'You have a visitor.'

Natalya stepped from behind the guard. She was dressed as she had been in the courtroom – smart KGB uniform, hair in a bun – and her face was grim and unsmiling. She carried a notebook in one hand and a small duffel bag in the other.

'I will be fifteen minutes,' she said to the guard. 'Stay close by. When I'm finished taking his statement, I will knock.'

'Be careful of him. He bit a guard's ear. He's a shit.'

'Don't go far,' she said.

The guard closed the door, locking it.

Natalya stared at Garin. She hadn't slept, her dark eyes were nervous, and she made a great effort to look composed. Her lips were pressed tight, which gave her expression a hint of menace. 'You look like an animal,' she said.

'What are you doing here?'

'Yes, what?!' She looked at the cell's interior doors. 'Are you alone?'

'Yes.'

She placed the duffel bag on the table. 'I am here to take notes on your case so there is a record for your trial. That is what I have told the guard. If he comes back, that is what I must be seen doing.' She unzipped the duffel bag. 'I don't feel responsible for you. This, you brought on yourself.'

His notebook and travel documents were inside the bag. She pushed them aside to pull out a Soviet Army captain's uniform, which she presented to Garin.

'You are Luca's size. Put it on quickly. If you walk confidently, no one will ask questions of a Soviet captain wearing the Order of the Red Banner. *Afganets.*'

Garin stripped his smelly clothing and pushed his arms in the sleeves of the wool jacket and thrust his legs in the pants, buttoning the tunic, his hands shaking. He swept his hair back and placed the high-crown cap on his head. 'Why are you doing this?'

She scoffed. She looked through the barred window and turned back to Garin. 'What happened in the courtroom after I left?'

'His defense was rejected.'

'What will happen to him?'

'You know. He'll be executed. He may already be dead.'

She flinched, and her mouth opened involuntarily at the sudden, shocking news. She covered her surprise with a deep, calming breath and fortified her expression with false bravery.

'Why haven't they let me go?' Garin asked.

'Why would they? You know too much.'

'And so do you.'

She shook her head. 'I am not under suspicion.' She looked at Garin accusingly. 'You conspired against Dmitry.'

'I did what I had to do.'

Her eyes were fierce. 'You lied. Everything you said was a lie.'

'He betrayed your father. He is the one who informed Talinov of the border crossing.'

Color left Natalya's face, and she stared at him, confused and disbelieving, but she knew the truth. Her face remained tough, but her hands began to tremble.

Garin had a great urge to comfort her, but he didn't. He felt the club in his hand, which he gripped threateningly, but there was dangerous sympathy in his heart. 'That is what you need to know,' he said. 'Yes, I lied. You want to know? I will tell you. But it is dangerous for you and dangerous for me.'

Garin heard the guard approaching. 'We set up Posner from the beginning,' he said. 'We used you. We used him. We needed to shift attention away from GAMBIT. Posner once worked for us – he worked for everyone, if it paid – but he was no longer useful. Or reliable. We used you to set him up. Now you know everything. It won't make things easier. The truth never makes things easier.'

She looked like she'd been punched, and she gasped audibly.

The guard was approaching. Garin lowered his voice. 'Are you coming with me?'

She handed him her nine-millimeter Makarov. 'You will need this.'

'You're not coming?'

'For what?' She stared at him. 'This is my country, my

215

home. Leave for what? An immigrant's life in a strange place? Chernenko is dead. Things will change.'

Garin heard determination in her voice, and he knew nothing he said or did would change her mind.

She smiled – an insolent smile. 'To be like you, a man without a country? I prefer to stay. I can be miserable here in my own home. I don't have to be miserable in Brighton Beach with the *zadroty*, still talking and plotting against what they left.' Her expression softened. 'Kiss me.'

'What?'

'You shouldn't leave believing I don't care for you.'

Garin heard the guard yelling at the man in the next cell. Urgency made a claim on him, but he did as she asked. He kissed her briskly, with urgent emotion that she returned.

She broke away, frightened by the power of the moment to change her mind. She presented her wrists. 'Tie me up. There's a car outside, a red Lada. Bogdan is driving. He is excited to play his part, so make him think he's important. He will drive you where you tell him.'

'This is stupid. Come with me.'

'It's not possible. The door is opening.'

Garin had stepped to one side so when the door opened, he was able to bring the club down on the unsuspecting guard's head, sending him to his knees. A second blow put him on the floor, and a low moan came from his throat. Garin tied his hands behind his back with his belt and wound a cloth over his eyes. A towel went in his mouth to silence him.

Natalya stepped forward. 'Now hit me.'

He was appalled.

'Do you want me to be tortured for being your accomplice? They won't be as kind as you. Hit me,' she snapped. 'You're an idiot. Do it.'

Garin was startled and numb, but he summoned courage.

He stared at her pleading eyes – earnest and angry and ready. He fought against his horror. When he opened his eyes, he looked away, but his pistol struck her jaw. Her face contorted in pain, and her scream resounded in the small room. Blood gushed from an obscene gash on her lower lip and sullied her uniform. More blood came from her broken nose. She fell to the floor beside the guard, drawn into a fetal position to protect against the next blow.

Outside on the street, a light rain had begun to fall, and somewhere there was the sound of briskly marching soldiers following their commanding officer's tyrannical bark.

Garin looked down at Natalya with pity and regret. Her pain was real; the blood was real; the loud cries for help were real; all that was false was her outrage.

Garin stepped from the room and looked both ways down the empty passageway. He walked in the direction that he knew would take him to the street.

25

ON THE TRAIN

BELORUSSKY STATION WAS THE perfect place to vanish. A main highway to the south started nearby, and there were always cars outside waiting to pick up or drop off relatives or friends. There was also an underpass from the street to the metro station, and a man could easily be anonymous in the crowd that moved to the train platforms. Northbound trains went to other principal stations in Moscow and ultimately to Leningrad and the Finnish border. Southbound trains traveled past towns dotting the countryside outside Moscow and then continued their long overnight journey to Uzhgorod.

Garin waited by a pillar, away from passengers pushing forward to board the train. He was chilly without an overcoat, but the Soviet Army uniform gave him the comfort of knowing he wasn't of interest to the trio of militiamen who scanned the crowd for deserters. Twice strangers had seen the Order of the Red Banner on his chest and smiled, and he'd looked back indifferently. He rubbed his hands together for warmth. Spring had arrived on the calendar, but temperatures fell sharply at night.

When he heard the clanging bell announce the train's departure, he stepped forward and took three steps into the carriage. He didn't look left or right. No innocent man needed to survey the platform to see if he'd been spotted. Then he was inside the train.

Almost immediately, the carriage shuddered and lurched forward, and the train picked up speed and settled into a comfortable rhythm. Garin headed toward the first-class compartment in the front of the train, moving down the aisle packed with travelers arranging their baggage in overhead compartments, who moved aside when he begged to pass, and in this way Garin arrived at the end of the car. He was stopped by a conductor who demanded his ticket. 'You're in back. Third class.'

Garin turned around, politely obliging the conductor, looking grateful for the direction, but once the conductor had passed through the carriage, Garin proceeded to the front of the train and Compartment 12. Garin moved his hands from one seat back to the next to steady himself, and twice he inadvertently touched a passenger. Each time the person's indignant expression vanished when he saw the red-and-gold pinned medal. No one seemed to care that he hadn't shaved in several days; no one noticed his insurgent stubble with wisps of gray, and no one recoiled at the swollen lip or his rank odor. He was a war hero returned from the front. He accepted the respect and let passengers think what they wanted. If asked, he had already decided that he would say he was on home leave and *fuck off* if he was unshaven and smelled.

He ignored family groups who settled into their seats for the thirty-two-hour journey, undoing twine from small boxes of bread, sausage, cured meats, and dried apricots, laughing or complaining in loud voices. His eyes picked out single men or a man with a male companion. KGB operated in teams of two on trains to the border. Sometimes the men were together, and sometimes they split up. Undercover teams rode most of the trains, and they remained unseen unless something came to their attention.

Garin moved slowly, lurching from one seat back to the next, apologizing to a passenger if he needed to but always keeping an eye out. His escape had surely been reported by now and an alarm raised.

He spotted Petrov in the second of the two first-class carriages, sitting in Compartment 12 with his family. They acknowledged each other, and Garin continued along the aisle until he reached the end of the car, where he lit a cigarette. Petrov joined him, and the two took a smoke together.

'So, you made it,' Petrov said.

They faced each other across the swaying, shuddering platform between carriages, which was open to the rails underneath. The rhythmic rumble of the train's wheels rolling along the railbed reverberated loudly in the narrow space. No one was there to hear them, and they spoke loudly to be heard.

'What about Posner?'

'He's out of the way.'

'*Mudak!*' Petrov spat.

Garin nodded at the compartment. 'Any problems?'

'She's okay. My rowboat will have been found overturned, and right now her parents will be fretting the possibility that we've drowned. You look official,' he said, nodding at the uniform. 'Some medal. You could be shot if you're caught wearing that.'

Garin nodded but did not smile. He confirmed the details of the plan, which he'd previously laid out. Repetition saved even the best plan from failure. Garin described the plan and then he did it a third time, demanding that Petrov repeat each step. The car would be waiting for them two blocks from the train station. The car's hidden compartment, Petrov's invitation to a sporting competition in Prague, the track suits he and Olga would be wearing. The smuggler's name. There would be a team of Americans waiting on the other side of the frontier. He would carry his film inside the lining of his leather jacket.

Garin looked directly at Petrov. 'A woman might join us.'

Petrov's eyes flared. 'You never mentioned a woman. Who is she? Does she know who I am?'

'If she boards, she'll get on at the next station. She will be no trouble.'

'If she boards?'

'We'll see.'

Petrov wasn't happy.

*

Garin joined Petrov, Olga, and the boy, Aleksey, in their first-class compartment, taking the fourth ticket.

Olga looked at him with nervous trepidation, which she masked with an awkward smile, and he responded with a pleasant nod. He wondered how much Petrov had told her and how much he had lied. Garin smiled to reassure her and make her feel at ease, and he looked at the boy, openly admiring a plush doll he held.

'He'll get a sedative when we get close to Uzhgorod,' Olga said. She turned to her son. 'Remember what I told you. When we get near the end we'll give you something to help you sleep.' She leaned over to her son. 'Darling, do you remember the game we're playing?'

'Yes, Mama, we're pretending that I'm a girl and my name is Nata. But how will anyone think I am a girl? I am a boy. Can't they see that?'

'Of course you're a boy,' she said.

'Oh, so you're a boy,' Garin said, playing along. 'I couldn't tell. I will keep your secret.'

'See?' Olga said. 'You are playing the game well. Let's see

how many people we can fool. You have a doll, a girl's name, and a girl's hat. You've already fooled this soldier, and he isn't easily fooled. Do you see his medal? He's a hero.'

'What if I don't want to play anymore?'

'We'll give you a pill to help you sleep.'

'This doll isn't my type,' he said.

Olga smiled. 'Pretend it is an action figure or an alien in disguise. I'll tell you a story about how much fun it is to fool people into thinking you are one thing when you are really a different thing.'

Garin saw that Olga had her son's attention.

The door opened, and a stocky conductor entered. He wore a dark blue uniform, a large leather belt across his chest, and the smugness of a minor official proud of his authority.

'Tickets.' He turned to Garin, who produced the fourth first-class ticket Petrov had bought. 'You're in the third-class car. I already sent you back. Are you a troublemaker?'

'He's with us,' Petrov said. 'He has a ticket.'

'He has two tickets. You can't have two seats. It's not permitted. We're sold out. I need to report this.'

Petrov produced several rubles from his pocket and added to the amount until the conductor was satisfied.

'Don't worry,' the conductor said. 'You're safe in this seat. Our patriotic soldiers deserve to be treated well.' He patted the child's head. 'Cute little girl you've got.'

*

Kaluga. The first stop on the Moscow main line south was two and a half hours into the journey. There was a large train station that was used for local traffic and passengers traveling to and from Moscow. The station was a two-story, rose-and-cream stucco building from tsarist times that sat astride the railbeds. Garin had risen from the compartment when he heard the conductor announce their approach.

He wasn't surprised when he didn't see Natalya among the small group waiting for the train. They boarded quickly, and when the five minutes allotted for the stop were up, the train lurched forward, and continued toward Uzhgorod.

'Well?' Petrov said.

'It is just us,' Garin replied.

'That's better. We don't need complications.' He gazed at Garin. 'Somehow you look disappointed.'

'No.' He pointed to his face. 'This is never what you think it is.'

'Be careful,' he said, and turned to his wife, who was alarmed at what she'd heard. 'Don't worry. Sometimes he doesn't know that his humor is lost on people.'

It was a long train ride. Garin knew he would have to sleep, but he found it hard to put Natalya out of his thoughts. He believed that she might change her mind, drive her car, and join him as they had discussed. She knew the plan, had agreed on the town, and had reasons to leave, even if she claimed she would rather stay. There was the possibility that she could escape the Soviet Union on her own and suddenly appear in the West asking for asylum. And there was another possibility. She had been arrested, now in Lefortovo Prison, or already dead.

He didn't dwell on the thought. She was gone from his life and that was the same as death – a type of death. The same as his wife. Garin took one last long pull on his cigarette and ground it into the arm's ashtray. *Fuck it.* The curse slipped from his lips.

Early-morning darkness was upon them, and he knew he had to sleep. Just when he was drifting off, a baby somewhere began to cry in another compartment, and when the child quieted, he heard riotous singing of two troublemaking drunks who pounded on each compartment door as they made their way through the carriage, exciting angry howls from sleeping passengers, and the noise woke the infant, who started to cry again.

Garin turned in his seat, adjusted his head against the headrest, and made a determined effort to ignore the noise. Once inside the quiet of his mind, he again began to fret the details of the coming day. Sometime in the middle of the night, he drifted off. It wasn't sleep as much as it was the suspension of wakefulness. He was aware of things entering his consciousness. He was aware of sounds, alert to the change in the train's rhythm. He heard the tapping of hammers as maintenance men tested the Krupp steel wheels for fractures. There was the explosive sound of air pressure slapping against their carriage as a high-speed train passed. He had wild dreams that he did his best to ignore.

*

Dawn came as glowing warmth through the window. Garin was aware of bright sunlight on his face. He sat up and saw Petrov, Olga, and the boy still asleep. The boy lay across his mother's lap. Petrov's mouth was open, his head leaned back. A great exhaustion and the uncomfortable worry of the next day's unknown kept them from stirring.

Garin looked out the window at the great steppes that disappeared to the far horizon. Then there was the restless rumble underneath as they crossed a trestle bridge over a surging river, and out the window he saw the beginnings of russet hills that glowed in the early-morning light. They had passed through Kiev, and now the landscape changed to fertile flatlands, scar, and ravine. They would be on the train all day, and half a second night, before ending the long journey.

Garin left the compartment for the passageway, lighting a Prima, which he drew on deeply. He gazed out the window at the passing landscape and contemplated the land of his father. He tried to imagine the man he had never met. It was at times like this that the American graft on his Russian heart gave him great pain.

The train made its slow, wending way south and west through terrain dotted with farm villages. He saw diesel-starved tractors with hoes being pulled by horses. A kind of serene stupidity came over him. The hours of travel had softened his face and brought him to a comfortable reckoning. He was lost in thought gazing at the passing landscape, and in the moment, he was a young boy again looking at the far horizon of his life, leaving behind the weary man living his future. The changing landscape and the train's rhythm subdued him. He had the face of a boy who knew the evil of the world and how he would cheat it.

26

UZHGOROD

THE CONDUCTOR ANNOUNCED THE train's arrival with three loud raps on the compartment's window, waking the sleeping family. They had succumbed to exhaustion during the thirty-two-hour journey, and sleeping quieted the anxiety of what lay ahead. They were arriving in predawn darkness. It was 2:56 a.m.

Petrov was startled awake by the sudden announcement. Outside, the night was punctuated by streetlamps on the outskirts of the border town. The train was slowing, and its steel wheels screeched on the sharp curve that carried it past warning lights and the clanging bell of a street crossing. There were three short bursts from the locomotive's whistle. Half-asleep passengers outside their compartment sat on their luggage and made sullen remarks. Only the boy, Aleksey, sedated, slept.

Garin leaned to Petrov and Olga and reminded them of what they had to do.

'No one knows we are here. If the border guards look at you, it doesn't mean they are looking *for* you. It is their job to stare and make you uncomfortable. The driver will be parked with his Mercedes two blocks from the station. You will know him because his trunk will be open.'

Uzhgorod was not a typical border town. It was the point of entry to a Warsaw Pact country, and no less heavily defended. Travelers crossing the border were rigorously challenged. Most of the traffic to and from Western Europe crossed the border at Chop, fifteen miles away, so the bulk of the movement at Uzhgorod was local business and civilians passing between Czechoslovakia and Ukraine, where wars had repeatedly altered the political boundary.

Uzhgorod Station's clock tower chimed three times in the darkness, marking the early hour, and everywhere tired, zombie-like men and women ignored the dozens of alert, gray-uniformed guards.

Garin emerged from the station's bathroom, where he had changed his clothes. He wore a gray business suit, narrow tie, black shoes, and wire-rim glasses, which he stopped to clean as he passed two border guards resting their arms on Kalashnikovs, and he confirmed the guards had no interest in him. Petrov left the station carrying his sleeping son on his shoulder, and Garin walked behind, Olga at his side, giving the appearance of a couple.

Garin found the driver and his parked Mercedes where he'd been told they would be. Streets in the medieval town were narrow cobblestone alleys that twisted in unpredictable ways along ancient routes built around old homes. Windows were dark at that hour, doors locked for the night, and the streets were empty.

'You're late,' the driver said. He looked skeptically at the family. 'This is the package? I was told there would be one.'

'Change of plans.'

'What's your name?'

'Alek,' Garin snapped. 'What's yours?'

'Boris. Okay. Plans change. A patrol drove by two minutes ago. Get in.'

Boris proceeded to remove a section of the back seat of his Mercedes S-Class. Garin made a judgment of the man as he worked, cigarette dangling from his mouth, grunting displeasure. Garin trusted the Agency's Czech contacts, but he knew that local smugglers were a special breed of men who worked for money and had no political loyalties. At the first sign of danger, they were quick to switch allegiances for their own good. Garin adjusted the nine-millimeter Makarov pistol under his belt.

'Throw that away,' Boris said. 'If they find that, forget about getting across the border.' Boris shrugged and added casually, 'Or you can keep the gun, but I'm not driving.'

Garin dropped the pistol through a sewer grate. He had stuffed his Soviet Army uniform into the covered wastebasket in the station bathroom, where he knew it would be found, but by that time, they would be across the border.

Boris hustled the family and its two bags into the car. He threw Olga's duffel bag into the trunk and followed with Petrov's, putting on a show of urgency. He directed Olga to get in the car. 'Up front,' he said. 'Next to me.'

'You,' he said to Petrov, 'in here.'

Boris had pulled the back seat forward to reveal a specially fabricated compartment that sat between the trunk's well and the back seat. It wasn't large, just enough space for a grown man and a child – or whatever the week's contraband. Petrov slipped in the small space and hunched against one side, his legs drawn to his chest. Aleksey, drowsy from the sedative, was placed in Petrov's arms, his small legs stretched forward.

'Keep him quiet,' Boris said. 'If he talks when the guards look in the trunk, they'll tear the car apart.' Boris looked at Petrov. He threw a handkerchief. 'If he looks like he is going to talk, hold his mouth shut. He's a nice kid. Don't make him an orphan.'

The space was cramped but ample, and air circulated through the sides of the back seat. Petrov took a deep breath as Boris pushed the false wall in place and reset the back seat.

Garin sat in the back behind Olga. 'I will tap once when we get to customs,' he said through the seat. 'Twice when we are across.'

'Names?' Boris asked. He glanced sideways at Olga. 'They will ask me at the border. You want me to look stupid? Two passengers who've paid me to drive them four hours to Prague and they haven't introduced themselves?'

Olga gave the name on the Soviet passport and identity card that Technical Services had created, and Garin did the same. Boyfriend and girlfriend. Sports enthusiasts visiting European competitions going on in Prague.

'I know the guard at the first checkpoint. That's where he will open the trunk and dogs will circle the car. He is Ukrainian, and I provide him tips on the side. Sometimes a girl. So he looks the other way. Just answer his questions and we will be fine.' He looked at Garin in the back seat. 'Do you want to listen to music? It might help. Everyone listens to music.'

The Mercedes had begun to move while Boris fiddled with the radio dial, and he confidently sped up as he sought a station, accelerating around corners without headlights.

'If we don't have music we might seem like we're smugglers,' Boris said. He played with the dial until he found a Czech station playing ABBA.

'We're six kilometers from the frontier. At the first checkpoint, we will be asked to get out. They check documents, car registration, ask a few questions, and they'll look in the luggage. If we are cleared, we go to the second checkpoint. They look at us again, look at the documents, sometimes they put a mirror under the car. I say hello. They may ask you questions, but don't offer anything. Yes and no. Understand? Then, if all goes well, they wave us through to the Czech side. It is sixty meters across no man's land. We're not safe until we are past the Czech border guards.'

Garin settled into the back seat and looked out at the dark streets. Dawn was hours away, and the streets were deserted. Clouds had moved in and dense fog limited visibility, but distant lightning pierced the mist.

*

They arrived at the first Soviet checkpoint, a cluster of three cinderblock buildings alongside covered lanes that led to the frontier beyond. Two tall streetlamps cast a dim glow through the fog and lit red-and-white stanchions that blocked the road. Military kiosks stood on either side of the checkpoint. One sign read *STOP*, and a second, *СТОП*.

Eighteen-wheel transports were parked at the far end of the largely empty lot, waiting for morning. A bright searchlight atop a tall, steel-girder watchtower swept the empty frontier.

Boris pulled into the rear of the line of waiting passenger cars. Two Volkswagens, a gray Volga sedan, and a silver Mercedes were stopped in front of them. A camouflage-uniformed border guard, his arms resting on a Kalashnikov hanging around his neck, observed a customs agent addressing a driver. He was alert but bored, far into his night shift, but his eyes had the menace of soldiers everywhere. An armored personnel carrier with light machine guns was parked behind the customs kiosk. Another customs agent stepped forward and waved the Volkswagens through the raised barrier.

Boris put his car in gear, moving forward until the guard raised his hand: 'Halt.'

Boris whispered to Olga without turning his head, 'Keep

quiet. I'll answer his questions.' Then he lowered his window. 'Good morning.'

'Papers, please.' The guard looked up after scanning them. 'Destination?'

'Prague.'

'Who are these people?'

'From Moscow. I'm driving them to the games.'

The guard lowered his head and illuminated Garin's face with his flashlight. 'Why didn't you fly?'

'Flights were sold out.'

The guard nodded. 'Wait here.'

27

CHECKPOINT

GEORGE MUELLER STOOD IN the darkened office on the
second floor of the Czechoslovakian Border Control
building and looked out the bay window at the strip of empty
frontier. Warmth had passed from the earth, and thickening
fog obscured the Soviet checkpoint sixty meters away. A
watchtower's searchlight played across no man's land, slowly
sweeping the razor-wire-topped, chain-link fence along the
road. Cool early-morning air brought with it wisps of ground-
hugging fog and misting rain, and farther off there were
lightning flashes from the approaching storm. The search
lamp's beam was leaden gray through the fog.

Mueller raised his 12x binoculars and studied the scene at
the Soviet checkpoint. Border guards were in the midst of a
shift change. Fresh guards stepping in for the ones ending their
duties, and there was a halt in activity as the new men took
over.

Mueller looked for movement through the shifting fog. The
candy-striped barrier had been raised, and a silver Mercedes
S-Class made its way toward the Czech side. Mueller saw the
car enter the sorrowful darkness of the frontier, but when he
looked through his binoculars he saw only the driver.

Where is Alek? He looked at his watch. *It's time.* The window was open for the light breeze, and it was open too for the rifle held by the black-ops Agency sniper who stood beside Mueller. The man observed the top of the watchtower through his German binoculars. His heavy-barrel .270 bolt-action Mauser rifle with laminated walnut stock and telescopic sight hung on his shoulder with a leather harness sling. The rifle was fitted with a Canjar trigger.

The man was tall, like Mueller, but heavyset, and the large rifle looked small and toy-like on his chest. He wore a black utility vest and tan fatigues without identifying markings. He dropped the binoculars onto his chest and raised his rifle, sighting the cross hairs on the Soviet sniper who stood atop the watchtower.

The Soviet marksman wore a black wool cap over thick hair that fell over his ears, and a kaffiyeh wrapped his neck, the ends tucked into his field jacket. His rifle hung around his neck, the barrel pointing down. He wore desert camouflage fatigues and an Afghan tour of duty service patch.

The Agency sniper had his Russian target in the scope's cross hairs. He knew the exact drop of his bullet in five-meter increments, and he calculated the distance it would have to travel. A clear shot across a short distance. It was the worsening visibility that was uncertain. Clouds were rolling in, coming intermittently, sometimes obscuring the target, and then unpredictably the air cleared, giving him a clean shot.

'Stand down,' Mueller said. 'It's not them. There are no passengers.'

Mueller glanced at the line of cars parked at the Soviet checkpoint, looking for a black Mercedes with Czech license plates, but the end of the line disappeared into fog.

Rositske stood behind Mueller, and beside him Ronnie Moffat, who wore a wool car coat and an anxious expression. Rositske handed Mueller another cup of coffee.

'Why don't you take a break?' Rositske said. 'I'll take over for a few minutes. You haven't slept since Washington. You're no good like this.'

Mueller ignored the offered coffee. 'They'll be here,' he said. 'The train arrived in Uzhgorod.'

'If they were on it.'

'They were.' Mueller turned. 'He's good at what he does. He'll get GAMBIT across. He'll come.'

'When?'

'When it's safe. There's no deadline. He's not running to catch an airplane. He'll wait until it feels right.'

'He might have been blown by the smuggler.'

'He doesn't get paid until he delivers. He won't risk his life, but I trust his greed.'

'What about Garin?'

Mueller paused. 'I'm talking about Garin.' Mueller nodded at the black-ops sniper at his side. 'That's why he's here. If there's a problem.'

A telephone rang. The one-note chime pierced the room's quiet and startled the four Americans. From another room came the urgent sounds of a man speaking Czech. A uniformed officer appeared in the corner office's door and nodded briskly at Mueller. Czechoslovakia and the Soviet Union were Warsaw Pact allies, but the Czech people still remembered the Soviet Army's brutal repression of the 1968 Prague Spring uprising. The Czech intelligence officer who approached Mueller had lost his only son to a Soviet tank tread.

'There may be a problem,' he said in English.

'What problem?'

'A Soviet transport aircraft landed in Uzhgorod airport an hour ago. The airport closes at midnight, but it was reopened for this airplane. Four passengers, three men and a woman, disembarked and took a waiting government sedan.'

Mueller considered the meaning of what he'd just been told. *An hour?* 'Where did they fly in from?'

'Moscow.'

Mueller rubbed his hands together against the chill and moved back to the open window. There was no backup plan. If the smuggler was stopped, they would be questioned, and Mueller had no idea if the wife's nerves would hold up under stress or if the child's cry would betray them. There was always a weak point in an operation – the single point of failure. It didn't reveal itself until the crisis moment.

Mueller considered the problem. If the car had been stopped, it was possible the waking son gave them away or the wife became nervous, triggering a search of the car. Or they might have seen a problem and abandoned the car, going on the run. They stood no chance against the border's defenses: two rows of razor wire, machine gun towers every two miles, land mines dotting the strip of land between chain-link fencing, and round-the-clock patrols with dogs. Escaping across the border on foot was a dangerous and often fatal mistake. The muscles on Mueller's neck contracted, and tension tingled his spine.

'It's too late if the smuggler has turned them in,' Rositske said. Mueller ignored his former deputy, but he was aware of Rositske standing at his side. They were both tired, both under stress.

Mueller knew he was facing his test – this was his operation, and the full weight of a failure would fall on him. Mueller turned, sensing Rositske's eyes on him, and the two men stared at each other.

'Did you really believe you could trust him?' Rositske snapped. 'A mercenary? He's no better than the smuggler. If he's desperate, he'll do whatever it takes to save himself.'

Old grudges between the two men rose up.

'You think you know him,' Rositske went on, 'but you don't.'

Mueller turned away. They both knew what would follow from a failure. Questions would be asked, a formal inquiry convened, and the careers of the men involved placed on hold until answers were given. He would no longer be in charge of his retirement.

Rositske added, 'The whole operation has been wrong from the start. The idea we could use one of their own against them. The game they're playing has changed. He will become a Soviet hero who turned in GAMBIT. Have you considered that we've been played?'

Mueller was ready to accept the mistake. It was possible that the best professional calculations applied to GAMBIT's exfiltration – the studied gnomic briefings on what little they knew of the inner workings of the KGB and Headquarters' meticulous effort to come up with a plan – were all in the service of a wildly ingenious enemy manipulation. But that didn't feel right to Mueller. There was a long silence as both men contemplated the possibility.

'The night isn't over,' Mueller said. His eyes moved to the open window, and then he suddenly turned back. 'He's not that kind, but if he is… so be it.'

'What kind is he?'

Mueller didn't get the opportunity to answer. The black-ops Agency sniper had stepped closer to the window, binoculars pressed to his eyes. 'It's him.' He handed Mueller the binoculars. 'Look.'

28

CZECHOSLOVAK FRONTIER

HONKING CAME FROM THE front of the line of cars at the Soviet checkpoint, and the sound was followed by the sharp clap of quickly moving boots on pavement, accompanied by grunted commands.

'Halt!'

Boris had pulled away from the second checkpoint, and he was driving through the empty stretch of frontier when the watchtower's beam found the Mercedes. The cry went up in a frantic chorus. 'Halt! Halt! Halt!'

'Keep driving,' Garin said from the back seat.

'And get shot?' Boris braked. 'You want to run? Go ahead. Take your chances.'

Garin opened his pocketknife and put the blade across the smuggler's throat. 'Keep driving.'

'My chances are better with them.' Boris pushed away Garin's hand contemptuously. 'Not every crossing succeeds. That is how I stay in business.'

He opened the car door and emerged into the searchlight's hot beam, blinking, his right hand at his eyes to block the brilliant illumination. Seeing gun muzzles pointed at him, he raised his hands in a show of surrender and waved peacefully at the two border guards approaching through the mist.

Boris had a meek, innocent smile and the contrite manner of the wrongly accused. He walked quickly, speaking Ukrainian, a language Garin understood well enough. *Shithead.*

Garin motioned for Olga to slide across the front seat and get behind the steering wheel. She was rigid with fear, her eyes wide, and her breath came in fits. Garin looked at her calmly, almost affectionately, and spoke in a gentle, coaxing voice. 'Do what I say. The life of your child depends on it. Do you understand?' His expression hardened. 'Drive toward the men standing ahead of us. Now!'

She nodded almost involuntarily.

'Don't stop. If guns are fired, keep driving. Stop for nothing.'

She nodded again, then moved across the front seat, sliding over the center console and gear shift, and dropped into the driver's seat. She clutched the wheel with nervous hands and gripped the gear shift, trembling.

'Good,' he said. 'I am getting out. Drive when I close the door.'

Garin stepped into the searchlight, squinting against the glare. Border guards, who'd taken Boris into custody, added Garin to their coverage. They sent Boris back to the Soviet checkpoint and turned their weapons on Garin, who retreated one step, and then a second step, and he slapped the Mercedes once when he heard Olga fumbling with the ignition.

Without an active intention on his part, and not through any obvious mistake, Garin found himself vaulted into a future he'd always known awaited him, where things could go very wrong – but they could also go right. Now, suddenly, that future was upon him. His mind calibrated and recalibrated the risks.

The answer came to him as he retreated from the car. A vexed sky let go a lightning bolt that was immediately followed by shattering thunder. The frightening rumble passed, but it diverted the attention of the border guards, and as darkness fell again, Garin pounded twice on the Mercedes. He saw the two young border guards turn their heads at the sound of the Mercedes' revving engine. Then its tires squealed in violent acceleration.

An urgent chorus of voices shouted, and an alarm went up. The confusion of the moment climaxed in a burst of automatic gunfire. One border guard had the presence of mind to lift his Kalashnikov and direct the weapon at the fleeing car, but he fired from his hip, so the hail of bullets hit the pavement in white puffs, other shots straying wildly toward the Czech customs hut, shattering a window. Czech guards ducked for cover. A second border guard carefully aimed his rifle, shattering the car's rear window and taking out the rear tires. One hissed as it deflated and the other burst, so the rubber flapped against the pavement, bringing the car to a halt. It was stopped short of the Czech border's raised barrier. All eyes settled on the car in no man's land. A precarious silence lengthened as everyone waited for a sign of life.

'Over here,' Garin shouted. He had crossed the few yards to the car, waving at the Czech guards. He peered in the window and then quickly opened the doors, helping a stunned Olga from the driver's seat. Petrov emerged, holding his frightened son. Garin faced the Soviet border guards, a human shield, giving the family time to retreat into the line of Czech guards, who opened their ranks.

Garin was alone in the frontier. A tense standoff between opposing armed forces ensued. Garin stared at the nervous Soviet guards pointing their weapons, and then he felt a presence at his side. Mueller had crossed the short distance and joined him in the open.

Garin heard his name called. It was a vaguely familiar voice from deep inside the thickening fog, a voice without provenance that had spoken his real name.

239

Behind the two Americans, and protected by the dubious comfort of the invisible political divide, Czech guards stood with their commanding officer. Rositske took a position on the front line, joining the drama. All were alert, all were anxious, and all were eager to protect their success. Months of planning, long nights of worry, and two days of extraordinary suspense on two continents were over. This was to be the victorious moment when Mueller and Rositske pulled Garin back to the caravan that would drive everyone to the waiting G4 executive jet, which would fly them to London and then on to Washington, DC.

Mueller put his hand on Garin's shoulder. 'Let it go.'

Garin ignored the command and peered through the fog, alert for the woman's voice. The purling blanket of mist diffused the light's beam and made it hard to recognize who was on the other side. Garin heard his name called a second time, and he knew her voice.

He stepped forward to peer into the puzzling haze. And then his name again, louder, pleading, luring him with dangerous bewilderment.

Mueller put a restraining hand on Garin's arm. 'Forget it. Let's go.'

Forty meters away the fog opened up and revealed a silver Chaika limousine that had stopped at an acute angle just inside no man's land. The rear door was open, and Garin saw Natalya. She stood erect at the door in her KGB uniform.

Garin heard her call his name again – a loud, harassing voice that came with a plaintive plea.

'Don't,' Mueller said.

Natalya wore the sullied uniform that she'd been in when he left her on the floor of the cell – her smart tunic and buttoned white shirt torn, and someone had tried to clean the bloodstains. Her cheek was swollen, her arm bent at a terrible angle, and her expression vacant. And then Garin heard pain in her voice. He wondered how long she'd held out before their brutality had gotten her to talk.

Her voice again. A melancholy pitch. There was a disembodied hollowness to her request that he help her. *A warning?* he wondered.

She was beaten but defiant. It was hard for him to look at her proud figure bent slightly from abuse and to see her pronounced limp when she stepped forward. She wore her pain bravely, and her clothes covered the bruises of her torture. She raised her hand to her eyes to look through the gauzy light.

Deputy Chairman Churgin stepped out of the silver Chaika and joined Natalya, gripping her elbow firmly. He held a nine millimeter Makarov service pistol in his other hand.

Churgin's presence was a startling surprise, but the value of Garin's professional training was its preparation for the unforeseen. Churgin's appearance caused Garin to rethink things. Vengeance laid its cold hand on his heart. He stared at Churgin through the fog, thinking about old wounds. Urgency stirred. Things were not playing out as he had expected. Ever since they'd arrived at Uzhgorod, he'd believed they would safely cross the Czech border and then he'd enjoy a glorious success.

'Let's go,' Mueller repeated. 'There is nothing we can do.'

Garin threw off Mueller's hand and stepped forward. There were only four of them in view now on the Soviet side, or five with the driver, hardly visible behind the windshield. The driver turned, and Garin saw Lieutenant Colonel Talinov behind the wheel. Deputy Chairman Churgin and Natalya were visible, as were the two nervous border guards, but he knew others were hidden in the eddying fog. Talinov remained in the car. The odds were terrible. That was Garin's thought as he stepped forward.

'You had less gray hair in your photographs,' Churgin said. 'I'm not the first one to make that observation. Posner said it, too. "He's gone gray. You wouldn't recognize him without his moustache."'

'But there's still a likeness to your photograph among the graduating class at Dzerzhinsky Institute. How clever you have been, Aleksander Leontyevich, thinking you could enter your country, do this business, and be gone before we were able to recognize you. Fortunately, Posner had his people compare the likenesses. When he knew you'd betrayed him, he did not hesitate to tell us what he had discovered. Your scar made the connection. I can't see it from here, but I'm sure I'll have a closer look when we're finished talking.'

Deputy Chairman Churgin pushed Natalya forward, squeezing her elbow. 'Ten minutes,' he said. 'Ten minutes earlier and we would have stopped you. The airport took too long to open, so we couldn't land.' He shook his head.

'We always knew you could be a risk. We trained you too well. We knew the mother's loyalty might not transfer to the son. You were an experiment. An American boy with Russian roots. Our Manchurian Candidate inside the CIA. But not all experiments work out.'

The deputy chairman continued to move forward, but even as he talked, his serpent eyes fixed on Garin and the Mercedes that was stopped short of the Czech border.

'A trade,' Churgin said. 'Her for him.' He nodded at Petrov, who stood among the Czech guards, holding his wife and son.

'That's not going to happen,' Mueller said. 'We've won, understand? This operation is over.'

'It's over!' Garin shouted at Churgin.

'For you,' he said. 'Not for her.'

Garin felt his anger stir. 'Me for her,' he said. 'A good trade. You'll have your pound of flesh.'

'No!' Natalya shouted. 'You're an idiot.'

'A good trade,' Garin repeated. 'A big prize to take back to Moscow. Show how this was a clever ploy to snare me. You'll become a Hero of the Soviet Union.'

Deputy Chairman Churgin contemplated the offer, and he evaluated the ten meters that separated the two small groups. Garin was a step ahead of Mueller, facing Churgin, and behind each side, security forces moved in the fog. The sounds of hustling boots filled the silence that fell over the small patch of earth. There was the feeling of truce in the air. An offer had been made, terms of the trade set, and with it came an unstable peace.

Mueller had taken a step forward and, unseen, lodged his .45-caliber Colt pistol in the small of Garin's back, under his belt. 'She's not worth it,' he whispered. 'You've lost your mind.'

Garin stepped forward with his hands raised over his head in surrender, but he kept his eyes on Churgin's face, and he also observed the vague forms moving through the fog on the Soviet side. Garin had no idea what he was going to do, but he embraced the uncertainty like an old friend who'd come to pay an unannounced visit. This was his life. He'd sworn he'd never do it again, but here he was with a taste for revenge, and it wasn't in his nature to give up a chance to balance the scales of old wrongs. But none of this was in his conscious mind; none of it a conscious choice. He was a wolf advancing on its prey.

Garin didn't see Natalya's left hand move until it had already struck Churgin in the windpipe, stunning him. Her other hand grabbed his pistol, and there was a violent scuffle. The stronger but stunned Churgin fought the weaker but fiercer Natalya for possession of the Makarov. In the brief moment of intense struggle, a shot rang out.

Churgin stepped away from Natalya with his pistol dangling from his hand, stunned. His free hand had gone to his throat, and he struggled with quick, sucking breaths. He stumbled backward, dazed, and in doing so, Natalya was left standing alone.

Her palms were crimson, and she looked at the wetness covering her hands. They had come off her side, where a widening stain darkened her gray tunic. Her startled eyes stared at the blood, and for a moment she seemed disbelieving – almost peaceful in shock. A protest fell from her lips. *No.* She raised her eyes.

Garin looked for encouragement in her face but saw only trauma and disbelief. She raised herself, trying to stand tall and carry her wound stoically.

Churgin pushed her forward, causing her to stumble, but she recovered a weak stride. 'This is what you want,' he cursed. 'Your little red sparrow with her broken wing. Take her. Perhaps she'll live.'

Garin stood absolutely still, watching for danger, looking for an opportunity to present itself. Time slowed. He considered a way through the terrible choices. Nothing he had ever done prepared him for this outcome. His eyes shifted to the Soviet border guards, who moved in the obscuring fog with weapons raised, and he felt vulnerable standing in the open beyond the searchlight. He looked at the two Americans, who held back, horrified but unwilling to help. Garin felt the cold steel of the Colt lodged against his back.

'Don't do anything stupid,' Churgin said. 'Make this easy.' He raised the pistol and pointed it at the nape of Natalya's neck. 'She's weak. She won't live unless she gets to a hospital. She is all yours. *Dolboyob.*' Fuckhead.

Garin slowly rose to his full height and marched toward Churgin with his hands over his head.

'Leave her!' Mueller shouted.

Garin moved through the ellipsis of light from the

watchtower's beam, which had shifted and dimly illuminated Churgin and Natalya on the empty stage. Misting rain had strengthened to a cold drizzle that came in a steady stream, wetting Garin's hair. Rivulets rolled down his face. Garin entered the beam's perimeter, joining the two Russians, and in approaching, he looked at Natalya for a sign that she would live. Her mouth had formed a protest, but the words were prisoners of her terror, and her eyes were wide with fear. She stared at him indignantly. Rain streaming down her pale face washed away her tears. In passing, their eyes met, and he nodded his instruction to proceed to safety on the Czech side.

Garin had gone several yards past Churgin on his way to the Soviet checkpoint, his eyes taking in the relaxed vigilance of the border guards. They had lowered their weapons to receive the surrendering man. Garin took it all in like a sentry scanning a battlefield, collecting intelligence. Then he appeared to stumble. He dropped to his knee, and his right hand reached behind for the Colt, releasing the safety. He was certain that he had to kill Churgin for the suffering he had inflicted.

Garin gathered the courage that was companion to his fear. This was how it would end, he thought. In his dreams, he had always tried to kill Churgin, but the man eluded his efforts. He wasn't dreaming a dream now – he was steps away from the monster.

He spun around with the pistol gripped in both hands, his arms extended, sighting the weapon on the back of Churgin's head. He walked forward, his eyes fixed on the man he'd sworn to kill, bringing human justice to a lawless place. He cursed his life, that it was for him to make things right.

On his third stride, he fired once. The bullet struck Churgin as he turned, and it entered his right ear and exited through his cheek. The KGB deputy chairman collapsed without protest and fell to the pavement, where he lay in a heap, unmoving.

Garin saw dark blood pooling from the obscene head wound and confirmed that Churgin was dead. He saw the startled border guards raise their weapons and he fired twice, hitting one in the arm. The other fell to his knees, clutching his thigh, where he'd been shot. Garin's fourth and fifth bullets shattered the windshield and struck Talinov in the shoulder.

A brief, eerie quiet settled on the patch of earth. One dead, three wounded. The suddenness of the assault and its consequences were frozen in a moment of time. Then the entire world seemed to rise up in mad confusion. The desolate border crossing came alive with the hysterical wail of sirens, frantically shouted orders, and the loud clip of boots and grunted commands. Two more arc lamps converged on the small area, helping to illuminate what had happened in the cocooning fog and obscuring rain.

Garin was at Natalya's side. She had slumped to one knee and held her side with a limp hand. Her face had lost color, her eyes were dim, and the pleasant sleep of death hung over her weakened body. He saw confusion in her eyes and a cold, leaden pallor on her cheeks. All around them was chaos, urgent voices in the suffocating fog. She struggled to speak through choking breaths.

'Quiet,' he said. He looked calmly into her eyes. 'You'll get us both killed.'

Natalya bled into her hands, and she went to lie down.

'Stand up,' he said, and then shouted, 'Get up!'

Garin lifted her into his arms, grunting at the weight. Their eyes met. She tried to speak again, but her voice was soft, and he didn't understand what she was trying to say.

'Don't give up,' he said encouragingly. 'You'll make it.'

She was heavy in his arms, but he found a way to manage, and he walked toward the safety of the Czech border. He glanced back, mumbling the prayer that always came to him in moments of danger. He moved at a steady pace, drawing in short breaths. His eyes blinked to clear the blurring rain from his vision, and he focused on the short distance to safety.

Garin shouted for help over the growing clamor provoked by the carnage; his body trembled against his will. He saw her eyes begin to close and snapped, 'Stay awake.'

At that moment, Garin seemed to sense a change in the danger, and he glanced over his shoulder at the mist-shrouded watchtower, but even as he did, he had begun to quicken his pace toward the waiting Americans. Garin shut out the siren's piercing wail and the chorus of hostile voices. He shaped his mind to the smallness of his world – the woman in his arms and the several steps to safety.

The Soviet sniper's first shot caught Garin in the thigh and seemed to thrust him forward; the second struck him in the shoulder, snapping his head back. He stumbled, somehow managing to take two more steps, but then he collapsed, dropping to the pavement and releasing Natalya from his arms. One more bullet in the rapid sequence tore into his skull, shattering it and covering Natalya in brain matter. She saw the grievous wound and struggled to crawl away from his body.

Mueller's mouth had opened in the hope that Garin would make it the last few steps to safety, but now his face was grim with horror.

The shooting stopped when the American sharpshooter found his target through the shifting mist, aligned the cross hairs of his scope, and fired a bullet into the Soviet sniper's forehead.

29

LANGLEY
1992

GEORGE MUELLER STOOD IN front of the wall of Vermont marble and looked out at the small crowd gathered under the reaching height of Headquarters' vaulted lobby. It was the Agency's annual ceremony honoring intelligence officers who had died in the line of duty. The subdued group consisted of families of the fallen, Agency staff, a few reporters, and the outgoing Director of Central Intelligence. Mueller, the newly appointed acting director, adjusted his reading glasses and looked at the somber gathering. It was a cold space of stone and glass that was warmed by the emotions of the people looking up at him, each with a private memory. They were there to grieve for the new black star chiseled into the wall of marble.

Mueller paused, acknowledging several familiar faces, and as he did, his eyes passed over the Agency's symbol set in stone in the lobby floor – a vigilant eagle perched on a crimson shield with radiating compass points. He adjusted his speaker's notes and consciously glanced behind at the marble wall. There was a slender, waist-high glass case attached to the marble, and sealed inside, like a reliquary, a leather parchment portfolio with the names of the fallen quilled in ink followed by a date. In a few cases, old missions continued to be classified and the entry had no name, only an asterisk. That was the case with the newest entry: * *April 14, 1985. Uzhgorod Border Crossing.*

'We owe each of these men a great debt,' Mueller said, opening his remarks. 'We honor their sacrifice and remember the role they played in the defense of our freedoms. And today is no different, except that it is the first of these occasions held in the aftermath of the Soviet Union's downfall. Many of the men and women represented on the wall behind me gave their lives in the service of our great struggle against totalitarianism, and we honor each of them today, but it is also fitting on this day that we make a place for a man whose actions, as much as the contributions of any single officer, helped defeat the Soviet Union.'

Mueller looked at the faces in the first row, acknowledging Rositske, Ronnie Moffat, Petrov and his wife, and three former directors of the Agency.

'Those who knew him respected him,' Mueller said. 'The man we are adding to the wall today, like most men, was imperfect. He could drink too much, he disobeyed orders, he forgot details, and he was bored by what he thought were the political nuances of our work. But given the opportunity, he ran crazy – and in retrospect, almost mind-boggling – risks. Although he was dedicated to our mission, he was not one of us. But he became one of us. He cared for people, cared for this country, and he risked his life so that others might live.'

Mueller read his prepared remarks, which he had typed himself, and he kept his eyes on the people he knew, but he was nevertheless conscious of a late arrival. When she entered and took a seat in the last row, alone, he took note, pausing briefly. One or two in the front row, seeing his momentary distraction, turned around to see what had caught Mueller's attention.

Thin, willowy, with a disagreeable expression, the woman claimed the last seat. Natalya had arrived late to go unseen, but her arrival had the opposite effect. Had she been in a 1950s

Hollywood film, she would have been played by a young Alida
Valli, who, not without vinegar in life, in film made a specialty
of sullen, romantic women. Natalya wore dark glasses and
folded her hands comfortably on her lap.

Mueller returned to his script.

*

'So who was he?' a young reporter asked Mueller.

His remarks over, Mueller was standing in the corner of the
lobby where drinks and refreshments had been set out on a
long serving table covered in white linen. The young woman
with an eager smile had her notebook open and her pen poised
to take down his response. Mueller was uncomfortable with
journalists under any circumstance, and her badgering was
out of place at the somber event and reminded him why he
distrusted journalists even more than politicians, who at least
had manners. But he was cornered.

Perhaps it was the reporter's innocent question, or perhaps
his doubts were stirred by the event's gravity, or perhaps it was
the passage of time that allowed him to make sense of what had
happened, and this reporter, who he'd never met, happened
to appear with her question when he was ready to share the
thoughts he'd formed after reading the diary found on Garin's
body. Mueller ate the olive from his gin martini and led the
reporter to one side, away from the subdued crowd.

'What's your name?' he asked.

'Elizabeth Runyon.'

'Well, Elizabeth, let's move away from the noise.'

People in the lobby still mingled in small groups, and the
official photographer recorded the event for the Agency's
newsletter. And it was when Mueller led Elizabeth past the
photographer that he happened to see Natalya standing alone

at the wall of Vermont marble. She was quiet, dignified, and unapproachable in her contemplation. She had raised her hand and was touching the newly carved black star.

'Well?' the reporter pressed. 'Who was he?'

Mueller turned back to the reporter. 'These ceremonies are always sad events for me,' he said. 'The men and women on that wall are like the men and women in Arlington – and it's easy to glorify their heroism. It's also important not to dress things up too much.' He smiled. 'Someone more eloquent than me said it best: Spying is like war. It's a dirty business. Shed war of its glory, which it gathers in the fullness of time when events are rewritten by writers like you, trying to imagine the battlefield for the rest of us. But shed war of its glory and a soldier's job is to kill. It's that simple. And so, shed espionage of its popular mythology, the spy's job is to lie, deceive, and betray trust. The only value to the soldier's killing, or the spy's betrayal, is the worth of the cause they serve.'

Mueller sipped his martini. He rarely drank martinis, but to honor the fallen man's memory, he'd asked for the drink that Garin had notoriously abused. He alone appreciated the small gesture of communion.

Elizabeth was assiduously taking down what Mueller had said, which produced in him a sense of importance and encouraged him. He had formed thoughts about Garin the man, Garin the spy, and the business of espionage, using his firsthand memories, interviews, and the diary, but he had not shared his thoughts. Now he was the head of the whole enterprise, and the martini helped him speak more freely, even candidly. Perhaps a bit cynically.

'Spies are mercenaries at heart,' he said. 'Like well-paid stuntmen, we do our tricks and then move offstage and are forgotten. Other case officers have great ambitions to do good in the world, but they never get the opportunity to leave their

251

mark. Peace intervenes. They too are forgotten. But when an ordinary man, such as the man we honored today, gives his life for a political cause and has an impact on the course of history, his story is worth telling – and we forget his lies, deceits, and betrayals.'

Mueller put away the rest of his drink, feeling loose. He turned away from the reporter and saw the crowd had thinned. He too went for his coat on the rack and saw there was one other that hadn't been claimed.

Natalya stood at the marble wall with her hand over her mouth, crying. The afternoon light had softened and deepened, washing the wall of black stars in a flaming sunset. He watched her until finally she stirred and took her coat from the rack. Mueller waited for her to approach. He stood in the center of the lobby on the radiating compass points of the Agency's shield. She walked with a ballerina's poise and carried her coat over her arm. He saw a brave, sad expression on her face. Mueller didn't think he had the strength, or the presence of mind, to have a conversation, but he found his voice when she stopped in front of him.

'He was a good man,' he said. 'He cared for you. He wouldn't admit it, but he did.'

She smiled a wan, forlorn smile. 'I don't need your lies to feel better.' She looked ready to say more, but she didn't, and she walked away. But coming to the lobby doors, she happened to turn. 'You're no better than he was. You're all the same.'

ACKNOWLEDGMENTS

This book would not have been possible without my agent, Will Roberts, whose keen editorial eye helped deepen the story and shape its characters. Katie McGuire, my editor at Pegasus Books, improved the manuscript with her subtle insights and sharp pencil. John Beyrle, US ambassador to the Russian Federation 2008-2012, provided invaluable assistance with street names, Moscow life, and Russian vocabulary that only someone who was a consular officer in the American Embassy in 1985 would have. I want to acknowledge the book's early readers, particularly Rae Edelson, Bruce Dow, and Josh Freeman. Special thanks to my fellow writers in the Neumann Leathers Writers Group – Mauro Altamura, Amy Kiger-Williams, Aimee Rinehart, Dawn Ryan, and Brett Duquette – who were the novel's first readers. Fred Wistow, Andrew Feinstein, Brendan Cahill, Kelly Luce, Helen Phillips, Lauren Cerand, Kevin Larimer, John Copenhaver, Susan Isaacs, Jayne Anne Phillips, Sarah Russo, Milena Deleva, Elizabeth Kostova, Polly Flonder, and Nahid Rachlin have been generous with their support and encouragement over the years.

Several books were indispensable sources of information about the Soviet Union and the interplay of the CIA and the KGB. They are: *Echoes of a Native Son* by Serge Schmemann (Vintage Books, 1997); *Spy Handler* by Victor Cherkashin with Gregory Feifer (Basic Books, 2005); *Bears in the Caviar* by Charles Thayer (Russian Life Books, 2015); *The Billion Dollar Spy* by David Hoffman (Anchor Books, 2016); *Mole* by William

Hood (Brassey's US, 1993); *Tower of Secrets* by Victor Sheymov (Naval Institute Press, 1993); *Next Stop Execution* by Oleg Gordievsky (Macmillan, 1995); and *The Master of Disguise* by Antonio J. Mendez (Harper, 2000).

I owe particular thanks to my sons, Joe and Arturo, who have helped me see the world differently, and my wife, Linda, gracious person, generous mother, loving partner, and expert on Shakespeare.

BECOME A
NO EXIT PRESS
MEMBER

BECOME A NO EXIT PRESS MEMBER and you will be joining a club of like-minded literary crime fiction lovers – and supporting an independent publisher and their authors!

AS A MEMBER YOU WILL RECEIVE

- Six books of your choice from No Exit's future publications at a discount off the retail price
- Free UK carriage
- A free eBook copy of each title
- Early pre-publication dispatch of the new books
- First access to No Exit Press Limited Editions
- Exclusive special offers only for our members
- A discount code that can be used on all backlist titles
- The choice of a free book when you first sign up

Gift Membership available too – the perfect present!

FOR MORE INFORMATION AND TO SIGN UP VISIT
noexit.co.uk/members